The Wrong Ben

By

Rosanne Baker

COPPER LIGHT
PRESS

www.copperlightpress.com

The Wrong Ben
Copyright © 2026 by Rosanne Baker
All rights reserved.

No part of this book may be reproduced, stored in a retrieval system, or transmitted in any form or by any means — electronic, mechanical, photocopying, recording, or otherwise — without the prior written permission of the publisher, except by a reviewer who may quote brief passages in a review.

This is a work of fiction. Names, characters, places, and incidents are products of the author's imagination or are used fictitiously. Any resemblance to actual events, locales, or persons, living or dead, is entirely coincidental.

Published by: Copper Light Press
CopperLightPress.com
ISBN: 979-8-9936451-2-4
First Edition

NEW YEAR'S EVE, TWO MONTHS EARLIER

Ben Rosen was three beers deep and seriously reconsidering his life choices when Maya threw a handful of pretzels at his face.

"Stop moping," she said. "It's New Year's Eve. You're supposed to be making resolutions, not excuses."

"I'm not moping." Ben picked a pretzel out of his hair. "I'm reflecting."

"You're hiding." Jake leaned back in the booth, holding a mug of beer and laughing. "You've used the phrase 'I'm fine where I am' four times tonight. I counted."

"Because I am fine where I am."

"You live in a tiny apartment you found on Craigslist," Maya said. "You're twenty-seven."

"Yeah, but I'm saving for my own place. I have a five-year plan.

You have a five-year plan and live like you're a college kid!" Jake laughed.

The three of them had claimed their usual corner booth at Murphy's, the dive bar two blocks from Lincoln Elementary, where they all taught. The place smelled like old wood and cheaper beer. A disco ball someone had hung in 1987 spun overhead, casting sad little sparkles across their table. This was their New Year's Eve tradition: Murphy's, mediocre wings, and the annual "what are we doing with our lives" conversation.

"I like my small apartment," Ben said.

"You don't even have real furniture," Jake pointed out. "Your bed frame is literally milk crates."

"It's minimalist."

"It's college-dorm vibes." Maya wasn't letting this go. She'd been on this kick for months now, ever since she'd bought a small starter house and suddenly decided everyone else needed to grow up, too. "When's the last time you went on an actual date?"

"I date."

"Coffee with someone from a teacher training seminar doesn't count. When's the last time you made a decision that scared you?"

Ben pulled at the label on his beer bottle. Twenty-seven years old with a master's degree, and he was still living like a college student. The money didn't help; thirty-eight thousand a year didn't exactly scream financial stability. But if he was honest, that wasn't really the problem. Plenty of teachers made it work. Maya made it work, and Jake had his own nicely furnished apartment. Ben just... coasted. Safe job. Safe life. No risks, no pressure, no expectations beyond showing up with goldfish crackers and construction paper.

"You know what your problem is?" Jake said, and Ben braced himself because Jake only started sentences like that when he'd been drinking. "You never actually left school. Elementary to middle to high school to college to grad school to... elementary school again. You've been in the same system your entire life."

"That's not a bad thing."

"It's not a good thing either. You're twenty-seven, Ben. When are you going to figure out what you actually want?"

"I like teaching."

"You like teaching because it's safe," Maya said, gentler now. "You like it because five-year-olds think you're amazing and you never have to prove yourself to anyone who matters."

That stung, mainly because it was true.

Ben had been coasting for years. Easy job. Easy roommates. Easy life. He didn't have a five-year plan, a retirement account, or health insurance that wasn't catastrophic coverage. His mom still did his taxes. His sister still reminded him about oil changes. He was perfectly happy to drift along, staying in his lane, never making waves.

Except lately, it had started to feel less like contentment and more like stagnation.

"New Year's resolution," Maya announced, pulling out her phone. "You're going to do something that scares you."

"I'm good, thanks."

"I'm serious. This year, you're going to take a risk. Make a big decision. Prove you're capable of adulting."

"I adult just fine."

"You asked me how to boil eggs last week."

"That was a specific temperature question…"

Jake grabbed Ben's phone off the table. "We're finding you a challenge. Something completely outside your comfort zone."

"Guys, no…"

"Too late." Jake was already scrolling. "We're looking at jobs. Real jobs. Grown-up jobs that require you to wear pants without elastic waistbands."

"I don't wear…"

"Holy shit. Listen to this one." Jake's grin was diabolical. "Executive Assistant to CEO. Tech startup in San Francisco. 'Requires organizational excellence, discretion, and the ability to anticipate needs. Ideal candidate will manage a complex calendar, coordinate with investors, and maintain a professional environment at all times.' It's for a wellness app called VibeGuide."

Maya leaned over to look. "That's perfect. That's like the anti-Ben job."

"Exactly," Jake said. "Corporate. High-stakes. It probably requires actual business casual."

Ben laughed. "What, you want me to apply?"

"Yes." Maya's eyes lit up. "New Year's dare. You apply for the most grown-up job we can find. Full professional application. See what happens."

"Nothing will happen."

"Probably not," Jake agreed. "But that's not the point. The point is you try. You put yourself out there. You do something that's not safe and comfortable and kindergarten-teacher-approved."

"This is ridiculous."

"You're ridiculous," Maya shot back. "Come on. What's the worst that happens? They ignore you? They reject you? You're already rejecting yourself by not even trying."

"I'll give you fifty bucks if you actually submit it," Jake added.

"Make it a hundred," Maya said. "I'm in too."

Ben looked at the job posting. Executive Assistant to a CEO. It was absurd. He had zero corporate experience. His resume was five years of teaching kindergarten and a summer job shelving books at the library. He wore cardigans with elbow patches. He color-coded with crayons.

But Maya was right, he never tried, he never risked. He stayed in his comfortable little bubble, convincing himself it was enough.

"Two hundred total?" Ben said.

"Two hundred total," they agreed.

"Fine." Ben grabbed his phone, something uncomfortable squirming in his chest. "But I'm doing this my way."

He opened his email and started typing.

To:

From:

Subject: Application for Executive Assistant Position

Dear Hiring Manager,

My name is Benjamin Rosen, and I'm applying for your Executive Assistant position. I have five years of experience managing complex environments, coordinating schedules for multiple stakeholders, and maintaining a positive workplace culture.

"That's actually pretty good," Maya said, reading over his shoulder.

"Shh. I'm not done."

In my current role, I oversee the day-to-day operations in a high-energy environment with 24 direct reports. I've developed organizational systems that maximize efficiency while prioritizing individual needs. My approach emphasizes clear communication, proactive problem solving, and creating spaces where people feel valued and supported.

Jake squinted at the screen. "Wait. Are you describing teaching kindergarten?"

"Technically accurate is the best kind of accurate." Ben kept typing.

I specialize in conflict resolution, crisis management, and keeping calm during high-stress situations. I'm skilled at anticipating needs before they arise and implementing creative solutions to complex problems.

"Is conflict resolution breaking up fights over crayons?" Maya asked.

"Crisis management must be dealing with the kid who ate glue," Jake smirked.

"Still counts." Ben was on a roll now, the beer making this seem like the funniest thing he'd ever done.

My organizational philosophy centers on positive reinforcement, clear systems, and treating everyone with respect, regardless of their role. I believe a strong workplace culture starts with small gestures of recognition and appreciation, and with creating environments where people want to show up every day.

He paused. That part was genuine. He did believe that. Teaching had taught him that people, even six-year-olds, especially six-year-olds, needed to feel seen and valued. Those gold stars and kind words mattered more than anyone wanted to admit.

Whatever. He was drunk. He kept going.

I'm proficient in calendar management (I currently maintain schedules for 24 individuals), email correspondence (average 50+ emails daily), and creating organizational systems that work for diverse personality types.

Additional skills include:
- Color-coded filing systems (highly effective)
- Conflict de-escalation (Five years' experience)
- Inventory management
- Crisis response (immediate and calm)
- Creating positive, supportive environments
- Making everyone feel like the most important person in the room

Maya was dying laughing. "Inventory management. You're putting snack inventory on a corporate application."

"It's a relevant skill."

"For a KINDERGARTEN class."

"For any workplace. Everyone needs snacks. I'm just brave enough to say it."

He attached his resume, the real one, listing his teaching experience, his master's degree, and his summer library job. Then he stared at the send button.

"You don't actually have to do it," Jake said quietly.

But Ben was thinking about milk crates and Craigslist roommates and the fact that he couldn't remember the last time he'd done anything that scared him. He was thinking about how he loved his job, but also how it was maybe too easy. How everyone expected nothing from him except showing up. How he'd been coasting so long, he'd forgotten what it felt like to actually try.

This application wouldn't go anywhere. But maybe that wasn't the point. Perhaps the point was proving to himself, and to Maya and Jake, that he was capable of more than just staying comfortable.

He hit send.

"Done." Ben set down his phone. "Can I have my two hundred dollars?"

"You actually did it." Maya looked impressed and concerned in equal measure.

"I can't believe you put inventory management for a snack cupboard," Jake said, still laughing.

"It's a gift." Ben finished his beer. "Now, can we please never speak of this again? I'm going to wake up tomorrow and die of embarrassment."

"To bad decisions and personal growth!" Maya raised her glass.

They toasted, ordered another round, and by midnight, Ben had entirely forgotten about the application.

He never expected to hear back. He never expected to get an interview. And he absolutely, positively never expected what would happen next.

But life, as Ben would learn, had a way of forcing you to grow up whether you were ready or not.

The trick was not running away when it did.

.

CHAPTER 1

Friday Morning

Mara Wright's apartment looked like it had been staged for a real estate photo shoot. Everything matched. Nothing was out of place. The living room was all grays and white: gray couch, white walls, silver picture frames with stock photos of beaches she'd never visited. The kitchen counters were clear except for a coffee maker and a bowl of decorative lemons that she'd never eaten. The bedroom was the same. White duvet, gray pillows, and no clutter anywhere.

It wasn't cold, exactly. Just careful, controlled, as if someone had designed it to show that a successful person had lived here, even though that person was rarely actually home.

She stood in front of her walk-in closet at 5:45 AM, staring at the rows of blazers. They hung black on the left, grays in the middle, and navy blues on the right. Below them, pants and skirts organized the same way. Everything dry-cleaned. Everything pressed. Everything ready.

She pulled out the black blazer first. This was the one she'd worn last month when she'd had to fire David from product management. It made her look harder. Colder. Like someone who could make difficult decisions without flinching.

She put it back.

The gray one was safe. Boring, but safe. Nobody had strong feelings about gray. But today wasn't a day for boring. Today was Richard Steele and 30 million dollars, proving that she deserved to run a company worth funding.

Navy blazer it is.

She laid it on the bed next to tailored black pants and a cream silk blouse. The blouse had a high neckline. The pants were fitted but not tight. Everything appropriate and everything correct.

Mara was thirty-two years old, five-foot-six, and size sixteen. She had dark brown hair, worn in a sleek bob that hit just below her jaw. Her face was round, something her mother had called "cherubic" when she was young and "full" now that she was grown. She had brown eyes and pale skin that flushed easily when she was stressed, angry, or embarrassed.

She wasn't thin. Hadn't been thin since college, before the startup life and the eighty-hour weeks and the stress-eating and the years of building something from nothing while forgetting to take care of herself. She'd made peace with it through expensive therapy and expensive clothes that fit properly and the grudging acceptance that she had bigger problems than whether men found her attractive.

But that peace was fragile. It cracked on mornings like this.

She checked her reflection in the full-length mirror. The pants smoothed her hips. The blazer created structure. Everything was as good as it was going to get.

Her phone buzzed on the white nightstand.

Mom: *Saw your interview in TechCrunch! So proud. You look beautiful. Have you been dieting? You look like you've lost weight. Love you!*

Mara deleted the message without responding. Her mother meant well. The concern was genuine. But the message was always the same underneath the words: Your body is my business. Your appearance requires monitoring. You look good, but let me find something to worry about anyway.

She walked to the bathroom, washed her face, and went through her makeup routine. Foundation. Concealer under her eyes to hide the five hours of sleep. Powder. Blush. Mascara.

The lipstick came last. Muted rose. The same shade she'd worn to every major presentation for five years. She'd bought six tubes because certain superstitions earned their place through repeated success.

Her phone buzzed again.

An email this time. Subject line in all capitals: URGENT: STEELE WANTS CHANGES TO DECK.

Her stomach dropped. She opened it.

Mara - Looking at projections again. Need customer acquisition cost broken down by channel. Also want clearer exit strategy scenarios. Can you add 3-4 slides? Meeting still on for 11 AM. - RS

Richard Steele. Lead partner at Arch Venture Capital. The man whose decision would determine whether VibeGuide secured the funding it required or whether Mara spent the next six months scrambling to prevent collapse.

Three to four slides. Four hours' notice.

She was already moving. Grabbed her laptop bag from the chair by the window. Phone charger. Portable battery. The lucky lipstick went into her blazer pocket.

Another buzz.

Chelsea: *Saw the Steele situation. Already in the office pulling CAC data. Breakdown by channel will be ready in 20 minutes. Hot water with lemon on your desk. We've got this.*

Mara felt something ease in her chest. Chelsea. Seven years of working together. Seven years of this exact dynamic: crisis emerging, Chelsea already solving it before Mara had to ask.

Mara: *Thank you. En route.*

She grabbed her keys and left.

***

The VibeGuide office was on the third floor of a converted warehouse in SoMa. Exposed brick walls. High ceilings with visible ductwork painted white. Polished concrete floors. Large windows and natural light, exactly like every other tech startup in San Francisco.

The main workspace was open plan, with desks in clusters, no cubicles. The walls were painted a soft gray-blue that matched the company logo. Motivational posters hung in white frames: "WELLNESS IS NOT A LUXURY." "SMALL STEPS, BIG CHANGES." "YOU ARE WORTH THE INVESTMENT."

Mara had approved of all of them. They tested well with users.

The office was quiet when she arrived. Chelsea was already there, sitting at the desk directly outside Mara's office. Chelsea's desk was organized but lived-in. A coffee mug that said "WORLD'S OKAYEST ASSISTANT" sat next to her keyboard. Photos covered the wall of her cubicle partition: Chelsea and her husband at their wedding. Chelsea and her sister on a hiking trip. The whole VibeGuide team at last year's holiday party, everyone wearing ugly Christmas sweaters.

A small succulent sat in a white pot near her monitor. It was thriving, somehow, despite the fluorescent lighting and Chelsea's repeated claims that she killed every plant she touched.

Chelsea herself was thirty-four, blonde, five-foot-eight, and thin in the way that seemed effortless. She wore dark jeans and a blue sweater today. Her hair was pulled back in a ponytail. No makeup except mascara.

She looked up when Mara approached. "Morning. The CAC data is almost done. Should be ready in five minutes."

"Thank you."

Mara walked into her office. It was smaller than people probably expected for a CEO. Just enough room for a desk, two visitor chairs, and a small bookshelf with business books she'd actually read. Her desk was glass and chrome. Nothing personal on it except a framed photo of her and her co-founder, Eliza, at their Series A celebration.

The white mug sat next to her keyboard. Steam rose from it. The temperature was perfect. Hot enough to be soothing, cool enough to drink immediately. Chelsea had been making it for seven years. She'd perfected the timing.

Mara set down her laptop bag and took a sip. The lemon was fresh, not bottled. Chelsea bought real lemons every Monday and kept them in the office kitchen.

Small things. That was the job, really.

Mara opened her laptop and started building slides.

***

By 7:43 AM, the new slides were halfway done, and Mara was starting to believe she could pull this off.

Chelsea appeared in the doorway holding a protein bar. She set it on the desk next to the now-empty mug and looked at Mara with an expression that said: Eat this, or I'm not leaving.

"I had hot water with lemon."

"That isn't breakfast." Chelsea's voice was firm but not unkind. She'd had this exact conversation approximately eight hundred times.

Mara picked up the bar. Unwrapped it and took a bite. It tasted like compressed sawdust with delusions of being chocolate, but she forced it down.

"Satisfied?"

"For now." Chelsea turned to leave, then stopped. "The exit strategy scenarios: multiple options or a single recommended path?"

"Three scenarios. Conservative, moderate, aggressive. Steele likes options."

"I'll pull the relevant data."

She left. Mara returned to the slides. By 8:50, the presentation was complete. She reviewed it twice, checking for typos, formatting inconsistencies, and anything that might undermine the content.

Everything was correct. The slides were good. Better than good.

But something felt off. Chelsea had been acting strange all week. Small hesitations before responding. A certain distance in her usual efficiency. And this morning she'd arrived even earlier than usual, prepared the data with extra thoroughness.

Mara stood and walked to Chelsea's desk.

"Do you have a moment?"

Chelsea looked up. Something flickered across her face. Anxiety, maybe, or resignation. "Of course."

She followed Mara into the office and closed the door behind her. Closed doors meant serious conversation.

Chelsea sat in one of the visitor chairs. She looked uncomfortable. Her hands were clasped in her lap. She wasn't making eye contact.

"Is something wrong?" Mara asked.

Chelsea took a breath. Let it out slowly. "I need to tell you something. I wanted to wait until after the pitch, but the timing doesn't work, so I'm telling you now."

Mara waited.

"Google offered me a position. Head of Executive Operations. Director level." Chelsea's voice was steady but quiet. "They made the offer last week. Asked for a response by this morning."

The words took a moment to process. Google. Director level. Chelsea was leaving.

Mara's face didn't change. She'd learned a long time ago how to receive bad news without showing a reaction.

"I see," she said. "I assume you accepted?"

"I did. I'm sorry about the timing. I know this is..."

"It's an excellent opportunity. Congratulations."

"Thank you." Chelsea's hands tightened in her lap. "I wanted to give you proper notice. Two weeks. That should provide enough time to hire and train my replacement."

"That's very professional of you."

"But there's a complication." Chelsea finally looked up. Her eyes were slightly red. "I spoke with HR this morning. Because I'm your executive assistant, and because I have access to sensitive information: board communications, investor details, strategic planning, their policy requires that I leave today."

The office felt very quiet suddenly. Mara could hear the clock on the wall ticking. The air conditioner humming. Distant voices from the main office.

"Today," Mara repeated.

"Security protocol. Anyone who reports directly to an Executive and resigns must depart the same day. They'll compensate me for the full two weeks, but I can't remain in the building or access company systems." Chelsea's voice cracked slightly. "I'm sorry. I wanted to give you time. I wanted to train someone properly. But I have to pack my desk and leave by the end of business today."

Mara absorbed this. Filed it in the part of her brain that handled crisis management.

"I'm aware of the policy," she said. "I approved it three years ago when we implemented our security protocols."

The irony wasn't lost on her.

"So, you're leaving today," Mara said.

"Yes. Karen from HR is coming at two to process my exit. I'll pack my desk, turn in my credentials, and sign the necessary paperwork." Chelsea's eyes were definitely wet now. "I'm so sorry, I wanted more time, I wanted to train someone properly, and make sure you were prepared."

"I'm prepared. I've been running this company for seven years. I'll manage."

It came out sharper than intended. Chelsea flinched.

Mara softened her tone. Fractionally. "That was unprofessional. I apologize. This is simply unexpected timing."

"I understand. And I really am sorry."

They sat in silence. Through the glass wall of Mara's office, the rest of the company went about their Friday morning. Priya from engineering walked past carrying coffee. Marcus from sales laughed at something on his phone. Tyler was gesturing wildly while talking to Sarah from Product.

Normal. Everything looked normal.

"Karen mentioned she's already working on finding a replacement," Chelsea said. "She's reaching out to Benjamin Rozen. He was the second-choice candidate when you hired me seven years ago. He's been working in executive support at tech companies since then. Very experienced. Karen thinks he'd be an excellent fit."

"I'm sure he would be."

Chelsea stood. "I should let you prepare for the pitch. You'll be excellent. You always are."

"Thank you."

Chelsea left, closing the door gently behind her.

Mara sat at her desk and allowed herself exactly thirty seconds of reaction.

Her hands were shaking. Just slightly. She pressed them flat against the cool glass of her desk and waited for them to steady.

Seven years. Seven years of professional partnership. Seven years of working together so closely they could finish each other's sentences, anticipate each other's needs, and function as a single unit.

She looked at the clock. Forty-five minutes until the pitch.

She didn't have time for this. She opened her laptop and reviewed her notes.

***

The conference room on the second floor was Mara's favorite space in the building. Floor-to-ceiling windows overlooking the city. A long table made of reclaimed wood. Modern, comfortable chairs. A large screen for presentations.

Mara arrived early to set up. She connected her laptop to the projector and tested it. Adjusted the lighting, filled the water glasses, and set out notepads and pens.

Everything was perfect. Everything was ready.

Richard Steele arrived at 11:04.

He was in his mid-fifties, tall, gray hair styled in a way that probably cost more than Mara's entire outfit. His suit was charcoal gray and perfectly tailored. He carried a leather portfolio that looked expensive and well-used. He wore a watch that probably cost more than most people's cars.

He didn't smile when he entered. Didn't apologize for being late. Just walked in like he owned the space and sat down at the head of the table.

"Mara." He set down his portfolio. Opened it. Pulled out a tablet. "Thank you for accommodating the last-minute changes."

"Not a problem. I've added the customer acquisition cost breakdown and exit scenarios you requested."

"Let's see them."

She presented.

Her voice was calm. Steady. Professional. She stood at the head of the table, using a remote to advance through slides. She didn't fidget. Didn't say "um" or "like." Didn't qualify her statements with "I think" or "maybe."

She just presented facts. Numbers. Analysis. Strategy.

This was what she was good at. This was what seven years of building a company had taught her. How to stand in front of powerful men who controlled millions of dollars and convince them that she deserved some of it.

Steele interrupted often. It was his style.

"Your customer acquisition cost for paid channels is higher than industry average. Why?"

"We're targeting working professionals aged twenty-five to forty with disposable income and existing wellness concerns. That audience requires more sophisticated targeting, which increases acquisition cost. However, our retention rates are thirty-seven percent higher than industry average, which means the lifetime value of each customer significantly exceeds the acquisition cost." She clicked to the next slide. A graph showing retention rates over time, the line climbing steadily upward.

"Your exit scenarios assume continued growth in the corporate wellness market. What if that market dips?"

"The corporate wellness market has shown consistent growth for the past eight years, even during economic downturns. Companies view employee wellness programs as cost-saving measures. But if the market did dip, our consumer base would provide diversification. Sixty-two percent of our users are individual consumers rather than corporate accounts."

The questions continued for ninety minutes. Steele probed every assumption. Mara answered every question.

She'd spent seven years building this company. She knew every metric, every detail, every risk and opportunity. This was her life. Her work. The thing she'd sacrificed sleep, relationships, and any semblance of work-life balance to create.

She wasn't going to let Richard Steele find a flaw.

At 12:30, Steele closed his tablet.

"This is good work, Mara. I'm impressed with the level of detail in your planning."

"Thank you."

"My team will review the materials and get back to you early next week with next steps. But I'll say this, you've built something solid here. The metrics are strong, the market opportunity is real, and you clearly have the operational discipline to execute."

This was the closest Steele came to expressing enthusiasm. Mara allowed herself a small internal moment of satisfaction.

"I appreciate that, Richard. I look forward to hearing from your team."

"Expect a call Monday or Tuesday. We'll want to discuss terms."

He stood. Shook her hand. His grip was firm and brief. Then he left, taking his expensive portfolio and his power to decide her company's future with him.

Mara stood alone in the conference room.

The city spread out beyond the windows. San Francisco in the early afternoon, all glass buildings and blue sky.

The pitch had gone well. Steele was interested. The funding was likely.

She just felt tired.

She packed up her laptop and walked back upstairs to the main office.

***

Chelsea was packing her desk.

Mara tried to work in her office, tried to focus on follow-up items from the Steele pitch, but she kept looking up through her glass wall.

One of Chelsea and her wife came down first. Then one of Chelsea and her sister. Then the whole team at the holiday party. Seven years of photos, removed from the cubicle partition and placed carefully in a cardboard box.

The "WORLD'S OKAYEST ASSISTANT" mug went next. Wrapped in tissue paper.

The succulent. The desk drawer full of emergency snacks, Band-Aids, and phone chargers. The stapler Chelsea had bought herself because the company-provided one jammed constantly.

Seven years of making a workspace into a space that belonged to someone. All of it going into a box.

People started coming by to say goodbye around one-thirty. Tyler arrived first with yellow roses. Priya from Engineering brought a card that the whole team had signed. Marcus gave Chelsea a bottle of wine. Sarah came by and just started crying. Chelsea hugged her, and Sarah's shoulders shook.

Eliza, Mara's CMO and closest thing to a friend, pulled Chelsea aside. They talked quietly for several minutes near the windows. Mara couldn't hear what they were saying, but she saw Chelsea wipe her eyes. Saw Eliza put a hand on her shoulder. Saw them both look toward Mara's office.

Then Eliza left, and Chelsea returned to packing.

At 2:00, Karen from HR arrived. Short gray hair. Black pantsuit. The professional expression of sympathy that came from years of processing departures.

The exit paperwork. The confidentiality reminder. The equipment return form. Chelsea read everything and then signed everything. At 2:15, she sealed the box.

She stood holding it. The box had "CHELSEA" written on the side in black marker.

Then she turned and walked toward Mara's office.

Mara met her at the door.

"Ready?" Mara asked.

Chelsea nodded.

They walked together to the elevator. The team had gathered in the common area without anyone organizing it. Soft applause started. A few people called out goodbyes.

"You'll be great at Google!"

"Don't forget about us little people!"

Chelsea smiled. Tried to hold it together. "Thank you for seven incredible years. This has been..." Her voice caught. She took a breath. "This has been the best job I've ever had."

The elevator arrived with a soft ding. Chelsea stepped inside. Mara followed.

The doors closed, cutting off the sound of the office. Just the two of them in the small metal box, descending.

Neither of them spoke.

In the lobby, Chelsea handed over her badge. The security guard scanned it. "All set. Good luck with your new position."

"Thanks."

Chelsea picked up the box.

"Well," she said. "This is it."

"Yes."

"Thank you for everything, Mara. For taking a chance on me seven years ago. For being an excellent boss."

"You were an excellent assistant. Google is fortunate."

Chelsea smiled. Small. Sad. "We're very professional, aren't we?"

"It's appropriate for the situation."

"What if I said I'm going to miss you? Is that professional?"

"It's acceptable."

"Then I'm going to miss you. A lot."

Mara allowed herself the slightest crack in composure. "I'll miss you as well."

"Take care of yourself," Chelsea said. "Eat lunch sometimes. Don't work every weekend."

"I'll take it under consideration."

"That's the best I'm going to get, isn't it?"

"Yes."

Chelsea laughed. It sounded wet. "Okay. I'm leaving now before I completely fall apart in your lobby."

She walked toward the exit. Stopped. Turned back.

"Mara? You're going to be fine. Better than fine. You're brilliant, and you've never needed me as much as you think you did."

"That's inaccurate."

"It's not. You just don't see it yet."

Chelsea pushed through the glass doors and stepped outside. The afternoon sun hit her blonde ponytail. She shifted the box in her arms and started walking down the sidewalk.

Mara stood in the lobby, watching until Chelsea turned the corner and disappeared.

Then she took the elevator back upstairs and returned to work.

***

The rest of Friday was spent in manufactured productivity. Emails. Metrics. Materials for Tuesday's board meeting.

At 4:30, Eliza appeared in Mara's doorway.

"Are you okay?"

"I'm fine."

"Liar." Eliza walked in uninvited and sat in one of the visitor chairs. She was thirty-three, tall, with dark hair in a messy bun, and heavy black-rimmed glasses. She looked like someone who had better things to do than worry about appearances, which was true. "Chelsea wasn't just personnel. She was your right hand."

"She was an excellent assistant. I'll miss her professional contributions."

"Mara."

"What?"

"You're allowed to be sad about this."

"Feeling it doesn't change the situation."

Eliza sighed. "Okay. How can I help?"

"Karen is searching for a replacement. She mentioned reaching out to Benjamin Rozen. If he's interested, we could potentially have someone start next week."

"And if this Benjamin Rozen doesn't work out?"

"Then we'll find someone else. There's no shortage of qualified executive assistants in San Francisco."

"There's a shortage of people who know you well enough to bring you hot water with lemon at the right temperature."

Mara didn't respond to that.

Eliza stood. "You're allowed to be sad. Chelsea mattered. That's okay to acknowledge."

She left before Mara could respond.

Mara sat at her desk, staring at her closed laptop.

Chelsea had mattered. Seven years of mattering.

But acknowledging that didn't change anything. Feeling sad didn't bring Chelsea back.

She opened her laptop and returned to work.

***

At 6:45 PM, Mara was alone in the office.

The space was different at night. Quieter. The overhead lights had motion sensors that turned off in unused areas, so only her office and the area immediately around it stayed lit. Outside, the city lights were coming on.

Her phone buzzed.

Karen: *Update on replacement search. Posted the position this afternoon. Already have 17 applications. Also left a message for Benjamin Rozen. He was our number-two choice seven years ago, very experienced in executive support at tech companies. If he's interested, we could potentially have him start next week. Will keep you posted.*

Mara: *Thank you for the rapid response.*

Karen: *Of course. I know this timing is terrible. We'll get you someone excellent as quickly as possible.*

Mara set down her phone.

She stood and walked to the window. Looked out at the city. Somewhere out there, Chelsea was probably home by now. Probably telling her wife about her last day. Probably excited about Google and nervous about starting something new, and maybe a little sad about leaving.

Somewhere out there, this Benjamin Rozen person was maybe getting Karen's voicemail and maybe considering whether he wanted to work for a CEO who'd built a thirty-million-dollar company but couldn't keep her assistant for more than seven years.

Her phone buzzed again.

Karen: *Benjamin Rozen called back! He's very interested. Can come in Monday morning for an interview and potentially start immediately if it's a good fit. This is excellent news. You're going to love him. Very professional, very experienced, exactly what you need.*

Mara: *That's efficient. Thank you.*

Karen: *Happy to help. See you Monday.*

Monday. A new assistant. Someone named Benjamin Rozen, who was very professional and very experienced.

Fine.

Mara grabbed her laptop bag and left the office. Took the elevator down alone. Walked through the empty lobby alone. Got into her car in the parking garage alone.

She drove home through Friday evening traffic. People everywhere, walking to restaurants, heading to bars, laughing with friends. Living lives that included things besides work.

Mara drove past them all and went home.

***

The apartment was exactly as she'd left it that morning. Gray couch. White walls. Everything in its place.

She changed into sweatpants. Ordered a salad from the place down the street that knew her order by heart. Ate it at the kitchen counter while reviewing materials for Tuesday's board meeting.

Normal Friday night activities.

Except everything felt slightly wrong. Slightly off-center.

At 9:30, she gave up on being productive. She washed her face, put on the expensive moisturizer that was supposed to prevent aging, and went to bed.

The bedroom was dark except for the streetlight coming through the window. She lay on the white duvet, staring at the ceiling.

Monday would come. Benjamin Rozen would arrive. The work would continue.

She just needed to get through the weekend first.

But as she lay there, alone in her carefully controlled apartment, she allowed herself one moment of honesty.

She missed Chelsea. Not just the professional support. Not just the efficiency. But the person. The relationship. The seven years of partnership that had made everything easier.

But missing Chelsea didn't change anything.

She closed her eyes and tried to sleep.

Outside, the city hummed and glowed and never stopped moving.

Inside, Mara lay alone in the dark, waiting for morning.

CHAPTER 2

Mara arrived at the office early Monday morning. Even earlier than usual. She'd been awake since five, lying in bed and staring at the ceiling, thinking about Chelsea's empty desk and the interview with Benjamin Rozen scheduled for nine.

The office looked the same as it had on Friday afternoon. Same gray-blue walls. Same motivational posters. Same desks arranged in clusters across the open floor plan.

But Chelsea's desk was empty. The cubicle partition, which had been covered in photos, now showed bare gray fabric. The space where the succulent had lived was just an empty desk. Even the coffee mug was gone.

Mara walked past it without looking too closely and went into her office.

She had thirty minutes before the interview. Thirty minutes to prepare. She opened her laptop and pulled up Benjamin Rozen's resume for the fifth time that morning.

Benjamin Rozen. Seven years of executive support experience at various tech companies. Started at a Series A startup, moved to a mid-sized firm, and is currently at a company going through rapid growth. Every position showed increased responsibility. His references were excellent. Karen had spoken to all three and reported back that he was professional, detail-oriented, and excellent at anticipating needs.

Perfect. He sounded perfect.

Mara needed perfect. She needed someone who could step into Chelsea's role and make everything function smoothly again. Someone who understood corporate environments and professional boundaries and how to support a CEO without constant handholding.

At 7:55, she walked to the kitchen to make hot water with lemon. The office was filling up. People arrived with coffee cups and bags, settling in at their desks and booting up their computers. Tyler was already talking loudly about his weekend. Priya scrolled through code on her monitor. Marcus typed aggressively on his phone.

Mara filled the electric kettle and waited for it to boil. Chelsea used to do this. Would have had hot water with lemon ready before Mara even arrived. But Chelsea was gone, so Mara made her own.

The kettle clicked off. She poured water into a plain white mug and added lemon from the container in the fridge, the one Chelsea had always kept stocked.

She was walking back to her office when Karen from HR appeared, slightly out of breath.

"Mara! Quick question before your nine o'clock."

"Yes?"

"Benjamin Rozen just called. He's running about fifteen minutes late. Traffic on the bridge. He apologized profusely. Very professional about it. I told him not to worry, these things happen."

"That's fine. Thank you for letting me know."

"He sounded great on the phone. Very polished. I think you're going to love him."

Karen hurried back to her office on the first floor. Mara returned to her desk and continued preparing for the interview.

At 9:14, she heard the elevator ding in the hallway.

Footsteps. Someone walking fast. Then Karen's voice, greeting someone in a friendly, but frazzled tone.

Mara stood and straightened her blazer. Navy again. Professional. Authoritative. First impressions mattered.

She walked out of her office to meet her new assistant.

And stopped.

The person standing at Chelsea's desk was not what she'd expected.

He looked young. Mid-twenties, maybe. He wore khaki pants that were too big, held up with a belt with a cartoon pencil buckle. The actual buckle was shaped like a pencil. It was yellow with a pink eraser.

His shirt was button-down, which was appropriate. Except it was covered in tiny dinosaurs. Little T-rexes and Stegosauruses scattered across light blue fabric.

Over the dinosaur shirt, he wore a cardigan. Not an everyday cardigan. This one was burgundy with leather elbow patches, and it looked like something someone's grandfather had owned in 1987 and then donated to Goodwill.

His glasses were wire-rimmed and slightly crooked on his face. One arm was held together with medical tape. Actual white medical tape wrapped around the hinge.

His hair was dark and messy, sticking up in the back like he'd forgotten to look in a mirror that morning.

He held a coffee mug shaped like an apple…a red ceramic apple with a green stem and a small brown worm poking out of one side.

He saw Mara, and his whole face lit up.

"Hi!" He set down the apple mug and stuck out his hand. "You must be Mara! I'm so sorry I'm late. There was an accident on the Bay Bridge, and traffic was completely stopped, and I left early, but not nearly enough apparently, but I didn't think."

He bumped his hip against Chelsea's desk. The apple mug wobbled. He grabbed for it, missed, and it tipped over. Coffee, thankfully in a sealed travel mug design, didn't spill, but the mug rolled across the desk and onto the floor with a loud thunk.

"Oh no. Sorry. I'm sorry. I'm a little clumsy in the mornings. Actually, all the time. My sister says I should wear a helmet." He crouched down to pick up the mug, and his glasses slid down his nose. He pushed them back up with one finger. They immediately slid down again.

Mara stared at him.

This couldn't be Benjamin Rozen. This couldn't be the experienced executive assistant with seven years of corporate experience and excellent references.

He stood back up, clutching the apple mug, slightly red in the face.

"Sorry about that. Fresh start. Hi. I'm Ben. Well, Benjamin, but everyone calls me Ben except my mom when she's mad, which is often because I keep doing stuff like…" He gestured at the mug. "…that. Anyway. I'm excited to be here. I brought cookies." He pointed to a container on the desk. "Snickerdoodles. I made them last night. Baking helps with interview anxiety. Studies show that…"

"I'm sorry," Mara interrupted. Her voice came out more sharply than intended. "There must be some mistake. You're Benjamin Rozen?"

"Yes! Well, technically Ben Rosen. R-O-S-E-N. No Z. Everyone expects a Z. Very disappointing when it's just an S."

"Ben Rosen with an S."

"Right. Not a Z. Common confusion. Happens all the time."

Mara's stomach dropped. "What's your current position?"

"Oh! I'm a kindergarten teacher at Lincoln Elementary. I've been there for five years. Best job ever. The kids are amazing. so much energy, very honest, sometimes brutally honest. Last week Emma told me my cardigan made me look like a depressed librarian, which was hurtful but also probably accurate." He laughed. Pushed his glasses up again.

Kindergarten teacher.

This was not the Benjamin Rozen with seven years of executive support experience.

This was the wrong Benjamin Rozen.

"Excuse me for one moment," Mara said.

She walked directly to her office, closed the door, and called Karen.

Karen answered on the first ring. "How's it going? He seems great, right?"

"Karen, that's not Benjamin Rozen."

"What? Of course it is. He introduced himself!"

"That's Ben Rosen with an S. R-O-S-E-N. He's a kindergarten teacher."

Silence on the other end of the line.

Then: "Oh no."

"Oh no?"

"Oh no. Oh no oh no oh no." The sound of typing. Frantic clicking. "I'm looking at the files now. We had two Benjamin Rosens apply for the position.

Benjamin Rozen with a Z. R-O-Z-E-N—that's the corporate one, the experienced one.

And Benjamin Rosen with an S. R-O-S-E-N—that's the... kindergarten teacher."

"And you called the wrong one."

"I called the wrong one. Oh my god. I'm so sorry. This is entirely my fault; we got a new HR system, and it must have put the wrong phone number on Benjamin Rozen's file. I didn't even notice, and IT is ironing out the glitches in the program."

Mara closed her eyes. Took a breath. "Can you call the correct Benjamin Rozen and see if he's still available?"

"Yes. Absolutely. Right now. I'll call him immediately and get this sorted out. Can you keep the kindergarten Ben there for a few minutes? I'll handle this."

"Fine."

Mara ended the call and walked back out to the main office.

Ben was still standing at Chelsea's desk, holding his apple mug, looking slightly nervous. He'd noticed her abrupt departure. His smile was smaller now, more uncertain.

"Is everything okay?" he asked.

"There's been a misunderstanding. HR will clarify shortly. In the meantime, please have a seat."

"Oh. Okay." He sat in Chelsea's chair. It squeaked. He looked down at it, surprised, then adjusted his position. The chair squeaked again. "Sorry. The chair seems upset with me."

Several people in the office had noticed the new person at Chelsea's desk. Tyler walked by slowly, staring openly at the dinosaur shirt. Priya glanced over from her desk, eyebrows raised. Marcus did a double-take at the cartoon pencil belt.

Mara returned to her office and waited.

Five minutes later, her phone rang.

"Mara, I have bad news." Karen sounded miserable. "I called Benjamin Rozen, the correct one, with the Z, and he's not available. He has been working at another company for years. He's no longer on the market."

"I see."

"I'm so incredibly sorry about this mix-up. This is entirely on me. I should have double-checked the number. I should have verified it, knowing we are having glitches with the new program."

"What's done is done. What's our next step?"

"I can start a new search immediately. Post the position again and reach out to recruiters. With Chelsea's experience requirements, it might take a little time to find the right candidate, but I'll move as fast as possible."

"How long?"

"Realistically? To find someone with Chelsea's level of experience? It could be two days or two weeks."

Two weeks. Two weeks without an assistant.

Mara looked out through her glass wall at Ben, who was now examining the desk drawer, pulling it open and closed experimentally, watching the mechanism as if it were fascinating.

"Two weeks is unacceptable, Karen."

"I know. I'm so sorry. But here's the thing," Karen's voice shifted, became almost pleading. "The kindergarten teacher, Ben Rosen, he's here, he applied for the position.

Technically, he passed our initial screening and his references were good."

"Karen, he's a kindergarten teacher."

"I know, but Mara, please hear me out. He has organizational skills. People management. A master's degree. Experience handling chaos, just different chaos. And he's available right now. Today. This minute."

"You cannot be suggesting..."

"Just for two days. Please, give me two days to search properly while he fills in temporarily. At least you'd have coverage for the immediate crisis, the board meeting is tomorrow, the Steele follow-up, you need someone at that desk."

Mara closed her eyes. This was unbelievable.

"He wears dinosaur shirts."

"I know."

"And his glasses are held together with medical tape."

"I saw."

"Karen, this is a terrible idea."

"I know, but it's the only idea I have right now. Please, two days. If he's awful, you fire him on Wednesday, and I'll keep searching. But if he's even marginally functional, he could buy us time. And Mara..." Karen's voice dropped. "You're going into a board meeting tomorrow. Richard Steele is calling this week. You can't do all of that with no administrative support. You know you can't."

She was right. Mara hated that she was right.

"Two days," Mara said. "And Karen, I need you to understand that if I fire him on Wednesday, that means I'm working with no assistant for potentially two more weeks. That's the trade-off you're asking me to make. Chaos now versus nothing later."

"I understand. And I'm going to search as fast as possible. But yes, that's the trade-off."

"Fine. Two days. Draft whatever paperwork you need. But make it very clear this is temporary and contingent on acceptable performance."

"Thank you. I'll have the offer letter ready in ten minutes. And Mara? I really am sorry about this whole mess."

Mara ended the call and walked back out to the main office.

Ben was now standing next to the desk, looking at the container of cookies he'd brought. He'd opened it and was rearranging them in a spiral pattern, moving each cookie with careful precision.

"Ben...There's been a misunderstanding with HR. They meant to hire a different Benjamin Rozen. Someone with corporate experience."

His face fell. "Oh. So, I should go?"

"Not exactly. HR has asked if you could stay temporarily. Two days. At the same time, they search for a permanent replacement. The position would be an executive assistant doing administrative support, calendar management, and basic office tasks."

His face transformed. It went from disappointed to delighted in under a second.

"Really? I can stay. For two days?"

"Two days. After that, we'll evaluate your performance. If it's not working, we'll part ways, and I'll manage without an assistant until HR finds someone qualified. If you're functional, you might stay longer while they continue searching. But I need you to understand that this is temporary. Very temporary."

"I understand! Temporary! I'm great at temporary! I once substitute-taught for six weeks. That's basically a professional temporary. I can totally do this, I'm very organized. I manage twenty-four kindergarteners every day. That's like herding chaos. This will be, well, different chaos. But manageable. Probably."

Mara had serious doubts about this decision.

But she didn't have a choice. The board meeting was tomorrow. Richard Steele would call this week. She needed someone at that desk, even if that someone wore dinosaur shirts and had glasses that were taped together.

"Your first task is to answer the phone when it rings and take messages. Can you do that?"

"Absolutely. I'm excellent at answering phones. I answer my phone constantly. Well, one phone. My phone. But the principle is the same, right?"

"Second task. Familiarize yourself with the calendar system. Chelsea left documentation in the desk drawer. Read it and figure out how to add appointments."

"Got it. Calendar system. Documentation. I'm great with documentation. I document everything. My sister says I over-document. She's probably right."

"Third task. Coffee. I drink coffee after nine AM. There's a coffee maker in the kitchen. Figure out how to use it."

"Coffee. Kitchen. After nine. Easy. I make coffee every morning. Well, usually I make it wrong, and it tastes like sadness, but I make it."

This was a terrible idea.

But she was committed now. Two days…she could survive two days.

"I'll be in my office. If you have questions, write them down and ask them all at once instead of interrupting constantly."

"Write down questions. Ask once. No constant interruptions. I can do that."

Mara returned to her office and closed the door.

Through the glass wall, she watched Ben settle into Chelsea's chair. He pulled out the documentation Chelsea had left: a neatly organized three-ring binder with color-coded tabs. Ben opened it and started reading, his lips moving slightly as he processed the information.

This was going to be a very long two days.

And if he failed, it would be an even longer two weeks alone.

***

By 10:30 AM, Ben had already caused three minor disasters.

First, he'd answered the phone wrong. The office line rang, and Ben picked up with: "Hello! VibeGuide! This is Ben! How may I brighten your day?"

Mara had heard it from her office and had closed her eyes and counted to ten.

The correct answer was: "VibeGuide, Ben speaking, how may I help you?"

Professional. Simple. Standard.

Not "how may I brighten your day?"

Second, he'd made coffee. Mara had heard the coffee maker gurgling, then Ben's voice saying, "oh no" very quietly. When she'd gone to investigate, the kitchen counter was covered in coffee grounds. The filter had apparently collapsed, dumping grounds into the pot. Ben was cleaning it up with paper towels, looking distressed.

"I'm so sorry. The filter betrayed me. I'll fix this. I promise. Coffee is coming. Eventually."

Third, he'd color-coded her calendar.

Mara hadn't asked him to do it. But when she'd walked past his desk, she noticed he had color-coded her calendar, and it looked like a rainbow of primary colors.

"What are you doing?"

He jumped and dropped a box of paperclips. They scattered across the floor in a metallic rain.

"Oh! Hi! Sorry. I was just…your calendar needed to be organized by types of meetings, it would be so much easier for you to tell what you have going on. I reorganized it by meeting type and aesthetic appeal. So, like, personal meetings are green. Shareholder meetings are red, because they are important, and client meetings are yellow because you need to prepare, and…" He stopped. "You didn't ask me to do this, did you?"

"No."

"Should I put it back?"

"Just finish what you started and then start reading Chelsea's documentation."

"Right. Yes. Absolutely. Finishing and reading. That's what I'll do."

Mara walked back to her office.

At 11:00, Tyler appeared in her doorway.

"What's with the new guy?"

"Temporary assistant. Two days."

"He's wearing dinosaurs."

"I'm aware."

"And he made a feelings wall in the break room."

Mara's head snapped up. "He made a what?"

"A feelings wall. Like, he put up a big sheet of paper and wrote 'How are you feeling today?' at the top. Then he put sticky notes and pens underneath. He told me it's for emotional processing. Said everyone needs a safe space to express feelings."

"He's been here for two hours."

"Yeah, and he's already trying to make us share our feelings. It's weird."

"I'll address it."

Mara walked to the break room.

Sure enough, there was a large piece of white poster board taped to the wall. "HOW ARE YOU FEELING TODAY?" was written across the top in cheerful block letters. Below it, a stack of sticky notes in various colors and a cup of pens.

Ben stood next to it, looking pleased with himself.

"What is this?" Mara asked.

"A feelings wall! Studies show that emotional expression in the workplace increases job satisfaction and reduces stress. People can write their feelings on sticky notes and post them anonymously. It creates a sense of community and shared experience."

"This is a corporate office, not a kindergarten classroom."

"But feelings are universal. Adults have feelings too. Sometimes, even more complicated feelings than kids. Like, yesterday I was feeling anxious about this interview, and I wrote it on a sticky note and posted it on my fridge, and it really helped."

"No feelings wall."

"But..."

"Ben, this is a professional environment. We don't post our feelings on the wall."

"Okay." He looked genuinely disappointed. "Should I take it down?"

"Yes."

"What if I made it optional? Like, no pressure, but it's there if people need it?"

"Take it down."

"Okay. Taking it down. Right now."

He started peeling the poster board off the wall. The tape resisted. He pulled harder. The paper tore.

"Sorry. The tape is very committed to the wall. This might take a minute."

Mara laughed to herself and returned to her office.

At 11:48, her phone rang. Internal line.

"Yes?"

"Mara, it's Priya. Is the new assistant supposed to be in the server room?"

"Why would he be in the server room?"

"I don't know, but he's in here. He said something about checking the temperature because servers need optimal conditions."

Mara stood up and walked to the server room. She found Ben standing inside, holding a small handheld thermometer, looking at the equipment with intense concentration.

"Ben, what are you doing?"

"Checking the temperature! Servers are very sensitive to heat. If they get too hot, bad things happen. I read about it online. Thought I should make sure everything's okay in here."

"That's not part of your job."

"Oh. Should someone be checking, though? Like, regularly? Because this seems important."

"The IT team handles server maintenance."

"Oh, good. That's good. They're probably much better at it than I am." He looked at the thermometer. "It's seventy-two degrees in here, by the way. That seems fine. I think. I'm really not sure what temperature servers like. I should probably leave now."

"That would be wise."

By noon, Mara had a headache.

Ben meant well. That was clear. He was enthusiastic, trying hard, and wanted to be helpful.

But he was also a walking disaster who had no concept of professional boundaries or corporate norms. He treated the office like an extension of his kindergarten classroom. Everything was an opportunity for improvement, organization, and emotional processing.

At 12:15, she saw him distributing something at people's desks.

She walked out to investigate.

Gold stars.

He was giving people gold stars!

Actual metallic gold star stickers, the kind teachers put on good homework!

"What are you doing?"

He turned, holding a sheet of stars. "Positive reinforcement! I gave Tyler a gold star for excellent email response time. Priya got one for solving that backend issue. Marcus got one for hitting his sales target.

"Ben, these are adults. Not kindergarteners."

"Adults like recognition, too! Everyone wants to feel appreciated. Gold stars are a simple, tangible way to say 'good job.' It's psychology."

Tyler walked by, a gold star stuck to his laptop. He saw Mara looking and shrugged. "I mean, it's weird. But also, kind of nice? I did respond to that email really fast."

"See?" Ben said. "It's working!"

Mara closed her eyes and took a breath. "Ben, come to my office, please."

He followed her, still holding the sheet of gold stars. She closed the door.

"Ben, you're very enthusiastic. I appreciate that. But you need to understand something about corporate environments. We have different norms here than in kindergarten classrooms."

"Right. More serious. More professional. I get that."

"Do you? Because in the last three hours, you've made a 'feelings wall,' checked the server room temperature, reorganized my calendar, and given grown adults gold stars."

"When you list it like that, it sounds like a lot."

"It is a lot. You're here to provide administrative support. Answer phones. 'Manage' my calendar. Handle correspondence. Not to reorganize the entire office according to kindergarten principles."

"Okay. I understand. Administrative support. Just the basics. No more organizational improvements."

"Correct."

"And no more gold stars?"

"No more gold stars."

He looked genuinely sad about this. "But people really liked them. Tyler said it made his day."

"Tyler is easily impressed."

"Still. It's nice to make people's days better, even in small ways."

Mara softened slightly. He meant well. That was the problem, really. He meant well and didn't understand why his well-meaning initiatives were inappropriate.

"Ben, I understand you want to help. But right now, the most helpful thing you can do is stick to the basic job responsibilities. Answer phones professionally. Manage the calendar. Take messages. Can you do that?"

"Yes. Absolutely. Basic responsibilities. I can do basic."

"Good. Now, please return to your desk and read the rest of Chelsea's documentation. I have a meeting in ten minutes."

"On it."

He left.

Mara sat at her desk and wondered how she was going to survive two days of this.

***

Monday afternoon was slightly better. Slightly.

Ben answered the phone correctly, or mostly correctly. He still said "VibeGuide, Ben speaking" with too much enthusiasm, but at least he'd dropped the "brighten your day" nonsense.

He figured out the calendar system. Added appointments where Mara requested them. Only made one mistake. He scheduled a meeting with an investor for 3 AM instead of 3 PM, but caught it himself and fixed it before Mara noticed.

He made coffee successfully on the second attempt. Brought Mara a cup without being asked. It was weak and slightly burnt, but it was coffee.

"I wasn't sure how you take it," he said, setting it on her desk. "So, I made it medium strength. If you want it to be stronger, I can remake it. Or weaker. I can make it any strength. I'm very flexible about coffee strength."

"This is fine. Thank you."

"You're welcome! Also, you have a meeting at three with Eliza. She confirmed. And Richard Steele's assistant called. Jennifer. She said Richard will call you tomorrow to discuss the next steps. I wrote down all the details." He handed her a sticky note with neat handwriting. "Also, I put a reminder in your calendar even though Jennifer said Richard would call you, because redundancy is helpful."

"That's actually very thorough. Thank you."

His whole face lit up. "Really? I did something right?"

"You did several things right."

"That's amazing! Wow. Okay. I'm going to go back to my desk and keep doing things right. This is the best day."

He practically bounced out of her office.

Mara looked at the sticky note. The information was clear and organized. The calendar reminder was appropriately titled. He handled the call professionally.

Maybe this wouldn't be a complete disaster.

At 3:00, Eliza arrived for their meeting. She stopped at Ben's desk first.

Mara could hear them talking through her glass wall.

"You must be the new assistant," Eliza said.

"Temporary assistant! I'm Ben. I'm here for two days while they find someone qualified, which is fine. Two days is good. I like temporary things. Very low pressure."

"What's with the dinosaur shirt?"

"Oh! I teach kindergarten, taught kindergarten. Past tense now, I guess. Maybe. For two days. Anyway, the kids love dinosaurs, so I have a lot of dinosaur shirts. This one's my favorite. See the T-rex? He's wearing a tiny party hat. Very festive."

Eliza looked at the shirt more closely. "That's actually kind of great."

"Thank you! Most people don't appreciate dinosaur fashion."

Eliza walked into Mara's office, closed the door, and immediately started laughing.

"Where did you find him?"

"HR mistake. They hired the wrong Ben."

"He's wearing dinosaurs and cartoon belt buckles."

"I'm aware."

"And he's adorable."

"He's temporary. He's been here for six hours and already made a feelings wall."

Eliza laughed harder. "A feelings wall? In a corporate office?"

"I made him take it down."

"That's amazing, I kind of love him."

"Don't love him. He's here for two days, and then Karen is finding someone qualified."

"Qualified is boring. This guy has a T-rex in a party hat on his shirt. That's not boring."

They spent the next hour reviewing the Q4 marketing strategy. Normal work discussion. Professional and productive.

Ben was color-coding something. She could see him through the glass wall, sitting at Chelsea's desk with a box of crayons, actual crayons, organizing something with all kinds of sticky notes and colors.

After the meeting, Eliza stopped at Ben's desk again.

"What are you doing?"

"Color-coding the paperwork I have to fill out!

"You're using crayons."

"They're very effective! And they smell good. This one's periwinkle. Smell it."

He held out a crayon. Eliza, to Mara's surprise, really smelled it.

"That does smell good."

"Right? Crayons are underrated in professional settings."

Eliza popped her head back into Mara's office. "Okay, I officially love him. Please keep him."

"He's temporary."

"He color-codes with crayons and offers people smell tests. That's the best thing that's happened to this office in months."

"That's concerning."

"I'm serious. Chelsea was great, professional, efficient, and perfect. But she was also kind of serious all the time. This guy is fun; the office needs fun."

"The office needs competent."

"Can't it have both?"

"He's not experienced enough."

After Eliza left, Mara returned to work. She tried to focus on tomorrow's board presentation, but she kept looking up at Ben through the glass wall.

He was singing while he worked. Some tune she didn't recognize, off-key and cheerful. His glasses kept sliding down, and he kept pushing them up with one finger, totally unconscious of the repetition.

At the end of the workday, most people started packing up. But Mara was still working. She always worked late.

At 6:15, Ben appeared in her doorway.

"Hi. I'm heading out, but I wanted to check if you need anything before I go."

"I'm fine. Thank you."

"Have you eaten today? Like, actual food? Not just coffee?"

"I had lunch."

"When?"

Mara tried to remember. "Around one."

"That was almost six hours ago. That's a long time. You should eat dinner. Food is important, especially if your brain is working very hard."

"I'll eat when I get home."

"When will that be?"

"Eight or nine."

"That's a long time to wait! What if I ordered you something? I could order food and have it delivered here. Then you could eat while you work. Very efficient."

"That's not necessary."

"But it would help. And I'm supposed to be helping. That's literally the job…helping."

He looked so earnest. So genuinely concerned about whether she'd eaten.

"Fine," Mara said. "There's a Thai place two blocks away. They deliver. Order whatever arrives quickly."

"On it! What do you like? Noodles? Rice? Spicy? Not spicy? I need parameters."

"Pad Thai. No cilantro. Not too spicy."

"Perfect. Pad Thai, no cilantro, mild spice level. Coming right up. Well, it will probably come in thirty minutes. Thai food takes time. But it's coming!"

He pulled out his phone and started searching for the restaurant. Twenty-seven minutes later, a delivery person arrived with Thai food. Ben brought it to her office. Set it on her desk with a napkin and plastic utensils.

"Pad Thai, no cilantro, mild spice level as requested. I got you spring rolls because everyone likes spring rolls. They're like universal food."

"Thank you. You can go home now."

"Are you sure? I can stay if you need help with anything."

"I'm sure. See you tomorrow."

"Okay. But Mara?"

"Yes?"

"You should go home soon, too. Working until nine isn't healthy. Studies show that overworking decreases productivity and increases stress, and you need sleep. Sleep is when your brain processes information and consolidates memories. It's very important."

"I'll keep that in mind."

"Okay. Just saying. As your temporary assistant. Temporarily caring about your wellbeing."

He left.

Mara sat at her desk with the Thai food and wondered what to make of Ben Rosen. He was chaos incarnate. Inappropriate, unprofessional, completely unsuited for a corporate environment.

But he'd also noticed she hadn't eaten and had ordered her food. Had stayed late to make sure she was taken care of.

Small things.

Different small things from Chelsea's small things. But still, small things that mattered.

She opened the Thai food and started eating. It was good. The spring rolls were excellent.

She ate, worked, and tried not to think about how the office felt different with Ben in it.

Tomorrow will be day two. One more day of chaos, and then Karen would find someone qualified.

Someone professional.

Someone who didn't wear dinosaurs, use crayons, or make feelings walls.

Someone appropriate for a CEO's assistant.

She finished the Thai food and went back to work.

Outside, the city darkened and lit up with evening lights.

And somewhere, Ben went home to wherever kindergarten teachers who wore cartoon belts lived, probably thinking he'd done a decent job on his first day.

He had no idea that Mara was already dreading tomorrow.

CHAPTER 3

Tuesday, Mara arrived to find Ben already at Chelsea's desk.

He wore different dinosaurs today. These were more scientifically accurate ones with muted greens and browns. The cardigan was olive green. The belt buckle was a cartoon stapler.

A cartoon stapler.

He looked up when she approached. "Morning! I brought more cookies. Chocolate chip this time. My sister says they're life-changing. She's biased, but I think they're pretty good. Want one?"

"No, thank you."

"Okay, but they're there if you change your mind. Also, your hot water with lemon is ready. I made it hotter today because yesterday's wasn't hot enough."

He handed her a mug. She took a cautious sip.

It was good. Truly good. The right temperature, perfect with fresh lemon.

"This is perfect."

"Really?" His whole face lit up. "On day two? That's amazing! Yesterday's was terrible, today's is perfect. I'm improving. This is very encouraging."

"Yes. Thank you."

"You're welcome! Don't forget that Richard Steele is calling you at 2 this afternoon. I set a reminder for 1:45 so you have time to prepare. I put a note with talking points I thought might be useful based on the meeting notes from last Friday. But you can ignore those if they're stupid. They might be stupid. I don't know venture capital stuff. I know kindergarten stuff."

She looked at the note. The talking points were quite good. Elementary, but relevant.

"These are helpful. Thank you."

"Really? They're not stupid?"

"They're appropriate."

He beamed like she'd given him a gold star instead of basic professional feedback.

At 9:30, the weekly team meeting started.

Everyone gathered in the conference room. Mara sat at the head of the table; her team arranged around her. Tyler from Marketing, Priya from Engineering, Marcus from Sales, Sarah from Product, and Eliza from Marketing. The core team.

Ben slipped in quietly and sat in the back corner with a notebook. The same cartoon-covered notebook he'd been using yesterday.

"What's he doing here?" Marcus asked.

"Taking notes," Mara said. "That's part of his role."

The meeting proceeded normally: Q4 strategy discussion, Metrics review, Project updates.

Halfway through, Priya explained a problem with the backend architecture. It was complex, technical, and boring to everyone who wasn't an engineer.

"Therefore, we're stuck," Priya concluded. "We can't move forward until we solve the integration issue but solving it requires more time than we have."

Everyone sat in silence, trying to come up with solutions.

Ben raised his hand.

Everyone turned to look at him.

"Yes?" Mara said.

"What if you broke it into smaller pieces?"

"What do you mean?"

"Like, instead of solving the whole integration problem at once, what if you tackled one piece at a time? Small chunks instead of one big overwhelming thing. We do that in kindergarten all the time. Big projects get broken into small, manageable tasks. Then kids don't get overwhelmed, and they actually finish stuff."

Priya frowned, thinking. "We can't really break backend architecture into discrete chunks. It's all interconnected."

"But you could break the testing into chunks, right? Like, test one feature at a time instead of testing everything together. Run them in parallel instead of sequentially."

The room went quiet.

"That could work," Priya said slowly. "We'd still need to integrate at the end, but if we ran parallel testing tracks instead of sequential…"

"Exactly!" Ben looked excited. "Everyone works on their piece independently, then you put it together. Like a puzzle. Or a class mural. Same principle, different scale."

Tyler laughed. "Did you just solve our backend problem with a kindergarten analogy?"

"I mean, maybe? Problem-solving is problem-solving, right?"

Priya was typing on her laptop, working through the implications. "This actually works. If we split into three parallel tracks, we could cut testing time by sixty percent."

"See?" Ben said. "Kindergarten wisdom strikes again."

The meeting continued. Ben took notes in his cartoon notebook. "Can I ask something else?"

"Go ahead," Mara said.

"The user feedback. The written responses from real people using the app. Where does that live? Like, physically? Because I've been thinking it would help to see it every day. Not in a spreadsheet. Just up on a wall somewhere. So you're always looking at who you're actually building this for." He paused. "We did that in my classroom. Put the kids' work on the walls so we never forgot who the room was for. Might be stupid at this scale."

"It's not stupid," Sarah said, writing something down.

Tyler was already nodding. "I could design something for the main workspace."

"Okay," Mara said. "Let's come back to it."

After the meeting, Tyler pulled Mara aside.

"Okay, the new guy is weird. But he might also be kind of smart?"

"He's temporary."

"You keep saying that, but he literally just solved our backend problem."

"He suggested breaking a complex task into smaller pieces. That's not revolutionary."

"But we didn't think of it. He did, in like thirty seconds."

Mara didn't have a response to that.

At noon, Ben appeared in her doorway with a sandwich, an apple, and a gold star sticker pressed to the apple's skin. "It's a fruit," he said. "Studies show…

actually, you know what, never mind the studies. Just eat." He left before she could respond.

At 1:45, her calendar reminder popped up. "STEELE CALL - 2:00 PM."

Below it, Ben had added: "You're going to be great. He's lucky to invest in you."

It was unprofessional, overly familiar, and not the kind of thing an assistant should put in a CEO's calendar. But it made her smile anyway.

At 2PM, Richard Steele called.

The conversation lasted forty-seven minutes. He asked more questions. She provided more answers. At the end, he said the words she'd been hoping to hear.

"We're prepared to move forward with the investment. My team will send over term sheets by the end of the week."

After the call, Mara sat at her desk and processed what had just happened.

They had funding! Arch Venture Capital was investing. VibeGuide was moving to the next level.

She should tell someone. Should celebrate. Should…

Ben appeared in her doorway.

"How'd it go? You were on the phone for a long time. That seemed good. Long calls usually mean good news. Or bad news. But your face doesn't look like bad news face. So I'm guessing good news?"

"We got the funding!"

"WHAT? THAT'S AMAZING!" He jumped, literally jumped up off the ground. "That's incredible! Congratulations! This is huge! You're getting thirty million dollars! That's so much money! That's like…" He paused, calculating. "…so many things! I don't even know what you'd buy with thirty million dollars! Probably not dinosaur shirts! Different stuff! Important stuff!"

He grabbed his gold stars and stuck one on her lapel!

Despite herself, Mara laughed. "Yes. Important stuff."

"We should celebrate! The team should know! This is big news!"

"We'll tell them at the next all-hands meeting."

"That's Friday. That's three days away. You have to sit on this amazing news for three days? That's torture."

"It's professional."

"It's sad, you should celebrate now, even just a little bit. Like, smile. Or do a small dance. Or eat a cookie. I brought cookies. They're very celebratory."

"I'm not going to dance."

"Okay, but what about smiling? That's very easy. I can teach you if you've forgotten how."

"I know how to smile."

"Prove it."

She smiled. Small, but genuine.

"There it is! A real Mara smile! I feel very accomplished right now."

"Go back to your desk, Ben."

"Going back to my desk. But I'm proud of you; this is a big deal. You should be proud, too."

He left.

Mara sat at her desk and tried to process the day.

Ben had solved their backend problem. Had brought her lunch. Had made her smile after getting the biggest funding win of her career.

And tomorrow was day three.

Except it wasn't supposed to be day three. Two days of Ben, then Karen would find someone qualified.

Her phone buzzed. Karen.

Karen: *Bad news. I haven't found a qualified candidate yet. Everyone good is already employed or not interested. I need more time. Can you keep Ben for a bit longer? Maybe through the end of next week? I promise I'm searching hard, but this is taking longer than expected.*

Mara stared at the message.

End of next week. That was nine more days. Eleven days total with Ben, his dinosaurs, his crayons, and his feelings wall.

Two weeks of chaos.

Two weeks of inappropriate kindergarten methods.

Two weeks of Ben.

She typed back: *Fine. But please prioritize finding a qualified replacement.*

Karen: *Absolutely. Thank you for being flexible. I know this isn't ideal.*

Mara set down her phone.

Two weeks.

She could survive for two weeks.

Right?

CHAPTER 4

Mara arrived at the office on Wednesday and immediately knew something was wrong.

The familiar scent of coffee brewing hit her first. Then the hum of the HVAC system kicking on, normal. But there was something else. A rustling sound. Paper moving, lots of paper.

She walked through the main workspace. The morning light streamed through the tall windows, casting long rectangles across the polished concrete floors. The exposed brick walls still had that industrial-chic look the landlord charged extra for. Everything looked the same as yesterday.

Except Ben's desk.

Ben was already there, which was fine; early arrival showed initiative. His coffee mug sat next to his keyboard, and his cartoon notebook lay open, covered in his neat handwriting.

But surrounding him, covering every available surface, spilling onto the floor in messy piles, were files and papers. Hundreds of papers. Old file folders in manila and new colored file folders. Documents with official letterhead. printouts of spreadsheets. Sticky notes in every color.

And Ben was organizing them with crayons.

Not just color-coding the file folders but drawing on them. Little colored symbols in the corners of official company documents. He had gold stars, circles, and triangles in waxy primary colors that would never, ever come off.

He sat cross-legged on the floor, surrounded by paper like a kindergartener at craft time, humming to himself while he drew a green star on what looked like a very important contract.

"Ben, what are you doing?"

He looked up. His glasses immediately slid down his nose. Today's shirt featured cartoon robots. The cardigan was mustard yellow, suggesting a complete absence of regret. His hair stuck up on the left side like he'd slept on it wrong and never noticed.

"Morning!" He scrambled to his feet, nearly tripping over a pile of folders. "I'm creating a comprehensive filing system. See, I was reading Chelsea's documentation last night. She was excellent at her job, by the way. She said to organize by date and category. But that's two-dimensional thinking."

He gestured enthusiastically with a crayon. A green one. It left a small waxy mark in the air as if he were conducting an orchestra.

"I'm adding a third dimension. Priority level. Red file folders mean urgent, yellow means important but not urgent, grey means informational, purple means follow-up needed, and orange..." He paused, looking at the orange file folders like he'd forgotten what orange meant. "Orange is for fun stuff. Like birthday cards and team celebrations."

"Why are there papers everywhere?"

"Oh. Right. I started by pulling everything out to see what we had. You know, get the full picture. But then I realized the filing cabinet drawers are organized alphabetically, which doesn't match the chronological system in the digital files, and alphabetical filing doesn't account for urgency, so I'm creating a hybrid approach that..." He stopped. Looked at Mara's expression. "I should have asked before pulling everything out, shouldn't I?"

"Yes."

"And I probably shouldn't be drawing on official documents with crayons."

"Definitely not."

The morning sun caught the waxy star he'd drawn on the contract, making it shimmer. It looked permanent. It looked like something that would require explaining to an irate lawyer.

"Okay. Learning. Growing. Improving." He looked at the paper explosion around him, hundreds of file folders, years of company records, all scattered across the floor like a tornado had hit a filing cabinet. "Should I put it all back?"

"Please."

"In the old system or the new hybrid system? Because the new system is much more efficient if you just..."

"Ben, put it back exactly how you found it."

"But it could be better..."

"Exactly. How. You. Found. It."

"Okay, putting it back exactly as found. No improvements." He looked at the mess. At the sheer volume of paper. At the filing cabinet across the room, which would need to hold all of it. "This might take a while."

"Take all the time you need."

Mara walked into her office and closed the door. Through the glass wall, she could see Ben crouching down, starting to gather papers. He picked up a stack. They immediately slid out of his arms and scattered across the floor again. His glasses slid down his nose. He pushed them up with one hand while trying to hold papers with the other.

It was 8:00 AM on day three, and Ben had already created chaos.

She went to boil some hot water. The electric kettle was sleek and expensive; Chelsea had programmed it perfectly, now Mara had to figure it out herself.

***

At 9:30, she had a video call with an investor in New York. Robert Yang had invested in VibeGuide's Series A and was considering increasing his stake with the Arch funding news. The kind of call that required absolute focus and professionalism.

At 9:28, Ben knocked on her door.

"Quick question. The video call in two minutes. Do you want me to sit in and take notes?"

"No, I'll handle it."

"Okay. Should I hold your calls?"

"Yes."

"Got it. Holding calls, I can do that." He paused. "What does holding calls mean exactly? Like, do I answer them and tell people you're busy? Or do I just not answer them? Or do I answer them and transfer them to voicemail? Chelsea's documentation wasn't super clear on that."

"Answer them, take a message, tell them I'll call back."

"Perfect. Answering, messaging, promising callbacks. I'm on it."

He left.

At 9:30 exactly, Robert Yang appeared on screen. Manhattan skyline behind him. Glass and chrome desk. Charcoal suit. The kind of face that made decisions about who got to build companies and who didn't.

"Mara, good morning."

"Good morning, Robert. Thank you for taking the time."

"Of course. I wanted to discuss the Arch funding and what it means for existing investors. Richard Steele doesn't invest lightly. This changes VibeGuide's trajectory significantly."

"I agree. We're excited about the opportunities it creates for..."

Behind Mara, the office door opened.

She didn't turn around. But she saw Robert's expression shift, his eyes tracking something behind her.

Then Ben walked into frame. Carrying her coffee mug. He set it on her desk with a gentle clink, gave her a cheerful thumbs up, and walked back out.

On screen, Robert paused. "Was that your assistant?"

"Yes, new assistant. He's still learning protocols."

"I see." Robert's tone was neutral, but his expression was not.

They continued for another twenty minutes. Productive. Professional. But Mara felt Robert's doubt sitting across from her the entire time, patient and quiet, like a third party who hadn't been invited.

After he disconnected, Mara sat at her desk and stared at the blank screen.

Then she walked out to Ben's desk.

"I said to hold my calls."

He looked up. "I did! No calls came through. One hundred percent call-holding success rate."

"I also meant don't interrupt me during video calls."

"Oh." His face fell, the kind of genuine disappointment that made him look about twelve years old. "I didn't think about video calls. I was bringing you coffee because you didn't have any, and I thought you'd want some, and I remembered you drink coffee after nine AM, and it was 9:31, so technically after nine, and I thought I was being helpful."

"Ben, when I'm in a meeting, any meeting, video or in-person, you don't come in unless it's an emergency. That's standard professional protocol."

"Emergency, got it. What counts as an emergency?"

"Fire. Medical crisis. The building is collapsing."

"So not coffee."

"Not coffee."

"What about juice boxes? I brought juice boxes. They're in the break room. Very refreshing. Probably not emergency-level though."

"You brought juice boxes to work?"

"Yeah. They're great for afternoon energy slumps."

"Ben."

"Right. Not an emergency. Got it." He pulled out his cartoon notebook and wrote something down. "No interruptions unless building collapses or fire."

"That's not exactly what I said."

"Close enough, though, right? I'm simplifying for memory purposes. My sister says I over-complicate things. She's probably right. She's usually right about most things. Very annoying how often she's right."

Mara walked back to her office. She had work to do.

***

Ben appeared in her doorway holding a thick stack of paper.

Not documents, not files, but printed user feedback forms, the kind the team had been analyzing in a spreadsheet for three weeks. Someone had printed the raw responses for a meeting last month and left them in the break room. Ben had apparently found them and read all of them. He'd highlighted things in three different colors and written notes in the margins in his neat, slightly childlike handwriting.

"Can I ask you something work-related?" he said. "Something actual work-related, not reorganizing-related."

She looked up. "Yes."

He came in and set the stack on her desk. "I've been reading these. The user feedback from the onboarding study. And I noticed something."

"What did you notice?"

"Everyone who drops out does it at the same place. The breathing exercise screen. Step four." He pointed to a cluster of highlighted comments. She could see the pattern even from across the desk. A dozen variations of the same complaint: Didn't know what to do. Felt lost. Wasn't sure if it was working. Gave up.

"Engineering has been looking at that. There's a known latency issue on that screen."

"It's not the latency." He pulled up a chair without being asked. Something in his voice made her wait rather than correct him. "I know because the people who dropped out on the fast connection have the same complaint as the people who dropped out on the slow one. They're not saying it was slow. They're saying they didn't know if they were doing it right."

Mara looked at the highlighted responses again.

He was correct. The language was consistent across all of them: Felt lost. Wasn't sure. Didn't know if it was working. Not a single complaint about speed.

"It's a feedback problem," he said. "Not a tech problem. In my classroom, when kids got quiet and stopped trying something, it was never because the activity was too hard. It was because nobody told them they were doing it right. They needed to know they were on track or they'd just stop." He nodded at her open laptop. "Can I show you something?"

She turned the laptop toward him.

He navigated to the onboarding flow. Hit the breathing exercise. Held his breath for the required four seconds. The screen sat there, elegant and minimal, doing nothing. No indication he was being tracked. No signal that the timer was running. Just a white screen with an animated circle and a countdown you had to stare at to notice.

"See?" he said. "I don't know if it's working or if I'm doing it right. Nothing is telling me I am, so I'd stop." He looked at her. "What if the screen just said something while it's happening? Something small. Like, you're doing great, or keep going. Not annoying. Just there."

The room was quiet for a moment.

"That's a UX problem," Mara said. "Not a backend issue at all."

"I don't know what UX means. But yeah, probably something like that."

She looked at the feedback stack. At his highlighted clusters. At three weeks of engineering hours aimed at the wrong problem because nobody had read the raw responses and asked the obvious question.

She picked up her phone and called Priya.

"The breathing screen drop-off," she said when Priya answered. "Pull up the raw feedback from the onboarding study. Not the categorized data, the actual responses." A pause while Priya found it. "Tell me what word appears most."

She could hear typing.

"Lost," Priya said. "Or variations of it. Huh."

"How long would it take to add real-time feedback to that screen? Text, something brief, while the timer runs."

"A day. Maybe less. It's basically a copy change and a trigger event."

"Put it on the sprint." She hung up.

Ben was watching her with the expression of someone who wasn't sure if he was in trouble.

"That was good," she said. Not easily. But honestly.

His whole face changed. "Yeah?"

"Don't make it weird."

"I'm not making it weird. I'm just. Okay." He stood and gathered the feedback stack, straightening it against her desk. "I'll put these back in the break room."

"You can keep them."

He looked at her for a second. Then he nodded once, like he understood something she hadn't said directly, picked up the stack, and left.

Mara turned back to her laptop. Stared at the breathing screen, still open. The minimal white circle. The silent countdown.

A kindergarten teacher had just found the problem that a team of engineers had been chasing for three weeks.

She closed the app and went back to work.

***

At lunchtime, Ben reappeared with a sandwich and a Honeycrisp apple.

"How did you know those are my favorite?" she asked.

"I pay attention." He set it on her desk and left before she could respond.

Mara looked at the sandwich. At the apple. At the evidence that Ben was paying attention to things she hadn't asked him to notice.

She ate both.

***

The Thursday board meeting started at 9:00 AM sharp.

Mara had been awake since 5:30, reviewing her presentation one last time. The slides were perfect. Every metric checked. Every projection defensible. Every answer to every potential question prepared and rehearsed.

The conference room looked good in the morning light. The windows faced east, so sunshine streamed in, making everything look clean and bright. The reclaimed wood table gleamed. Fresh water glasses sat at each seat. The screen at the front of the room was ready, waiting for her laptop connection.

Five board members arrived by 8:58.

Gerald came first. Mid-sixties, silver hair, dark gray suit, tie that cost more than Ben's entire wardrobe. He always arrived early and always found something to criticize.

Behind him came Patricia, the only woman on the board. Late fifties, steel-gray bob, the kind of sharp intelligence in her eyes that made people think twice before saying something stupid. She'd been Mara's biggest advocate in the early days.

Then Robert from yesterday's video call. He nodded at Mara but didn't smile. Still judging. Still wondering.

Then David and James, both venture capitalists, both wearing the Silicon Valley uniform of expensive jeans and quarter-zips over button-downs.

And finally, Richard Steele. He walked in at 8:59, precisely one minute before the meeting started. Never early. Never late. He sat at the head of the table like he owned it.

Maybe he did.

At 9:00, Mara connected her laptop and started the presentation.

"Good morning. Today I'll be reviewing Q3 results, Q4 projections, and the implications of the Arch funding for our growth strategy."

At 9:02, the conference room door opened.

Everyone turned.

Ben walked in carrying a tray. Six coffee cups balanced precariously on it, wobbling as he walked. He wore a cardigan covered in tiny cats. Orange tabbies and gray Persians scattered across purple fabric. His khaki pants bunched over his shoes. His glasses sat crooked, the tape coming loose on one side.

He froze in the doorway. The coffee cups wobbled dangerously.

Yesterday, he'd thought bringing coffee to a video call was helpful. A board meeting, he'd reasoned on the way upstairs, was a longer meeting with more people, which meant they'd be more tired, which meant they'd need coffee more, which meant this was a better idea than yesterday, not a worse one. This logic had seemed sound in the elevator.

It did not seem sound now.

"Morning, everyone!" His voice came out too loud, too cheerful for a board meeting. "I brought coffee. I wasn't sure how everyone would take it, so I made a variety. There's regular, decaf, and one with extra espresso for anyone who needs a boost." He walked carefully to the table and set down the tray. The cups rattled. "I brought cookies too."

He pulled a container from under his arm. Opened it. The sweet smell of fresh-baked oatmeal raisin filled the room.

"Very hearty and healthy. Oatmeal has complex carbohydrates that provide sustained energy. Unlike simple sugars, which cause crashes. Very important for long meetings."

The board members stared at him. Then at the cookies. Then at Mara.

Richard Steele picked up one of the coffee cups. Took a sip. His expression didn't change, but Mara saw the slight disappointment around his eyes.

"This is very weak."

Ben's face fell. "Oh no. Is it? I made it medium strength. Should I make it stronger? I can remake it. How strong do you like it? Like, scale of one to ten? With ten being espresso and one being brown water?"

"That won't be necessary," Mara said. Her voice came out sharper than she intended. "Ben, thank you for the coffee. You can return to your desk now."

"Right. Yes. Returning to my desk." But he didn't move. He stood there looking at the board members with a concerned expression. "But if anyone needs anything, I'm right outside. Just call me. Or wave. I'll probably see you wave through the glass. I'm very observant. Usually. Sometimes. I try to be."

He backed toward the door. Bumped his hip against the door frame. The coffee cups rattled on the tray he'd left behind.

"Sorry. I'm a little clumsy. My sister says I should wear a helmet. She's joking. Mostly. Okay. Leaving now. Have a great meeting. You're going to do great, Mara!"

He gave her a double thumbs-up.

Then he left, pulling the door closed behind him.

The room sat in silence for a moment.

Gerald spoke first. His voice was carefully neutral. "That's your assistant?"

Mara felt her face getting hot. "Temporary assistant. HR is searching for a permanent replacement."

"He's very... enthusiastic."

"He's transitioning from a different industry, so he is still learning corporate norms."

Patricia reached for a cookie. Bit into it. Her eyebrows raised slightly. "These are actually really good."

Mara started the presentation again. Walking through Q3 results: customer acquisition up 17%, retention up 22%, revenue growth exceeding projections by 11%. Professional. Prepared. Exactly what they needed to hear.

Through the glass wall, she could see Ben at his desk, juggling phone calls that had apparently all arrived at once. He was writing on sticky notes, talking, losing the sticky notes, retrieving them, talking again. The scene had the quality of a man trying to keep multiple small fires from becoming one large one.

She kept presenting.

The meeting ended. The board approved the growth plan. Signed off on the Arch funding terms. Everything was professionally fine.

But Gerald pulled Mara aside afterward. He stood too close, using his height to intimidate, a classic power move. Mara held her ground.

"Mara, I understand you're in a transition period with staff. These things happen. But presentation matters. Especially now. VibeGuide is about to scale significantly with the Arch funding. We need professionalism at every level. Including reception."

Reception. He'd called Ben reception.

"I understand. HR is actively searching for a permanent replacement."

"Good, make it a priority. I'd hate for something as trivial as an incompetent assistant, cats and all, to undermine investor confidence."

After the board members left, Mara walked to Ben's desk.

He looked exhausted. His hair was messier than usual. His glasses sat sideways. Sticky notes covered every surface, the desk, the monitor, and even one stuck to his cardigan.

"That was intense," he said. "So many phone calls. I didn't know board meetings generated so many phone calls. Is that normal?"

"Yes. That's why it's important to handle them efficiently."

"I tried. I really tried. But some of them were talking very fast and using words I didn't understand. One person mentioned synergies, and I had to ask them to explain what that meant, and they seemed annoyed. What even is a synergy? Is that a business word or a made-up word?"

"It's a real business term."

"Oh. What does it mean?"

"It means when two things work together to be more effective than they would be separately."

"That's just working together. Why not just say we're working together?"

"Because businesspeople like complicated words."

"That's silly." He looked at her, then seemed to remember something. "Oh no. The board meeting. I walked in during the board meeting with coffee and cookies. That was wrong, wasn't it?"

"Yes."

"I thought the board members might be hungry. Meetings are long. People get hungry during long meetings. That's just biology. Food helps brain function." He paused. "And yesterday, with the video call, I thought bringing coffee was wrong because it was just two people, and interrupting a conversation between two people is rude. But a big meeting with lots of people seemed different. I had reasons."

"Board meetings are formal, Ben. You don't interrupt them with coffee service regardless of how many people are in the room. There are protocols. Professional standards."

"So, what should I do?"

"Read Chelsea's documentation, all of it. There's a section on meetings and appropriate staff behavior. Study it."

"Okay. I'll read it tonight. All of it. I promise. I'll take notes, I'll make flashcards, I'll create a study guide, whatever it takes." He looked genuinely miserable. "I keep messing up. I don't mean to. I'm trying so hard to get this right, but I keep doing things wrong."

Mara softened slightly. He looked like a kid who'd just realized he'd failed a test he thought he'd aced.

"Just read the documentation. Learn the protocols. And Ben?"

"Yeah?"

"Maybe don't wear the cat cardigan to work anymore."

"But it's my favorite cardigan. The cats are smiling. See?" He pointed at a particularly cheerful orange tabby on his sleeve. "Happy cats."

"Exactly."

After she returned to her office, Mara reminded herself of Gerald's words. Incompetent assistant. Undermine investor confidence.

He was right. Ben was undermining her credibility. Every meeting he crashed. Every inappropriate outfit. Every failure to handle basic tasks. She was fighting to be taken seriously as a young woman CEO. Ben made that fight harder.

* * *

By Friday at 3:00 PM, Mara had made a decision. She was going to fire Ben.

The week had been a disaster. He'd ruined documents with crayons, interrupted a video call, and crashed a board meeting. He couldn't answer phones properly, spilled coffee, and gave people gold stars like they were kindergarteners.

Karen hadn't found a replacement yet, but that was fine. Mara would manage alone. She'd managed before Chelsea. She could manage again.

She was drafting the termination email to HR when Priya appeared in her doorway.

Priya was thirty-one, rail-thin, with dark hair always pulled back in a ponytail. She wore jeans and a VibeGuide hoodie today. She looked exhausted, the kind of exhaustion that came from debugging code for ten hours straight.

"Got a minute?"

"Of course."

Priya came in and closed the door. Sat in one of the visitor chairs. Mara noticed she was wearing a gold star on her lapel. Where everyone could see it.

"Are you firing Ben?"

Mara paused mid-typing. "What makes you think that?"

"Tyler saw you, through the window, emailing HR. He told Sarah, and Sarah told me. The office gossip mill is very efficient. So, are you?"

"He's not working out. You saw the board meeting yesterday. Gerald's concerns were valid."

"Gerald is always concerned about something. Last quarter, he was concerned about our logo font. He said it looked 'too playful' for enterprise clients. The man finds problems in everything."

"This isn't about Gerald. It's about Ben being inappropriate for the role."

Priya leaned back in the chair and crossed her arms. "Okay. Can I say something? And you can tell me if it's not my business, but I'm saying it anyway."

"Go ahead."

"Don't fire him."

"Priya..."

"Hear me out. Yes, he's weird. Yes, he wears dinosaurs and cats and whatever other cartoons he owns. Yes, he crashes board meetings and probably doesn't know what half the business jargon means. But Mara, the team loves him."

"The team doesn't understand professional standards."

"The team understands that they're happier. Sarah told me yesterday that she's actually enjoying coming to work again. Tyler said the same thing. Even Marcus, Marcus who complains about literally everything, said Ben makes the office feel less corporate and more human."

"We are a corporation. We should feel corporate."

"Should we? Or should we feel like a place where people want to work?" Priya adjusted her glasses, the gesture she always made when preparing an argument. "Look, Chelsea was great. Professional, efficient, perfect. But she also made this place feel sterile. Everything was serious all the time. Ben makes it fun. He brings cookies and gives people gold stars, and he does it because he cares. The team responds to that. It's what we built this app around."

"Caring isn't enough. I need competence."

"He found the onboarding problem on Tuesday. That was competent."

"He noticed a pattern in user language. That's not the same as solving it."

"But we didn't notice it. He did, in an afternoon, reading printouts from the break room because he wanted to understand the product." Priya stood up. Walked to the window and looked out at the city. "You know what I realized yesterday? I've been working here for three years. Three years. And before Ben, I couldn't remember the last time I genuinely laughed at work. Like, really laughed. Not polite meeting laughter, real laughter."

"When did you laugh?"

"Ben was trying to fix the coffee maker. Couldn't figure out which button did what. He pressed every button in sequence. The machine made this horrible grinding noise, and he jumped back and yelled, 'I'M SORRY' at the coffee maker. Like he'd hurt its feelings. It was the funniest thing I'd seen in months."

Despite herself, Mara smiled slightly.

"See?" Priya said. "That's what I mean. He makes things lighter. And yeah, he's not great at the assistant stuff. You're right about that. But maybe he doesn't need to be your assistant. Maybe he needs to be just Ben."

After Priya left, Mara sat at her desk and stared at her computer screen.

The termination email was drafted. She just needed to send it.

But Priya's words stayed with her. The team loves him. The office is better with him in it.

Did that matter? Should that matter?

At 4:00, she walked to the kitchen. The break room looked different from how it was on Monday. Small changes. The coffee supplies were organized in a way that actually made sense now: cups near the machine, stirrers in a container next to them, sugar and cream in a neat row. Someone had hung a plant in the window, a Spider plant with trailing vines. The chairs were arranged to encourage conversation instead of facing away from each other.

Ben changes.

Sarah from Product was at the counter making coffee. She was twenty-seven, short, with bright pink streaks in her black hair. She looked up when Mara entered and smiled. A real smile. Genuine. The kind Sarah hadn't given in months.

"Hey. Tyler's almost done with the design for the feedback wall. The one Ben suggested in the meeting on Tuesday. We're putting it in the main workspace."

"That's good."

"Right? He thinks like a teacher, not like a tech person. But sometimes that's exactly what we need."

Mara made her coffee and walked back to her office.

Everywhere she looked, she saw evidence of Ben's influence. Priya was humming at her desk. Priya, who usually worked in intense silence. Marcus laughing at something on his phone instead of scowling at spreadsheets. Tyler wearing not one but three gold stars on his laptop, seemingly proud of all of them.

The office felt different. Lighter. Happier.

But different and lighter weren't professional. They weren't appropriate for a company about to scale significantly with thirty million dollars in new funding.

***

At 5:00, most people started packing up.

Ben packed up his things: the cartoon notebook, the thermos shaped like a penguin, the jacket that was three sizes too big for him and made him look like a kid wearing his dad's clothes.

He stopped at Mara's office door and knocked quietly.

"Have a good weekend. And Mara?"

"Yes?"

"I know I messed up this week. The board meeting, the video call, all of it. I'm trying to get better." His expression was completely sincere.

He left before she could say anything else.

Mara sat at her desk, looking at the termination email on her screen.

Then she closed it without sending it.

She'd give him the weekend.

Think about it more.

Decide on Monday.

Maybe.

CHAPTER 5

Mara arrived on Monday determined to be objective about Ben.

She'd spent the weekend thinking, making lists, weighing pros and cons with the kind of systematic analysis she'd use for any business decision.

PRO: The team liked him. Measurably liked him. Office morale was demonstrably higher.

CON: He was unprofessional. Repeatedly. Consistently. Almost impressively unprofessional, given how much he was trying.

PRO: He occasionally saw things nobody else did. The onboarding feedback. The user feedback wall. The supply closet was better now, she'd noticed, even if nobody had asked him to touch it.

CON: Meaning well wasn't enough. Couldn't be enough. Not when you were trying to run a real company with real investor expectations.

She'd come to no conclusions, just more confusion.

Ben was already at his desk when she walked past. He looked different today. Still inappropriate, but differently inappropriate.

He wore a button-down shirt covered in tiny books. Little leather-bound volumes scattered across light gray fabric. His cardigan was forest green and less wrinkled than usual. His pants were still khaki, but they'd been ironed. Normal belt this time.

His glasses were still taped together, but the tape looked fresh and carefully wrapped.

"Morning! Good weekend?"

"Fine. Yours?"

"Great! I went to the museum with my sister Jade. They had an exhibit on ancient Rome. Did you know Roman concrete was better than modern concrete? Their buildings from two thousand years ago are still standing, while our modern stuff starts crumbling after fifty years. History is wild." He paused, switching gears without taking a breath. "I spent yesterday reading all of Chelsea's documentation, the whole thing, cover to cover. It took six hours. I made detailed notes and created study guides with color-coded sections. I'm ready to be better this week. Much better. Significantly better. Measurably better."

"That's good to hear."

"I brought muffins today, blueberry. I made them last night. Baking helps me process information. It's like meditation but with flour."

Despite herself, Mara almost smiled.

The morning proceeded almost normally.

Ben answered phones correctly this time. Mostly correctly. He said "VibeGuide, Ben speaking" with only slightly too much enthusiasm. He managed the calendar without significant errors. Added a 2 PM appointment with a venture capital firm, set an alert, sent a reminder. She noticed she kind of liked the color-coded appointments. She could just glance at them now and know what kind of meeting was coming up.

He brought her coffee at exactly 9:07, the right temperature and strength.

"Here you go. Medium-strong, no sugar, splash of cream. I asked everyone last week how you take your coffee. Conducted informal surveys. Gathered data. Very scientific."

"You asked people how I take my coffee?"

"Yeah. Tyler said black, but Priya said you sometimes add cream, and Eliza said you vary it based on how tired you are. I went with medium-strong with cream as a safe bet. Was I right?"

"You were right."

"YES!" He fist-pumped. "Coffee success! I'm getting better at this! Professional competence is happening!"

***

At 11:30, she had a meeting with Eliza about Q4 marketing strategy.

Ben knocked before entering and waited for permission.

"Sorry to interrupt. A package arrived for you, and it requires a signature. Do you want me to sign or should I bring it in?"

"You can sign."

"Got it. Signing. Being helpful. Not interrupting unnecessarily. Following protocols." He paused. "Also, you have a 12 PM with Sequoia Capital. They're fifteen minutes early. Should I tell them you're running on time or offer them coffee in the lobby?"

That was exactly right, exactly what Chelsea would have done.

"Offer them coffee. Tell them I'll be ready at noon."

"On it!"

He left.

Eliza stared at the closed door. "Was that Ben being competent?"

"Apparently, he spent yesterday studying Chelsea's documentation."

"Wow, character growth, I'm impressed."

"Don't be too impressed. The week's not over yet."

Later that day, Karen called with an update on the assistant search.

"I've interviewed five candidates. None are right. One wanted fifty percent more than we budgeted. One had availability issues and couldn't start for two months. One seemed great until I checked references and found out she'd been fired from her last two positions. One is moving to New York next month. And one just gave me bad vibes. I can't explain it, but something was off."

"How much longer will this take?"

"At least another week, maybe two. The market is really competitive right now. Every tech company is hiring, and everyone wants experienced executive assistants. I'm being thorough because you need someone excellent."

After the call, Mara processed what that meant.

Two more weeks minimum. Two more weeks of Ben or two more weeks alone.

She'd keep him a little longer. Chaotic coverage was better than none.

At 5:36, Ben appeared in her doorway. Still wearing the book shirt, but more wrinkled now. Glasses slightly crooked again. Hair stuck up on one side.

But he looked pleased with himself.

"I managed the whole day without major disasters! No interrupted video calls. No crashed meetings. Proper phone protocol. Successful coffee delivery. I even handled that weird situation with the delivery guy who couldn't find the office." He paused. "Okay, one of those messages might have been slightly wrong. I wrote down 'Mr. Stevens called about the thing' when I should have written 'Mr. Stephens called about the Thompson contract.' But that's like ninety-five percent right. The phonetics were correct even if the spelling wasn't."

"That's progress."

"Right? Progress! I'm improving! Evolution is happening! Next week I'll be even better!"

"I hope so."

"You won't regret keeping me. I promise. I'm going to prove that kindergarten teachers can do professional jobs. Well, sort of professional. Professional-adjacent. Professionally trying."

He left, practically bouncing.

Mara sat at her desk and wondered what she'd gotten herself into.

Two more weeks of this.

At least.

CHAPTER 6

The invitation arrived three weeks ago, back when Chelsea was still here to manage these things. "Women CEO's in Tech Leadership Summit - Networking Dinner." Black tie optional. Hotel Pinnacle downtown. Cocktails at 7, dinner at 8.

The kind of event Mara usually avoided because networking felt performative and exhausting. Because standing in a room full of successful people meant being constantly aware of how she measured up. Constantly conscious of her full figure. Constantly wondering if people were looking at her and thinking "CEO" or thinking something else entirely.

But Eliza had insisted. "You need to be visible. Richard Steele will be there. Other investors. Potential partners. Plus, free food."

So here Mara stood at 5:45 PM on Tuesday, in front of her closet, having the same argument with herself she had before every professional event.

The bedroom was dim. Evening light filtered through the sheer curtains, casting everything in soft blue-gray. Her apartment was quiet except for the distant sounds of the city. Cars were honking, someone's music, the rhythm of other lives happening.

She pulled out the black dress first. Held it up to her body in the mirror.

Too severe. She looked like she was attending a funeral. Or an execution. Possibly her own execution, given how this week was going.

She put it back.

The blue one came next. Navy blue, knee-length, structured but boring. Professional. Unremarkable. Safe.

Safe meant invisible, and invisible at a networking event meant wasted time.

She put it back.

The burgundy one hung in the back. She'd bought it six months ago for a board dinner and never wore it. Too bold, she'd decided that night. Too much.

She pulled it out now. The fabric was beautiful: a silk blend with a rich, deep color like good wine. The cut was elegant. V-neck but not too low. Sleeveless. It hit at the knee. It would fit well, she knew. It would emphasize her waist and skim over her big hips without clinging.

But sleeveless. Her arms.

She held the dress up and looked at herself honestly. The color worked. The cut was flattering. She knew that objectively. But sleeveless meant her arms exposed. Soft, rounded, everything the wellness industry said a wellness CEO shouldn't be. She thought about the room she was walking into. Corporate Women, CEOs. Derek Morrison's, because she saw his name on the attendee list.

She put the burgundy dress back and pulled out the blue one again.

Safe. Boring, but safe.

She laid it on the bed next to her navy blazer. Maybe the blazer would help add structure and authority. It would be coverage.

But the blazer over the dress looked ridiculous. It looked like she couldn't decide if she was going to a business meeting or a party.

She tried the burgundy dress one more time. Held it up. The rich color caught the evening light through the window.

It was beautiful. She would look beautiful in it.

But beautiful wasn't the goal. Professional was the goal. Appropriate and worthy of being taken seriously.

She put on the blue dress and carefully did her makeup. The rose lipstick, more eyeliner than usual, and blush to add color. All over the foundation to even everything out. Then to finish it off, mascara. The routine was comforting in its familiarity.

She looked at her reflection. She looked fine. Professional. CEO-appropriate.

Boring.

At 6:42, her phone buzzed. Eliza.

Eliza: *Leaving now. Meet you there at 7:30 Remember—you're a badass CEO who just got $30M in funding. Act like it. Stop stressing about what to wear. You look perfect in everything.*

Mara looked at her reflection one more time. The blue dress. The safe choice.

She grabbed her bag and left before she could change her mind again.

***

The Hotel Pinnacle was exactly what its name suggested. It was tall, expensive, and covered in glass that reflected the city lights. The kind of place where they charged forty dollars for a cocktail, and nobody blinked.

The ballroom was on the third floor. Mara took the elevator up, smoothing her dress, checking her reflection in the mirrored walls. The elevator was empty except for her. She watched herself rise through the building, getting smaller and smaller in the reflection.

At 7:08, the elevator opened.

The ballroom was already filling up. Two hundred women and men in professional attire. Some in dresses, some in pantsuits. All networking, laughing, and exchanging business cards. The room buzzed with conversation, clinking glasses, and the energy of ambitious people trying to make connections.

Large windows along one wall showed the city at dusk. The chandeliers overhead cast warm light. Tables were set with white linens and sophisticated centerpieces: orchids and candles in glass holders. A bar stretched along the far wall, already crowded with people ordering drinks.

Mara got a glass of white wine and found a corner where she could observe without being observed.

This was her least favorite part of being CEO. The performance. The small talk. The constant awareness of being evaluated. Every conversation was an opportunity, and every introduction was a test. Say the right thing. Laugh at the right moment. Be impressive but not threatening. Confident but not arrogant. Female but not too female.

She sipped her wine and watched.

Most of the women looked younger than her. Thin. Wearing clothes that fit perfectly. Laughing easily. They moved through the room as if they belonged here. Like, networking was fun instead of exhausting.

"Mara Wright?"

She turned.

A man stood there. He was tall, maybe six-two, with dark hair styled in that effortlessly perfect way that probably required expensive product and thirty minutes in the bathroom. His suit was charcoal gray and fit like it had been custom-made for his body. His shirt was crisp white. His tie was silk and probably cost more than her entire outfit.

He smiled. The kind of smile that came from years of getting precisely what he wanted.

"Yes?"

"Derek Morrison. I run WellPath." He extended his hand. His grip was firm, confident, exactly the right amount of pressure. "The competing wellness app? Probably your biggest competitor, actually."

He said it like it was charming. Like competition was flirting.

"I've been wanting to meet you for a while," he continued. "Your TechCrunch interview last month was impressive. Really impressive. You handled those questions about women in tech leadership beautifully."

Derek Morrison. She knew the name. Everyone in the wellness app space knew WellPath. They launched two years ago with massive funding. They were growing fast, taking market share, and doing everything right.

And Derek Morrison looked exactly like someone who succeeded in Silicon Valley. Polished. Confident. Handsome in a generic successful-person way. The handsome that came from good genetics, expensive grooming, and the knowledge that doors opened when you walked toward them.

"Thank you," Mara said. "WellPath is doing well from what I've seen."

"We're managing." He took a sip of his drink, something amber in a crystal glass, probably expensive whiskey. "But VibeGuide is the one to watch. Arch funding is no small thing. Richard Steele doesn't invest in just anyone. You must have really impressed him."

"We have strong metrics."

"You do, I've been following your growth." He leaned in slightly, his voice dropping to something more intimate. "And I have to say, meeting you in person? Even more impressive than I expected."

The compliment landed differently than his earlier ones. More personal. His eyes held hers a moment longer than purely professional.

Mara felt heat creep up her neck.

"That's kind of you to say."

"Not kind, honest." His smile shifted, became warmer. "How's the wellness space treating you? It must be interesting, navigating all this as a woman CEO. The dynamics can be... complicated."

"It has its challenges."

"I bet." He studied her face like he was genuinely interested in her answer, not just making conversation. "You're handling it well, though. Better than well. I've been watching your trajectory. The way you've positioned VibeGuide in the market, the partnerships you've built...it's smart work."

"Thank you."

"I mean it. There's a lot of noise in this space, but you've found a real angle. Corporate wellness programs with individual crossover. It's a good strategy." He paused, then added with that smile, "Though I'll admit, it makes competing with you more challenging. You're tougher competition than I expected."

Was he... flirting?

The tone wasn't quite business. The way he stood, angled toward her. The eye contact that lasted just a beat too long. The compliments that felt personal alongside the professional ones.

But why would Derek Morrison flirt with her?

He could have anyone. Women who looked like they belonged in this room, who wore sleeveless dresses without thinking twice, whose arms were toned from expensive trainers, and whose bodies fit the Silicon Valley ideal.

Unless he wasn't interested in her that way at all. Unless this was a strategy. Charm as competitive intelligence. Flattery as a way to lower her guard.

He worked for a competing company. This could all be performance.

But then his expression softened, became almost shy. "Listen, I know this might be forward, but I'd really like to continue this conversation sometime. Away from all this." He gestured at the room. "Somewhere we can actually talk without performing for investors and potential partners."

Before Mara could respond, there was a commotion near the entrance.

People turning, murmuring, someone laughing.

Mara turned to look.

And her stomach dropped.

Ben had just walked into the networking event.

He was wearing khaki pants that were somehow even more wrinkled than usual. A button-down shirt covered in tiny planets. His cardigan was gray and threadbare. His backpack, an actual backpack, covered in pins, completed the picture.

He saw Mara across the room and his whole face lit up. He waved an enthusiastic, completely unselfconscious wave and started walking toward her.

Mara felt her face getting hot.

No. No, no, no. This wasn't happening.

"Oh no," she whispered.

Derek followed her gaze. His eyebrows raised. "Friend of yours?"

"My assistant."

"Your assistant came to a Women in Tech event?" He sounded amused, as if this were entertaining rather than mortifying.

"He wasn't supposed to."

Ben reached them slightly out of breath. Up close, she could see the backpack read 'MR. BEN'S CLASSROOM' in rainbow letters. His shoes were gym sneakers.

"Hi! Sorry, I'm late!" He was genuinely breathless, like he'd run here. "I wasn't going to come, but then I saw the invitation on your desk when I was putting away files, and I thought maybe you needed help. Like, networking support. Or moral support. Or just someone to talk to if conversations get awkward because networking is really hard and you do so much hard stuff alone, and I thought maybe I could help."

He stuck out his hand to Derek. "I'm Ben. Mara's assistant. Well, temporary assistant. Very temporary. Like maybe a week or two more temporary, possibly less if I mess up, which is still possible. I'm trying not to, but it could happen."

Derek shook his hand, barely concealing his amusement. "Derek Morrison. I run WellPath."

"Cool! Wellness apps are great. Very important for mental health. Though..." Ben's face turned serious. "I have to be honest, VibeGuide is better. Just objectively. Better user retention metrics. Better engagement rates. Better customer satisfaction scores. I read about it in that TechCrunch comparative analysis. Very impressive stuff Mara's doing."

Oh God.

Mara wanted to disappear. To sink through the floor. To be literally anywhere but here, watching her assistant, her temporary, inappropriate, planet-shirt-wearing assistant, tell her direct competitor that her company was better than his.

Derek's smile didn't waver, but his eyes sharpened. "Interesting perspective."

"It's not perspective, it's data. Numbers don't lie. Well, they can lie if you manipulate them wrong, but these numbers seem legitimate. A third-party analysis is very credible." Ben looked genuinely concerned that Derek might have his feelings hurt. "But I'm sure WellPath is also good! Just maybe not quite as good? Which is okay! Second place is still impressive!"

"Ben," Mara said quietly. Firmly. "Can I talk to you for a moment?"

"Sure!"

She took his arm, gently but with clear intent, and pulled him toward the windows. Away from Derek and away from the crowd.

"What are you doing here?"

"Providing support! I thought you might need..."

"This is a professional networking event. For executives...You can't just show up uninvited."

"Oh." His face fell. The enthusiasm drained out like someone had pulled a plug. "I didn't think about that, I just thought you might be nervous. These events are so stressful. You and all these successful people have to talk and say impressive things, and I thought maybe if I were here, you'd feel less alone."

Mara felt something twist in her chest. He'd come because he thought she needed support. Because he'd noticed she didn't like networking. Because he was trying to help.

But that didn't make it okay.

"Ben, you're wearing a planet shirt."

He looked down at his shirt like he'd forgotten what he was wearing. "These are planets. Educational planets. Saturn is my favorite. See the rings? Very distinctive."

"They're not appropriate for a black-tie optional networking event."

"Oh. What's black-tie optional?"

"It means you should wear either a suit or something equally formal."

"I don't own a suit. I was a kindergarten teacher who never had to wear suits. We wore things that can get paint on them and still be okay."

"And you need to leave. Right now. This is highly inappropriate. Everyone saw you arrive. Everyone saw you tell my competitor that his company is worse than mine."

"But it is worse! The data…"

"That's not the point. You can't just show up uninvited to professional events wearing cartoons and insulting people's companies."

His face did something complicated. Hurt, embarrassed, and confused all at once. "I was trying to help."

"I know. But you can't help by showing up uninvited. That's not how professional support works. That's not how any of this works."

He nodded slowly. Looked down at his planet shirt and at his wrinkled khakis. At his sneakers that absolutely did not belong at this event.

"Okay. I'm sorry. I was trying to, but you're right, I shouldn't have come. I'm going. Sorry for embarrassing you."

He left. Walked toward the elevator with his backpack and his planets and his completely crushed expression.

Mara stood there, face hot, aware that people had noticed her assistant showing up inappropriately dressed and had heard him tell Derek Morrison that WellPath was objectively worse than VibeGuide. They had watched her dismiss him as if he were a child who'd misbehaved.

She returned to Derek, who was watching with barely concealed amusement.

"That was your assistant?"

"Temporary assistant, HR made a mistake. He's only here for two more weeks."

"Interesting hiring choice. Very...unconventional." He took a sip of his expensive whiskey, then his expression shifted. Softened. He looked at her with something that might have been admiration. "Though I have to say, the way you handled that? Very impressive. Direct but not cruel. Clear boundaries. That's good leadership."

Mara blinked. She'd expected more mockery. More amusement at her expense.

"Thank you," she said carefully.

"I mean it." He stepped slightly closer. Not invasively close, but enough that she could smell his cologne. Something expensive and subtle. "You carry yourself well under pressure. It's attractive."

Attractive.

The word hung in the air between them.

Mara's brain stuttered. Had he just called her attractive? Professionally attractive, meaning her leadership style? Or actually attractive?

"That's... kind of you to say."

"I'm not being kind. I'm being honest." His smile changed, became warmer, more personal. "I've been watching you work the room tonight. You're good at this, even though I can tell you hate it."

"How can you tell?"

"The way you hold your wine glass. Like it's armor. The way you scan for exits. The slight relief on your face when someone ends a conversation first." His eyes held hers. "I do the same thing. Networking is exhausting when you'd rather be working on actual problems instead of performing competence for strangers."

Mara felt something flutter in her chest. He understood. He got it.

"Exactly," she said.

"So here's what I'm thinking." He shifted his weight, angled toward her slightly. The body language was unmistakable. "We should grab dinner. Not networking dinner, actual dinner. The kind where we can get to know each other without all this..." He gestured vaguely at the room. "Performance."

Dinner. He was asking her out for dinner.

Derek Morrison, who looked like he'd walked out of a magazine spread on Successful Tech Entrepreneurs. Derek Morrison, who ran a competing company. Derek Morrison, who was standing close enough that she could see the precise line of his jaw and the way his eyes crinkled slightly when he smiled.

He was asking her for a dinner date.

Why?

The question arrived fully formed in her mind, sharp and insistent.

Why would he be interested in her?

She was a size sixteen in a room full of size twos and fours. She'd chosen the boring blue dress because the beautiful burgundy one would have shown her arms. She was good at her job, yes, but Derek Morrison could have coffee with anyone. Could date anyone. Probably did date people who looked like they belonged in fitness ads.

"I know this great place. Tiny spot, nobody knows about it. He paused, and his smile became almost shy, almost vulnerable. "I'd really like to take you there. If you're interested."

Mara's heart did something complicated and stupid.

This was exactly what she'd always wanted. Someone successful, polished, and appropriate, showing genuine interest. Someone who looked right, who fit in these spaces, who represented the kind of life she was building.

Derek was everything right, and he was looking at her as if she were someone worth pursuing.

Maybe he was interested, maybe she was exactly his type, maybe he liked smart, capable women who ran their own companies. Maybe her size didn't matter to him, and maybe she was overthinking this.

Maybe, for once, something good was happening.

"I'd like that," she heard herself say.

His smile widened. Genuine pleasure crossed his face. "Yeah? Perfect." He pulled out his phone. "Give me your number, and I'll text you."

She gave him her number and watched him type it in. She watched him send a text that made her phone buzz in her clutch.

"There. Now you have mine too." He looked at her with something warm in his eyes. "I'm really looking forward to this, Mara."

The way he said her name made something flutter in her chest again.

"Me too."

"I should let you get back to networking. Though if you want to skip out early, I won't judge. These things are brutal after the first hour." He leaned in slightly. "Text me if you need a rescue excuse. I'm very good at fake emergencies."

He walked away, leaving Mara standing alone with her wine glass and a text message from Derek Morrison and the dizzy, uncertain feeling that something significant had just happened.

She stayed for dinner, because leaving early would look weak. Eliza came, and they made small talk with people whose names she forgot immediately. She exchanged business cards she'd probably never use. She performed the role of a Successful CEO even though she felt anything but successful.

But the whole time, part of her brain was thinking about Derek Morrison saying, "I'd really like to take you to dinner" with that almost-shy smile.

The whole time, she was aware of people glancing at her. Were they judging her for her figure, or were they judging her for her inappropriate assistant? Or were they noticing that Derek Morrison had asked her to dinner?

At 9:15, she left.

She drove home through San Francisco streets that sparkled with nightlife and people having fun. People who weren't thinking about professional image, investor confidence, or whether their assistants' cartoon shirts undermined their credibility.

She sat in her apartment. The carefully arranged, perfectly coordinated apartment that looked like a showroom, and she tried to process what had happened.

She pulled out her phone and looked at the text. "Looking forward to dinner. 😊 "

A smiley face. He'd used a smiley face.

This was what she'd always wanted. Someone appropriate, someone who fit, someone who made sense in her carefully constructed professional life.

Tomorrow she'd talk to HR about Ben. Explain why he needed to go. Make them understand that good intentions weren't enough. That caring wasn't a qualification.

That this had to end.

But tonight, just for tonight, she let herself feel something that might have been hope.

Derek Morrison wanted to have dinner with her.

And maybe, just maybe, that meant something good was finally happening.

CHAPTER 7

On Wednesday, Mara arrived at 8:30 with a plan.

The office was quiet. Most people didn't arrive until nine. Just her and the early birds. Priya was at her desk already deep in code, Marcus was in the kitchen making coffee, and Sarah was in the break room eating something that smelled like peanut butter.

And Ben. Already at his desk. Wearing a different shirt today, tiny books instead of planets, but the same defeated expression from last night.

He looked up when she passed. "Morning."

"Morning."

"I'm really sorry about yesterday, the networking event. I shouldn't have..."

"We'll discuss it later. I have a team meeting at nine."

She went into her office and closed the door.

At 9:00, she gathered everyone in the conference room. Tyler, Priya, Sarah, Marcus, and Eliza. The core team.

Ben sat at his desk outside, visible through the glass wall. He wasn't invited to this meeting. He seemed to understand why.

Mara stood at the head of the table. Professional. Composed. She'd rehearsed this.

"I wanted to discuss my assistant situation. As you know, Ben has been filling in temporarily while HR searches for a permanent replacement. I appreciate his enthusiasm, and I know many of you have enjoyed working with him. But I don't think it's working out. Last night, he showed up uninvited to a professional networking event wearing inappropriate attire. He told our direct competitor that their company was objectively worse than ours. It reflected poorly on the company and on me personally."

She took a breath. This was the hard part.

"I think it's time to let him go. Karen is still searching for a qualified replacement. It might take another week or two, but I'd rather manage alone than continue with this situation."

Silence.

Tyler spoke first. He leaned back in his chair, arms crossed. "Wait. You're firing him because he went to a networking event?"

"He wasn't invited. He showed up wearing a shirt covered in planets. In front of other high-powered CEOs and competitors."

"But he was trying to help," Sarah said. Her voice was quiet but firm. "He told me this morning he thought you might need support. He was worried you'd be nervous."

"That's not his job. His job is administrative support, not showing up uninvited to events and insulting our competitors."

"Okay, but he's trying to learn," Priya said. She took off her glasses, cleaned them on her shirt, and put them back on. The gesture bought her time to think. "He's been reading all of Chelsea's documentation. He stays late studying protocols. Yesterday, he handled the complicated investor call perfectly. He's genuinely trying to get better."

"Trying isn't enough. I need competence. I need someone who understands professional norms without having to study them like a foreign language."

"He solved our backend problem," Priya pointed out. Again. She wasn't letting that go.

"One lucky suggestion doesn't make up for…"

"Constant inappropriate behavior, yeah, we know," Tyler interrupted. "But here's the thing. He also reorganized the supply closet, and it's actually better now, like measurably better, Sarah timed it. We save an average of two minutes per supply run. That's four hours per month across the whole team. Four hours of productivity that didn't exist before."

"He brought cookies to a board meeting."

"And Patricia loved them," Marcus said. He'd been quiet until now. Marcus was the most corporate member of the team, with a Fortune 500 background, always wore suits, and never used emojis in Slack. "I saw her take three cookies. Then she came by Ben's desk after the meeting and asked for the recipe. They talked for like ten minutes about oatmeal-to-flour ratios and the importance of real butter. Patricia smiled, Mara and I've worked with her for two years, and I've never seen her smile."

Mara stared at Marcus. "You're defending Ben?"

"I'm saying he has value. Just not as your assistant."

"Exactly," Sarah said, leaning forward. "He's terrible at being a traditional assistant. But he's amazing at making people happy. Making the office feel less like a corporate grind and more like a place where humans work."

"Look," Eliza said. She'd been quiet, letting others speak first. Now she leaned her elbows on the table.

"Chelsea was perfect at the job. Professional, efficient, organized. Never made mistakes. Never overstepped. Never wore cartoon animals."

"Right," Mara said. "Exactly."

"But she also made this place feel kind of cold. Kind of sterile. Everything was metrics and deadlines and professional distance. There was no joy. No warmth. No sense that anyone actually cared about each other as humans instead of just coworkers."

Mara felt defensive. "That's professional. That's appropriate."

"Is it?" Eliza spread her hands. "Or is it just what we've been taught appropriate looks like? Because I've been thinking about it since Ben started. Before him, how many times did people stay late working together just because they wanted to? Not because there was a deadline, but because they enjoyed being here?"

"We're not a social club, we're a company."

"We're a company made of humans. Humans who work better when they're happy, when they feel valued, when someone notices if they've had lunch." Eliza looked at her seriously. "We are creating an app about making company culture better. And Ben does that. He notices, he cares, and yeah, he does it in weird ways with gold stars and cookies and feelings walls. But people respond to it."

"The office is measurably happier," Priya added. "I've been tracking it. Employee satisfaction survey scores are up seventeen percent since Ben started. Seventeen percent in two weeks. That's statistically significant."

"You've been tracking employee satisfaction?"

"I'm an engineer. I track things. That's what I do." Priya pulled up something on her laptop. "Look. Sick days are down. People are staying later voluntarily. The Slack channels are more active, with actual, helpful collaboration rather than just work updates. Bathroom graffiti is more positive."

"You're tracking bathroom graffiti?"

"Data is data." She smirked.

Mara sat down. Looked around the conference room at her team. All of them looked back at her with the same message.

Don't fire Ben.

"So, what do you suggest?" she asked finally. "I need a competent assistant. Someone who understands corporate environments. Someone who doesn't show up to networking events in planet shirts. Ben clearly isn't suited for that role."

"Then make him a different role," Tyler said. "Keep him, but not as your assistant. Give him something else."

"Like what?"

"I don't know. Culture coordinator? Employee experience manager? Chief happiness officer? Whatever job title makes sense for someone who makes the office better just by existing."

"That's not a real position."

"Why not?" Sarah leaned forward. "We have positions for Marketing, Engineering, and Sales. Why not a position for culture? For making sure people actually want to work here? For preventing burnout and maintaining morale, and creating an environment where people do their best work?"

"Because that's not how companies function."

"Maybe it should be," Priya said. "Studies show that employee satisfaction directly impacts productivity, retention, innovation, everything. If Ben makes people happier, that has measurable business value. You could track it. Make metrics. Turn it into a data-driven position with actual ROI. Add it to the app!"

Mara sat in silence.

Create a new position. Keep Ben, but in a different role. Hire a real assistant for herself.

It was absurd, unprofessional, not how real companies operated.

But her team was unified. Completely unified in a way she'd never seen them before.

"I'll think about it," she said finally.

"Think fast," Tyler said. He wasn't joking. "Because if you fire him, I'm starting a petition. And I'll get signatures, lots of signatures. I've already drafted it. Want to see?"

"You drafted a petition?"

"Yeah. Google Form. Very professional. Thirty-seven responses so far."

"We have fifteen employees."

"I expanded the sample size by asking the cleaning crew, the security guard, and the barista downstairs. People have opinions."

Despite everything, Mara almost smiled.

After the meeting, she sat in her office, staring out the window at the city.

Create a position for Ben. Do this absurd, unprofessional thing that made no logical sense.

But her team loved him. The data showed improvement. Even Patricia, impossible-to-please Patricia, had smiled about oatmeal cookies.

Maybe Tyler was right. Maybe it should be how companies operate. They were creating an app, maybe it would be good for the company?

She opened her laptop and started typing.

***

By Friday at 2:00 PM, Mara had done something she never thought she'd do.

She'd created a position that didn't exist in any corporate playbook.

She called Karen.

"I need you to draft a new position description."

"For the assistant role?"

"No. For Ben. A different position. Manager of Employee Experience."

Silence. Then: "I'm sorry, what?"

"The team wants to keep him, strongly wants to keep him. But he's not suited to be my assistant, so I'm creating a new role. Something focused on office culture, employee satisfaction, and workplace environment. All the things he's actually good at."

"Mara, that's not a standard position. I'd need to create a whole new job description from scratch, determine salary range, reporting structure, and performance metrics. Get board approval. This is... unusual."

"I'm approving it. And I'll handle the board if they have questions. Just draft something. Make it official. Make it real."

"Okay, you're the boss."

"Fast-track finding me a new assistant, too. Find someone qualified. Someone professional who understands corporate environments and doesn't wear cartoon animals to work."

"I think I might have someone. Margaret Baker. She interviewed yesterday. She's amazing. Twenty years of executive support experience at major tech companies. Extremely professional. Impeccable references. Available to start Monday."

"Perfect. Hire her."

"Done. Are you going to tell Ben about this?"

"Yes. This afternoon."

After the call, Mara walked to Ben's desk.

He was eating a turkey-and-cheese sandwich. He saw her and nearly choked.

"Sorry. Eating at my desk. I know that's probably unprofessional. I'll finish in the break room."

"Ben, I need to talk to you. My office."

His face went pale, really pale, the color drained out like someone had pulled a plug.

"Oh no. This is it. You're firing me. I embarrassed you at the networking event, and now I'm fired. I understand. I deserve it. I should never have shown up wearing planets. That was wrong on so many levels. I'm sorry."

"Ben, just come to my office."

He followed her, leaving his sandwich behind. He looked like he was walking to his own execution.

She closed the door. Gestured to the visitor chair.

He sat.

"I'm not firing you."

"You're not?"

"No. But I am making a change. You're not suited to be my assistant, and this week proved that. The networking event. The video call interruptions. The board meeting cookies. You're trying hard, but this isn't the right role for you."

"Okay. So, I'm leaving?"

"No. I'm creating a new position for you: Manager of Employee Experience. It would focus on office culture, employee satisfaction, and workplace environment. Things like your user feedback wall idea. The supply closet optimization. Making sure people are happy and engaged. All the things you're actually good at."

He stared at her. Literally just stared. Mouth slightly open. Glasses crooked.

"Wait. What?"

"The team wants you to stay. They've made that very clear, repeatedly, with data and petitions. Tyler has a petition."

"Tyler has a petition?"

"With thirty-seven signatures."

"We have fifteen employees."

"He got creative and asked the cleaning crew, the security guard, and multiple baristas." Mara almost smiled. "The point is, you're not a good assistant. But you are good at making people happy. At improving culture. At making this place feel less like a corporation and more like somewhere humans actually work."

"You're creating a position just for me because the team likes me."

"Yes."

"Because I make people happy."

"Yes."

"Even though I'm terrible at answering phones and organizing files and not interrupting video calls."

"Yes."

"And you're hiring someone else to be your actual assistant."

"Margaret Baker. She starts on Monday. Twenty years of experience. Very professional. Probably doesn't own any cartoon shirts."

Ben sat there processing this. His hands twisted together in his lap.

"That's the nicest thing anyone's ever said to me in a professional context."

"Don't let it go to your head. You'll still need to follow some protocols. No showing up to events uninvited. No interrupting important meetings. No feelings walls without approval from me first."

"Got it. Protocols. I can learn protocols. I've been studying. I'm getting better at protocols."

"And Ben?"

"Yeah?"

"Thank you. For trying so hard. For caring about this place even when I was ready to fire you multiple times. For making the team happier. That matters. I didn't realize how much it mattered until this week."

He smiled. The real smile. The one that lit up his whole face and made him look like he'd just won something important.

"You're welcome. And Mara? Thank you for not giving up on me. I know I've been a disaster. Like an ongoing disaster. A disaster in progress. But I'm going to be so good at this new job. Employee experience management is going to be my thing. I'm going to make this office so happy. People are going to be like 'why are we so happy' and the answer will be 'because of Ben.'"

"Let's start with modest goals."

"Modest happiness. Got it. Reasonable levels of joy, sustainable morale improvements."

After he left, practically skipping back to his desk, Mara sat in her office and wondered what she'd just committed to.

She'd created a position that didn't exist. For someone with no qualifications. Because her team liked him and he made them happy.

It was absurd, unprofessional, and not how real companies were supposed to operate.

But maybe that was okay. Maybe different was good.

She pulled out her phone and texted Eliza.

Mara: *I'm keeping Ben. New position - Manager of Employee Experience. Margaret Baker starts Monday as my actual assistant.*

Eliza: *THANK GOD. Tyler was about to escalate his petition to the local news. He had a press release drafted.*

Mara: *A press release?*

Eliza: *"Local Tech CEO Fires Beloved Employee Despite Petition." He was going to send it to TechCrunch. I'm not joking.*

Mara: *Tyler is insane.*

Eliza: *Tyler is invested; there's a difference. But I'm glad you kept Ben. The office would have revolted, and it works with the vibe of our App.*

Mara looked through her glass wall at Ben. He was at his desk, typing something on his laptop. Probably drafting ideas for his new role and making lists of ways to improve office culture.

His glasses were still crooked. His shirt was still covered in tiny books. He still looked completely inappropriate for a corporate environment.

But he was smiling, and she could see other people smiling too. The office felt different, lighter. Maybe that was worth keeping.

Monday would bring changes. Margaret Baker would start. A real assistant. A professional assistant. Someone who understood corporate norms and wouldn't show up to events wearing planets.

And Ben would start his new role. Whatever that actually meant.

Everything would be different.

But maybe the whole point was to be 'different.'

Mara closed her laptop and went home.

The weekend stretched ahead. Time to think, process, and prepare for Monday and whatever came next.

Outside her windows, the city moved forward. Friday evening traffic, people going out, living their lives. And somewhere, Ben was probably celebrating his new position. Probably telling his sister Jade and probably making cookies to bring in on Monday.

Mara smiled despite herself.

This was going to be interesting.

CHAPTER 8

Mara arrived at 7:53 AM and found Margaret Baker at Chelsea's old desk.

Not Ben's desk. Chelsea's desk. The desk that belonged to Margaret now.

Margaret looked like she'd stepped from a professional assistant catalog. Mid-fifties. Sleek black hair in a perfect bun. Charcoal suit, crisp white blouse. She had designer glasses with angular black frames, no tape, no dinosaurs, and no wrinkled cardigans.

She looked like what a CEO's assistant should look like.

The desk had changed, too. Ben's scattered sticky notes were gone. His crayon-coded files had vanished. Everything sat at perfect right angles. A single pen holder with matching pens. A leather-bound planner open to today's date. A digital clock showing seconds ticking by.

Professional. Organized. Perfect.

Margaret glanced up. Her expression stayed pleasant but neutral. The kind you'd give any colleague at any workplace.

"Good morning, Ms. Wright. Your 9 AM with the design team is confirmed. Conference room B is prepared."

Ms. Wright. Not Mara. So formal, yet it was exactly what she asked for.

Margaret walked into her office three minutes later. "Your agenda is in your inbox. I've prioritized emails by urgency. The investor report is queued for review. Will that be all?"

"Yes. Thank you."

"You're welcome."

Margaret left. The door clicked shut.

Mara sat at her desk. Everything was perfect.

So why did something feel wrong?

***

The design meeting ran until 10:15.

Margaret appeared at 10:17 with a reminder. "Your ten-thirty is in thirteen minutes, conference line ready, and documents on your desktop."

No comment about the meeting running long, no question about whether Mara needed water, no break offered.

Just efficiency.

She left.

At 10:30, the call started. At 11:15, it ended. At 11:16, Margaret appeared with the next item.

The morning proceeded like machinery.

Efficient. Productive. Perfect.

At 12:30, Mara realized she hadn't eaten.

She walked to the kitchen for coffee. Margaret sat at her desk typing. Didn't look up when Mara passed.

The kitchen sat empty, quiet. The coffee maker clean and ready. Counter clear. Everything in its place.

Mara filled her mug. Through the doorway, she could see the main workspace. People at desks. Sketching. Typing. Working.

And Ben.

He sat at his new desk across the office. The "Manager of Employee Experience" desk. Just a regular desk in a different spot.

His glasses were different. New frames, sitting straight, no tape. When had that happened?

Mara walked back to her office.

She tried focusing on the investor report Margaret had queued. The numbers. Focus.

But she kept glancing through her glass wall at Ben's desk.

He talked to Tyler. Gestured with his hands. Tyler laughed.

Ben pushed his glasses up with one finger. They didn't slide back down because they fit. Because they weren't held together with tape.

Why was she noticing this?

Why did it matter?

Mara forced her eyes back to the screen.

Work.

Focus.

***

Mara woke at 5:30 AM on Tuesday, after dreaming about spreadsheets.

Sad. Probably meant she needed a vacation.

She dressed and left for the office.

She looked at herself in the mirror.

Professional, put together, hiding curves. Boring.

She left for the office.

Margaret was at her desk when Mara arrived. Different suit. Dark blue. Same perfect posture. Same neutral expression.

"Good morning, Ms. Wright. Your eight AM with accounting is confirmed. The Parker contract requires a signature. I've flagged relevant pages."

"Thank you."

Mara went to her office. Her mug appeared three minutes later. Margaret left without speaking.

The morning proceeded like Monday. Meetings at their scheduled times, documents prepared, everything is running with mechanical precision.

At 11:30, Mara felt stressed about something.

She couldn't figure out what.

Metrics were good, meetings productive, everything according to plan.

But something felt…off. Wrong. Missing.

She stood and walked to the window. She looked out at the city. San Francisco in late morning. Glass buildings. Blue sky.

Behind her, Ben's voice carried from the main office.

"No, I'm serious. You've been coding for three hours straight. Walk around the block. Get air. Your brain will thank you."

"I'm almost done with this function."

"The function will still be there in fifteen minutes. You won't be functional in fifteen minutes without a break. That's a programmer joke. Get it? Function. Functional."

Sarah laughed. "That's terrible."

"I know. But you're smiling, so I win. Now take a break before I make another joke."

Mara smiled too.

She caught herself. Stopped.

Why was she smiling? Ben wasn't even talking to her. He was just being Ben to someone else.

She returned to her desk and tried to concentrate on her work.

***

Wednesday morning, Mara heard crashing sounds from the break room.

Then water, lots of water.

She jumped up and walked quickly out of her office.

Water poured from the break room, flooding across the concrete floor.

Ben stood in the middle of the chaos, holding a watering can. Soaking wet, and surrounded by tipped-over plants.

"I can explain," he said.

Tyler appeared with his phone out, already filming. "Please do explain. This I need to hear."

"I was watering the plants."

"With what appears to be a fire hose?"

"It was just a watering can. But the faucet." Ben gestured helplessly. "I asked facilities about replacing the plants last week. They said budget constraints. So I thought I'd save them. The internet said they needed more water. I was trying to give them more water. The faucet had different ideas about the definition of 'more.'"

Water continued spreading across the floor. Priya jumped up from her desk. "It's heading for the servers!"

"TOWELS!" Marcus yelled. "Someone get towels!"

The office erupted into organized chaos. Sarah grabbed towels from the supply closet, Priya started moving equipment, and Marcus ran to find the water shut-off.

Ben stood there, dripping, looking apologetic and ridiculous.

"I was trying to help," he said to no one in particular. "Everything here is grey and perfect and efficient. I thought some green might help; the plants looked sad."

Mara stared at him. At the flood. At the dying plants he'd tried to save with his own time and effort because he wanted the office to be less gray.

Something in her chest did a weird flip.

"Towels," she said. She grabbed some from Sarah. Dropped to her knees and started soaking up water.

Ben stared at her. "You're helping?"

"The servers are expensive. Move faster."

He dropped down next to her. Started mopping. "For the record, this isn't how I wanted to impress you today."

"How did you want to impress me?"

"I made cookies. They're in my desk. Chocolate chip. Very impressive cookies. But now they're overshadowed by my water disaster."

She laughed, while mopping up a flood Ben created.

Margaret appeared in the doorway. She surveyed the scene. Her expression didn't change.

"I'll call facilities," she said. Then left.

Twenty minutes later, the water was contained. Facilities arrived with industrial fans. The plants sat in sad, soggy piles.

Ben stood there. His shirt was plastered to his chest, his hair dripping. Glasses somehow still in place.

"I'm sorry," he said to Mara. "About the flood, and the plants, and the general chaos."

"The plants were dying anyway," she said.

"Were they?"

"They were brown."

"I thought that was their natural color."

"It wasn't."

"So I mercy-killed already-dying plants with excessive hydration?"

"Something like that."

He smiled. Small. Grateful. "Thanks for helping clean up."

"Thank Margaret, she called facilities."

"I will. But I'm thanking you for getting on your hands and knees to save servers from my well-intentioned incompetence. That's really nice."

She looked at him. Dripping. Earnest. Completely Ben. Trying to make the office less gray. Less perfect. More alive.

"Go change," she said. "You're leaving puddles."

"Going. Changing. Becoming less aquatic." He started backing away, slipped slightly on the wet floor, but caught himself. "Still graceful. Still impressive. Nailing this."

He left.

Tyler appeared at Mara's side. "So. That happened."

"That happened."

"You helped clean up."

"I did."

"You laughed."

"I did."

"While he was dripping wet and apologizing for trying to save sad office plants."

"Tyler."

"I'm just observing. Making observations. Completely neutral observations." He showed her his phone. "Also, this video has already been shared in the group chat seventeen times."

Mara walked back to her office. Her pants were wet. Her blazer was damp. She'd just spent twenty minutes on her knees mopping up Ben's plant disaster.

And she couldn't stop smiling.

She should be annoyed. This was chaos. Unprofessional chaos.

So why was she smiling?

***

At 2:15, raised voices carried from the main workspace.

Mara looked up from her laptop.

Tyler and Priya stood at the whiteboard. Clearly arguing. Something about the app architecture. Their voices got louder.

"Your approach is going to create lag," Tyler said. Voice tight. "I'm telling you, we need to restructure the backend first."

"And I'm telling you that's going to take six weeks we don't have," Priya shot back. "My solution works now. It's not perfect, but it's functional."

"Functional isn't good enough."

"Neither is your theoretical ideal that won't exist until Q2."

Other people were watching now. The tension spreading across the workspace. This was escalating.

Margaret appeared in Mara's doorway. "Should I intervene?"

Mara started to stand.

Then Ben walked over to Tyler and Priya.

"Okay," he said. Calm. The same voice he probably used when kindergarteners fought over crayons. "Here's what we're going to do. Tyler, you get the blue marker. Priya, you get the red marker. You each get two minutes to explain your approach without interruption. After that, we find the compromise."

Tyler blinked. "Are you serious?"

"Completely serious. Blue marker. Two minutes. Go."

Something about Ben's tone made Tyler take the marker. He started drawing on the whiteboard. Explaining his backend restructure idea.

Priya crossed her arms. Started to interrupt.

Ben held up one hand. "Red marker gets her turn next. Let the blue marker finish."

Priya's mouth snapped shut.

Tyler finished. Stepped back.

Ben handed Priya the red marker. "Your turn. Two minutes."

Priya explained her approach. Drew her architecture. Tyler fidgeted but stayed quiet.

When she finished, Ben studied the whiteboard. "Okay. Tyler's approach is better long-term. Priya's approach works short-term. So, we do Priya's solution now to hit the deadline, but we schedule Tyler's restructure for Q2. You both get what you need. Different timelines. Problem solved."

Tyler and Priya looked at each other.

"That actually works," Tyler said slowly.

"I can live with that," Priya agreed.

"Great. Now shake hands before I make you hug it out. That's not a joke. I will make you hug."

They shook hands. Both smiling now.

The tension dissolved.

Ben walked back to his desk like nothing had happened.

Mara stared through her glass wall.

He'd just mediated a technical argument using kindergarten conflict resolution tactics.

And it had worked.

Margaret still stood in Mara's doorway. "That was unexpected."

"That was Ben," Mara said.

Margaret returned to her desk without commenting.

Mara sat there thinking about Ben calmly mediating a fight. Using children's techniques on adults. Making it work through sheer earnest confidence.

He wasn't just chaotic. He was effective. In his own strange way, he was actually good at this.

She pulled up her email and tried refocusing on work.

She failed completely.

***

Thursday afternoon, Mara reviewed budget allocations while losing the battle against a headache.

She should take a break. Walk around. Get air.

Instead, she kept working.

At 4:15, someone knocked.

"Come in."

Ben entered holding water and two ibuprofen tablets. "Thought you might need these. You've been rubbing your temples for thirty minutes, classic headache indicator."

She stared at him. "How did you know?"

"I pay attention, and your office is glass; I can see you from my desk." He crossed over to her and set the water down. "Observation skills are part of the job."

He held out the ibuprofen.

One tablet slipped from his fingers and bounced off her desk.

"Shit." He dropped to his knees. Peered under her desk. "Sorry. It went under there somewhere."

"I can get it."

"No, I dropped it, I'll find it." He squinted into the shadows. "Why is it so dark under here? This is where tablets go to die."

Mara sighed. She got on her hands and knees beside him. "Move over."

"I said I've got it."

"And I said, move over. I know where everything is under my own desk."

They were shoulder to shoulder. Both peering into dusty space beneath her credenza. The office felt small. Quiet.

"There," Ben pointed. "By your left hand."

Mara reached at the same time he did.

Their fingers brushed.

Both froze.

The touch lasted maybe a second. Barely contact. But Mara felt it everywhere.

"Sorry," Ben said. Voice quiet. "Did you get it?"

She couldn't speak. Couldn't move. Her hand was touching his hand, and everything felt very still and very loud at the same time.

"Mara?"

She grabbed the pill, pulled back, and sat on her heels.

Ben was already standing and offering his hand to help her up.

She looked at his hand. At his palm. At the same hand that had just touched hers under the desk.

She took it.

His palm was warm. Slightly callused. He pulled her to her feet with unexpected ease.

They stood much closer than necessary.

A strand of hair fell across her face. Ben reached up. Stopped. His hand hovered near her cheek.

"You have hair," he said softly.

"I'm aware I have hair."

"I meant in your face. Specifically." His hand suspended between them. "Can I…"

"Can you what?"

"Fix it, the hair, it's right there."

She should say no. Should step back. Should maintain professional distance.

"Okay," she whispered instead.

Ben tucked the strand behind her ear, his fingers barely grazing her temple.

His hand lingered. Just a second. Just long enough for her breath to catch.

His hand was so close to her face. His eyes were so blue. Everything felt very still and very loud at the same time.

She could kiss him. The thought arrived fully formed. She could lean forward six inches and kiss him and find out what that would feel like.

"There," he whispered.

"Thank you."

"You're welcome."

Neither moved. The setting sun caught the edges of his new glasses and turned everything gold and warm.

Her heart was racing. She could hear it. Could he hear it? Could he tell what she was thinking?

"You have good hair," Ben said suddenly. Then his eyes went wide. "I should have mentioned that when you asked about my makeover. Your hair is great. Very..."

He trailed off.

The spell broke.

Mara raised an eyebrow. "Very what?"

"Professional. I was going to say professional."

"My hair is professional."

"Extremely. The most professional hair I've seen in an office. Well, except for Margaret's hair. That's like. Too perfect. Not a hair out of place." He took a step back. Nearly stumbled over her visitor chair. "I'm leaving now before I compliment any other body parts inappropriately."

"Body parts?"

"Hair! I meant hair. Which is technically a body part, so that's accurate. But I wasn't. I'm not..." He grabbed the doorframe. "Take the ibuprofen, drink the water. Take a fifteen-minute break or go home. The work will be here tomorrow."

"I need to finish this."

"No, you don't. You need to take care of yourself." His composure was completely shattered. He backed toward the door. "That's more important than budgets. I'm leaving now before I overstep any more than I already have. But Mara? You look tired. Please go home."

"Ben..."

"Goodnight!"

He fled.

Mara sat at her desk. Stared at the ibuprofen in her palm. Her temple still tingled where his fingers had touched. Her hand still felt warm where his palm had been. Her heart was still racing, and he'd touched her hair. Called it professional. Possibly the worst compliment in history. Somehow it made her want to smile.

She took the ibuprofen. Drank the water. Packed up her laptop.

But she couldn't stop thinking about the moment under her desk. When their fingers touched. When everything went still.

When she'd wanted to kiss him.

At 5:03, she walked past Margaret's desk.

Margaret looked up. "Leaving early?"

"Yes. See you tomorrow."

"Have a good evening."

Mara walked to her car, trying to understand why perfect felt wrong.

Why a man who flooded break rooms and mediated conflicts with kindergarten tactics and complimented her professional hair felt right.

CHAPTER 9

Mara woke on Friday thinking about Ben.

This was becoming a pattern.

Thinking about him. The ibuprofen. The hair. The way their fingers had touched. The way he'd noticed her stress.

She got dressed. Navy blazer, black pants, the uniform.

She looked at herself in the mirror. Wondered when getting dressed became about hiding her figure. About not being seen.

The burgundy dress hung in the back of her closet. The one she'd almost worn to the networking event. Beautiful color. Sleeveless design.

She pulled it out. Held it up.

Too bold. Too much. Too risky for a Friday at the office.

She put it back. Wore the navy blazer.

At the office, Margaret sat at her desk. Same perfect posture. Same neutral expression.

"Good morning, Ms. Wright. Your nine AM is confirmed. The Anderson contract is ready for review."

"Thank you."

Mara went to her office. Water with lemon appeared. Perfect temperature. She drank it and felt nothing.

***

At 11:30, the team lunch started.

Ben had organized it. Pizza from three different places. Tables were set up in the break room, a playlist of what he called "upbeat work-appropriate music." Mostly '90s pop songs.

Everyone gathered. Tyler. Priya. Sarah. Marcus. Eliza. The whole team is laughing, eating, and looking happy.

Mara stood in her doorway watching.

Ben moved through the group like a social coordinator. Making sure everyone had food, introducing new hires to established members, and telling jokes that made people laugh.

He looked different from three weeks ago. New glasses. Styled hair. Plain blue shirt that fit.

But still Ben. Still making people smile. Still caring in that genuine way that couldn't be taught or faked.

"You're doing it again," Eliza said, appearing at Mara's side.

"Doing what?"

"That thing where you stand in your office and stare at people like a museum curator. Except you're not looking at everyone, you're looking at one specific person."

"I'm observing team dynamics."

"Sure. Team dynamics." Eliza's mouth twitched. "How long have you been standing here?"

"I just walked over here."

"Mara. I've been watching you watch him for five minutes. That's bordering on creepy boss territory."

Heat crept up Mara's neck. "I'm not watching him specifically, I'm watching the whole team."

"Right, the whole team, that's why you smiled when he laughed at Tyler's joke."

"I didn't smile."

"You absolutely smiled. Small smile. Corners went up. I saw it." Eliza studied her. "So what's going on? And don't say nothing because we've been partners for six years. I know your nothing face. This isn't it."

Mara glanced back at the break room. Ben pulled out a container of cookies. Oatmeal raisin. Passed them around and made sure everyone got one.

"Do you miss Chelsea?" Mara asked.

Eliza blinked. "Sometimes. Where's this coming from?"

"Margaret is perfect. Everything Chelsea was, but more efficient. Better organized. more professional. She doesn't make mistakes, she doesn't forget things, she doesn't need training."

"Okay. And?"

"And I should be happy about that." Mara crossed her arms. "We hired her for a reason. She's doing exactly what we need."

"But?"

"There's no but. She's great."

"Mara. You just gave me the 'she's great but' speech without the but. What's bothering you?"

Mara watched Ben with his container of cookies, making sure everyone got one.

"He's different now," Mara said. "Professional, put together. He fits here."

Eliza followed her gaze. Her expression shifted. "Oh."

"What?"

"Nothing. Just. Oh." Eliza's smile grew. "Ohhhh."

"Why do you keep saying oh?"

"No reason. Just making observations about team dynamics." Eliza pushed off the doorframe. "You should eat lunch. Pizza's getting cold."

"I have a budget review at two."

"Budget review will still exist, come on, five minutes. The company won't implode if you eat pizza." Eliza grabbed her arm. "Plus, as your partner, I'm concerned about your nutrition. You had coffee for breakfast, that's not a food group."

"It should be."

"It's not. Come eat."

"Eliza…"

"Mara. Get in that break room and eat lunch with your team. I'm not asking as your friend. I'm telling you as your partner. Employee morale includes CEO morale."

Mara let Eliza pull her into the break room.

The team made space. Someone handed her a plate with pizza. Tyler said something funny about the Anderson contract, and Sarah showed her a design mockup.

Normal lunch conversation. Nothing special.

But across the table, Ben caught her eye. Smiled. That genuine Ben smile that made his whole face light up.

"Saved you the last oatmeal raisin," he said and slid the cookie across the table. "I know they're your favorite."

"How did you know that?"

"You mentioned it once. Three weeks ago, during a conversation about not interrupting meetings with cookies." He shrugged. "I pay attention."

Mara took the cookie. "Thank you."

"You're welcome."

Beside her, Eliza made a small sound. Might have been a laugh. Might have been a cough.

Mara looked at her. Eliza was focused on her pizza. Very focused.

"What?" Mara asked.

"Nothing. Just choking on pepperoni. I'm fine. Totally fine." Eliza took a long drink of water. Eyes dancing with amusement. "Great pizza. Really great."

Mara bit into the cookie.

She could still feel where his fingers had touched hers yesterday. Could still feel the warmth of his hand. Could still remember the moment when she'd wanted to kiss him.

And now he was sitting across from her. Remembering that she liked oatmeal raisin cookies from a conversation three weeks ago. Paying attention to details nobody else noticed.

She tried ignoring the knowing look on her business partner's face.

Failed.

***

At 3:00 PM, Mara's phone buzzed.

Derek: *Dinner Next Friday? I know a great place in Nob Hill. Very exclusive.*

Mara stared at the message.

Dinner at an exclusive restaurant. This was good. This was what she was supposed to want.

She typed back: *Sure, Next Friday sounds great.*

Professional. Safe.

Derek: 7 PM Aphrodite. I will text you the address.

She set down her phone.

Ben sat at his desk typing on his laptop. New glasses caught the afternoon light. Hair slightly messy again, like he'd run fingers through it while thinking.

He looked up.

Their eyes met through the glass.

He waved. Small. Casual. She waved back, then forced herself to look away. Focus on work. But she couldn't stop thinking about yesterday. About their hands touching. About almost kissing him. About Derek being appropriate and Ben being chaos.

About perfect feeling wrong and wrong feeling right.

***

After most people had left for the weekend, Mara sat at her desk reviewing the Anderson contract for the third time. Words blurred together. She reached for another pretzel from the container.

A knock on her door.

"Come in."

Ben entered. Holding his cartoon notebook and a folder. "Budget approval needs your signature. Margaret said it's urgent."

"Thanks." She took the folder. Started reading.

He didn't leave, just stood there shifting weight between feet.

She looked up. "Was there something else?"

"Can I ask you something? "Do you like working with Margaret?"

The question surprised her. "She's very efficient."

"That's not what I asked."

Mara set down her pen. "She's professional. Organized. Everything runs smoothly."

"But do you like it?"

She thought about it. About perfect water with lemon at the perfect temperature. About meetings starting exactly on time. About efficiency, professionalism, and everything being right. About Margaret not noticing headaches, not bringing ibuprofen, and not having silly banter.

"It's what I need," she said.

Ben nodded slowly, like he was processing something. "Okay."

"Why are you asking?"

"No reason, just curious." He backed toward the door. Stopped. "For what it's worth? I think you deserve someone who notices when you're stressed. Even if they're chaotic about it."

He left before she could respond.

Mara sat there. Staring at the budget approval. Thinking about Ben noticing her stress. Bringing her ibuprofen. Touching her hair. About him asking if she liked it.

She signed the budget approval. Packed up her laptop and left for the weekend. And couldn't stop thinking about Ben's question.

CHAPTER 10

Mara woke up Monday morning humming. Actually humming. Like a person who hummed, which she was not.

She stopped mid-tune and sat up in bed, horrified.

When had she started humming? And more importantly, what was she humming?

She replayed the melody in her head.

Oh god. It was the alphabet song. The one Ben had been singing to Tyler last week when explaining his new filing system. The one that went "A-B-C-D-E-F-G, that's where customer files should be."

She was humming Ben's ridiculous alphabet song. This was a problem.

She got dressed. Navy blazer, black pants. Reached for her kitten heels and stopped.

The burgundy flats were at the back of the closet. She'd bought them six months ago and never worn them. They were too casual, too much like a person who had hobbies. She put them on.

In the mirror: navy blazer, black pants, burgundy flats. Almost the same. Slightly different. She left before she could talk herself out of it.

***

At the office, Margaret was already at her desk.

139

"Good morning, Ms. Wright. Your eight-thirty with the board is confirmed. And the quarterly report is prepared."

"Thank you, Margaret," Mara said, then paused. "And thank you for everything you do. You're very efficient."

Margaret blinked. "You're welcome."

Mara walked into her office feeling weird about the exchange. When was the last time she'd actually thanked Margaret? Or Chelsea? Or anyone?

Ben thanked people constantly. For everything. "Thanks for existing, Tyler." "Thanks for that email, Priya." "Thanks for being you, Marcus."

She was turning into Ben.

This was a problem. An amusing problem to have.

Mara opened her email. Margaret had already flagged her emails by urgency. Forty-seven new messages since Friday. She started triaging. Urgent. Important. Can wait. Delete.

At message thirty-two, she realized she'd been sorting them by color in her head. Red for urgent, yellow for important, green for can wait, blue for delete.

She had asked Margaret to change her appointments and messages back to black and white, and now she was seeing them like a kindergarten color-coding system.

Like crayons.

She was literally thinking in crayons now.

"Oh my god," she said out loud to her empty office.

Through her glass wall, she could see Ben at his desk. He wore a blue shirt today. His new glasses caught the morning light. He was gesturing animatedly at something on his screen, probably explaining a concept to himself.

He looked up and caught her watching. He waved with his whole arm, big, enthusiastic. Entirely inappropriate for an office setting.

She found herself waving back the same way.

What was happening to her?

***

At noon, Mara heard Ben's voice from the main workspace.

"No, I get that part, you click the cell. That makes sense. But why does it have letters AND numbers? Why can't it just have one coordinate system? This is unnecessarily complicated."

She looked up. Ben sat at his desk with Tyler leaning over his shoulder. They were both staring at Ben's laptop screen.

"Because that's how spreadsheets work," Tyler said. His voice was patient, as if he were explaining something to a child. "Letters for columns. Numbers for rows. A1. B2. C3."

"But why?"

"Because Excel said so."

"That's not a reason. That's just accepting chaos."

"Excel is not chaos. Excel is order. Excel is beauty. Excel is life."

Ben squinted at the screen. "Excel is a headache."

Mara walked over to Ben's desk. "What are you doing?"

Both men jumped.

"Learning Excel," Ben said, looking slightly panicked. "Or trying to. Tyler's teaching me, and it's going terribly. I'm very bad at this."

"You're not bad at it," Tyler said. "You're just fighting it. Stop fighting the spreadsheet, let the spreadsheet happen."

"I don't understand what that means."

Mara looked at the screen. Ben had created a spreadsheet with employee names in column A and random numbers in column B. In column C, he'd written "How do I make this add???" in the actual cell.

"What are you trying to do?" she asked.

"Employee satisfaction tracking. I did a survey last week. Got numerical responses. Now I need to calculate averages and trends and all that data stuff." He gestured at the screen. "But Excel hates me. Look. I tried to make it add these numbers. It just…It shows the formula, not the answer. Why does it show the formula?"

Tyler sighed. "Because you put a space before the equals sign."

"I WHAT?"

"Look." Tyler pointed. "You typed space-equals-SUM. You can't have a space. It has to be equals-SUM."

Ben stared at the screen. "A space. A single space broke the entire thing."

"Yes."

"That's the most ridiculous rule I've ever heard."

"That's Excel, baby."

Mara watched Ben delete the space. The formula calculated, and his eyes went wide.

"It worked! It did the math!" He looked up at Tyler. "I did math!"

"The computer did math. You just told it to."

"I'm a genius."

"You deleted a space."

"A genius space-deleter, that's my new title." Ben turned to Mara. "Did you see that? I made Excel do math. This is the best day of my life."

"It's a basic formula," she said. But she was smiling.

"It's MY basic formula." He looked back at his screen with pride. "What else can it do?"

"So many things," Tyler said. "So many things you're not ready for."

Ben returned to his spreadsheet and started creating formulas. He made mistakes. Tyler corrected him. He tried again.

Mara watched him work. Watched his face scrunch up in concentration. Watched him mutter to himself. "Okay. Equals. Then SUM. Then parentheses. Then the range. No spaces. No spaces anywhere. Excel hates spaces."

"Can it make graphs?" Ben asked suddenly.

"Charts," Tyler corrected. "We call them charts."

"Can it make those?"

"Yes."

Ben's eyes lit up. "Show me."

Tyler guided him through creating his first chart. When the bar graph appeared, Ben gasped.

"Look at that! It's a BAR GRAPH! I made a bar graph!"

"You did."

"This is the best day of my life."

"It's a bar graph."

"IT'S MY BAR GRAPH." Ben stood up and gestured at his screen. "Everyone! Come look at my bar graph!"

"We're working," Priya called back.

"But it's a BAR GRAPH!"

"We've all made bar graphs, Ben."

"But this one is MINE, and it's BEAUTIFUL."

Mara walked back to her office. She sat at her desk and watched Ben and Tyler work.

He caught her watching and gave her two thumbs up and the biggest grin she'd ever seen.

He was learning, adapting, and becoming part of the corporate world in his own Ben way.

And it was the most endearing thing she'd ever seen.

***

At 2:15 on Tuesday, Ben appeared in her doorway holding his laptop.

"Can I show you something?" he asked.

"Of course."

He came in. Set his laptop on her desk. Pulled up his spreadsheet. "I finished the employee satisfaction dashboard, the one Tyler helped me with."

The spreadsheet was impressive—clean formatting, clear charts, data that told a story. Employee satisfaction had increased 34% since Ben started. Team collaboration was up. Sick days were down.

"This is excellent," Mara said, looking at the numbers.

"Really?"

"Really. The board will be impressed."

Ben beamed. "Tyler said I should add one more chart showing the correlation between morale initiatives and productivity. But I don't know how to do that yet. I'll learn tomorrow."

"You learned a lot today."

"I learned that Excel is both my greatest enemy and my best friend. It's a complicated relationship. Very emotionally charged." He closed his laptop.

Mara sat at her desk. Thinking about Ben learning Excel. About his enthusiasm for bar graphs. About him asking for help without embarrassment.

About how much she liked watching him grow.

CHAPTER 11

Wednesday afternoon, Mara found herself in the break room making coffee when she heard a crash from Ben's desk.

"I'm okay!" Ben called out immediately. "Nothing's broken! Well, the stapler is broken."

Tyler's voice: "Did you just throw the stapler?"

"It attacked me first. It was self-defense."

"Staplers can't attack people."

"This one could; it had aggressive energy. It is a very hostile stapler. We're all safe now."

Mara walked out of the break room to see Ben holding a mangled stapler while Tyler was laughing at him.

"What happened?" she asked, unable to stop herself.

"Stapler malfunction," Ben explained. Seriously. "I attempted to staple the Peterson report, but the stapler had other ideas. There was a struggle. I won." He held up the broken stapler like Hamlet holding a skull. "To staple or not to staple. That is the question."

"You broke it," Tyler said, still laughing.

"The stapler broke itself. I was merely present during its self-destruction."

"You threw it at the wall."

"I placed it firmly against the wall. With velocity. There's a difference."

Mara felt a laugh building in her chest. An actual laugh. At work. During office hours. She tried to hold it back.

Failed.

Laughed.

Everyone stopped and looked at her.

"Did she just laugh?" Priya whispered from her desk.

"She laughed," Tyler confirmed, grabbing his phone to film. "Documented. Time-stamped. Historic moment."

"You documented that I laughed?" Mara protested, still smiling.

"Most of the time, you make polite professional sounds that approximate laughter," Ben said, grinning at her. "That was an actual laugh, big difference. We're making progress."

"We're not making progress. You broke a stapler."

"We're making emotional progress. The stapler was a necessary casualty in your journey toward joy."

Tyler posted something on his phone. "Group chat is losing their minds. 'CEO laughed at the broken stapler. Ben's influence is complete. We're in the endgame now.'"

"I'm firing all of you," Mara said, but she was still smiling.

"You're giving us gold stars," Ben countered. "And probably cookies. Because that's what you do now. You're 'fun Mara,' and we love 'fun Mara.'"

"I'm not 'fun Mara.'"

"You're wearing burgundy flats. You organized the snack shelf with labels forward. You bought oatmeal raisin cookies. You're humming when you walk. You're absolutely 'fun Mara.'"

"I don't hum." Mara wanted to be mortified. She wanted to be professional. Wanted to maintain CEO dignity. Instead, she laughed again. Truly laughed. At herself. At Ben's ridiculous singing. At Tyler's documentation of her downfall into fun Mara.

"I'm going back to work," she announced, still smiling. "You're all impossible."

"We're delightful," Ben called after her. "Embrace it!"

She went back to her office and squeezed the cat stress ball while smiling at her color-coded sticky notes.

Something had definitely shifted.

***

After the office started emptying for the evening, Mara sat at her desk and tried to return to the quarterly projections she'd been ignoring since noon.

She made it approximately two paragraphs before she looked up.

Ben was still at his desk. Most people had already packed up, but he was hunched over his laptop, one hand in his hair, muttering something she couldn't hear. Working late because he cared about finishing, not because anyone had asked him to.

She looked at the quarterly projections.

She looked back at Ben.

She closed her laptop and walked across the office before she could talk herself out of it.

"Hey," she said.

He looked up. The expression on his face when he saw her standing there was so unguarded it almost made her take a step back. "Hey."

"I'm going out for coffee and a scone. That place on the corner." She paused. "Do you want to come?"

He stared at her for a second. "Like, right now?"

"Yes, right now."

"For work…or..."

"Not for work."

Something shifted in his expression. He closed his laptop immediately. "Yeah. Let me get my jacket."

They walked down together. The evening air was cool, and the street was loud with end-of-day crowds. Ben reached for the coffee shop door, misjudged it completely, and walked right into it.

"It opens outward," he said.

"I saw that," she giggled.

"The door surprised me."

"Doors do that sometimes."

He laughed, and she laughed too, and she thought: this is why. This is exactly why.

They sat at a corner table with their coffees and scones and talked about nothing in particular. His weekend plans, which involved doing something fun with his sister. Her plans, which involved working, probably. He made a face at that. She made a face at his face. It lasted forty minutes. They walked back upstairs, and Margaret looked at both of them with an expression that conveyed nothing and understood everything.

Mara went back to her office and sat down. She didn't return to the quarterly projections. She just sat there for a moment, aware of something she couldn't quite name. Not happiness exactly. Something quieter. Like a door she hadn't noticed had been standing open, and she'd finally walked through it.

***

Ben was finally leaving when he stopped by Mara's door.

"You're still here," he said.

"So are you."

He didn't come in. Just stood there in the doorway. Hands in his pockets. Looking at something over her shoulder instead of at her.

"Margaret mentioned your dinner tomorrow night," he said. "With Derek Morrison, at Aphrodite, that fancy place in Nob Hill."

"Yes."

"That's good. Great. He seems..." Ben trailed off. "Professional."

"He is."

"Right. Professional." He finally looked at her. "Are you excited about it?"

The question landed wrong. Too careful. Like he was trying very hard to sound casual and failing.

"It's just dinner," Mara said.

"Right. Just dinner. With a successful tech executive who's very polished and appropriate and probably doesn't trip over his own feet or throw staplers." He smiled. But it didn't reach his eyes. "Should be nice."

Something in her chest tightened. "Ben..."

"I should let you finish up." He started to turn. Then stopped. "Can I ask you something? And you can tell me it's none of my business. Which it probably isn't. But I'm asking anyway."

"What?"

"Do you like him? Derek. Not in a professional networking way, genuinely like him?"

Mara opened her mouth. Closed it. "I don't know him well enough to answer that."

"But you're going to dinner with him."

"Because he asked. Because he's appropriate. Because..." She stopped. Hearing herself. "Because it makes sense."

Ben nodded slowly and looked at the floor. "Makes sense, that's good, it is important to make sense." He pushed his glasses up. "I just wanted to make sure you actually wanted to go. That you weren't just doing it because you think you should."

"Why do you care?"

The question came out sharper than she meant it to.

Ben looked at her. Really looked at her, and for a long moment, he didn't say anything.

"Because," he said finally. His voice was quiet. Careful. "I've noticed that every time Derek's name comes up, you get this look. Like you're bracing yourself. Like you're putting on armor." He paused. "You don't look like that when we have lunch together, or when you're laughing at my broken staplers. You look like yourself."

Something in Mara's chest cracked open.

Ben made her feel like herself. The realization hit her. When had his presence become the thing that made her relax instead of perform?

"Derek is who I should be dating," she said quietly. "If I'm dating anyone." She looked at him, at the concern in his expression. The way he was standing there, like he genuinely cared about her answer. "He's successful, established, and he fits."

"Fits what?"

"My life. My world. The corporate world." She heard herself saying it and hated how it sounded. Clinical.

Strategic. "It makes sense to say yes when someone like that asks you to dinner."

Ben was quiet for a long moment. "Okay."

"Okay?"

"Yeah, if that's what you want. I just wanted to make sure you actually wanted it, that's all." He started backing toward the door. "I should let you finish up."

"Ben..."

"Hope you have a good time. Really." He smiled. But something about it looked sad. "See you Monday."

He left before she could say anything else.

Mara sat at her desk. Staring at the empty doorway.

Ben looked sad. Not angry. Not jealous. Just sad. Like he'd asked a question he didn't want to hear the answer to and got exactly what he expected.

She pulled out her phone. Looked at Derek's last message confirming their reservation.

But Ben was the one who knew she hummed. Who noticed when she was stress-organizing. Who brought her ibuprofen and attacked staplers. Who learned Excel with pure joy and celebrated bar graphs.

Ben was the one she'd been thinking about all week.

When did that happen? When had Ben become the person she looked for in the office? The one whose opinion mattered. The one who made her feel like herself instead of like she was performing?

Oh.

Oh no.

She was falling for Ben. Had been falling for him for weeks, maybe even before that, and she'd been so focused on what made sense, on what was appropriate, that she hadn't noticed until now.

But it didn't matter. Derek was the one she should date. Derek fit in her world. Ben was her employee, her friend, someone who worked in a kindergarten a month ago.

Dating Ben would be complicated. Messy. Potentially a disaster.

Dating Derek made perfect sense.

So why did the thought of dinner tomorrow make her want to cancel?

Mara packed up her laptop and went home more confused than she'd been all week.

***

Friday evening, Mara pulled out the burgundy dress. Maybe the dress had been waiting for the right occasion all along.

The dress fit perfectly. It emphasized her curves and made her feel confident. She did her makeup with the rose lipstick and looked at her reflection.

Bold. Real. Herself.

She left for the restaurant feeling something that might have been hope.

Aphrodite was beautiful, with soft lighting and minimalist elegance. Derek was already there. When he saw her, his smile was warm. Genuine.

"Mara. You look absolutely stunning."

"Thank you."

He led her to a table in the back corner. Private. Quiet. Romantic, even.

"I asked for this spot," he said. Settling across from her. "Away from the crowd. I wanted to talk without networking interruptions."

That was sweet. Thoughtful.

A server appeared. Derek asked what wine she preferred before ordering. Small thing. But it mattered.

"So," Derek said, leaning forward slightly. "Tell me something that has nothing to do with work. What do you do when you're not being CEO?"

Mara laughed. "Honestly? Not much. I've been so focused on building VibeGuide that I haven't had time for much else."

"That's what I figured. You strike me as someone who's all in when you commit to something." His eyes were warm and interested. "But there must be something. Hobbies? Guilty pleasures?"

"I used to paint. Watercolors. Nothing serious. Just for fun."

"Used to?"

"Haven't had time in about three years."

"That's a shame. You should make time. Life can't be all work." He took a sip of wine. "Although I get it. Building a company is consuming. But you also need to remember to live. Otherwise, what's the point?"

It was exactly what Eliza had said, and what Ben had implied.

The food arrived. Tiny portions. But Derek was engaging. Asked about her family. Her background. Listened when she talked.

This was going well. Really well.

"Derek Morrison!"

A woman in a designer dress appeared at their table. Mid-forties. Perfectly styled. The kind of woman who looked like she belonged in Aphrodite.

"Catherine! Hey!" Derek stood and kissed her cheek. "How are you?"

"Wonderful. Just closed the MindfulCo acquisition and I am celebrating with the team." She glanced at Mara with polite curiosity. "Sorry to interrupt your date."

"Not a date, Catherine. This is Mara Wright, CEO of VibeGuide. We're discussing some potential collaboration." Derek gestured between them. "Mara, Catherine Bell. She runs WellPath Ventures."

Collaboration. Not a date.

"Nice to meet you," Mara said. Her stomach dropped slightly.

"You too. VibeGuide, I've heard great things. Strong metrics on that Series B." Catherine smiled. "Well, I'll let you two get back to business. Derek, let's grab coffee next week and catch up."

She winked at him.

"Absolutely. I'll text you."

Catherine left with a flirty smile. Derek sat back down completely unbothered.

"Sorry about that. Catherine's well-connected in the wellness space. Good person to know." He picked up his fork. "Where were we? Right. So, I've been thinking about this a lot. I really do see significant potential for collaboration between our companies."

Collaboration. Between companies.

"What kind of collaboration?" Mara asked carefully.

"Strategic partnership. Morrison Tech has enterprise distribution. Corporate wellness contracts. Infrastructure. VibeGuide has an incredible product and strong consumer traction. Blend our apps, and we could dominate the mental wellness space." He was animated now. Excited. "And beyond the business synergy, I think we'd work well together. You're sharp. Driven. You understand what it takes to succeed."

"Thank you."

"There's just one thing I want to be direct about." He set down his fork and met her eyes. "If we're going to do this, if we're going to build something significant together, we need to think about optics. Brand image. How we present ourselves to investors, to the media, to enterprise clients."

Mara got a chill all of a sudden. "What do you mean?"

"The wellness industry is competitive. The companies that win have founders who embody the brand, and who look like success, vitality, and health." He smiled. Sympathetic. "You're brilliant, Mara. Your business acumen is excellent. But if we're going to partner, if you're going to be the face of a major wellness platform, we need to think about the complete package."

There it was.

"You're talking about my weight."

"I'm talking about optimization. Brand alignment." His voice was smooth. Practiced. Like he'd thought about how to say this. "Look, I'm being honest because I respect you. The most successful wellness CEOs are fit. They inspire confidence. It's not shallow. It's strategic. Six months with the right trainer, the right nutritionist, and you'd be magazine-ready. Partnership-ready."

Mara's hands gripped her napkin under the table. "Partnership-ready."

"Exactly. I'm not saying this to be cruel. I'm saying it because I see potential…massive potential. VibeGuide is great. You're great. But if you want to compete with WellPath, with Headspace, with the major players, you need to consider how the market perceives you." He leaned forward. "I can help with that. I know people and resources; we could build something extraordinary together. A true partnership."

"A business partnership."

"Yes. A strong business partnership between equals. Two CEOs building something bigger than either of us could alone." He paused. "Personally, I tend to keep my dating life separate from business. Cleaner that way. But a partnership? That could be incredibly powerful."

The words landed like ice water.

He'd never been interested in dating her. This was never a date. The private table wasn't romantic. It was hidden away from people. And the compliments weren't genuine; they were a prelude to critique. He wanted a business partnership. But only if she lost weight first.

"I need to use the restroom," Mara's stomach turning.

She stood up on legs that felt mechanical and walked to the bathroom.

Inside, she looked at herself in the mirror. The burgundy dress, the rose lipstick, the body she'd worn proudly tonight because she'd thought maybe, finally, someone saw her as enough.

But he'd never wanted to date her. This was never a date. She splashed some water on her face and reapplied her lipstick. Then she made a decision.

When she returned to the table, Derek was checking his phone, already mentally onto the next thing.

"I'm going to go," Mara said, not sitting down.

He looked up, surprised. "What? We haven't talked through the partnership structure."

"That's because there isn't going to be a partnership."

"Mara, if I offended you, I apologize. I was trying to give you honest feedback, the kind of advice a real partner would give."

"A real partner wouldn't tell me I need to lose weight to be worthy of working with them. A real partner wouldn't introduce me to their contacts as a colleague when this was supposed to be a dinner date. A real partner wouldn't see me as a project that needs fixing."

Derek's expression shifted. Harder. "I was trying to help you. Do you know how competitive this industry is? How many CEOs would kill for the kind of honest feedback I just gave you? How many women would jump at the chance to be with me?"

"I don't need your feedback, Derek. I don't need your partnership, and I definitely don't need someone who thinks I'm not good enough for him." She picked up her purse. "VibeGuide is doing fine without Morrison Tech, and I'm doing fine without you."

"You're making a mistake. This kind of opportunity doesn't come around often."

"You're right. Thank goodness."

She walked away, leaving Derek sitting at his private table with his expensive wine and his business partnership pitch.

Outside, she got in her car and sat in the darkness.

Wow, what a jerk.

She drove home thinking about the word optimization and what it had felt like to hear it.

Her phone buzzed.

Ben: *Hope dinner went well. Here if you need anything.*

She looked at the message. At Ben's constant, steady presence. Ben, who'd never once looked at her like she needed fixing. Who brought her cookies. Noticed her stress. Made her laugh. Celebrated bar graphs with pure joy.

Mara: *Dinner was terrible. Derek's an asshole. Never seeing him again.*

Three dots appeared immediately.

Ben: *Whoa! Want to talk?*

Mara: *Not tonight, but thank you.*

Ben: *Okay, but seriously, you deserve way better than a terrible dinner. You deserve someone who sees how amazing you already are.*

Mara stared at the message.

Someone who sees how amazing you already are.

Not someone who sees potential if she changes. Not someone who wants a partnership with conditions.

Someone who sees her as enough.

She went to bed thinking about Derek's words. About optimization. Brand image. Being "partnership-ready."

And about Ben, who had never once suggested she needed to be anything other than herself.

Who thought bar graphs were miracles.

Who looked sad when she said Derek made sense.

For the first time, Mara wondered if she'd been choosing wrong all along.

CHAPTER 12

Saturday Mid-Morning

Twenty minutes after Mara texted Eliza about the Derek disaster, Eliza burst through the door holding wine, cheese, and what appeared to be a voodoo doll.

"Is that supposed to be Derek?" Mara asked.

"I made it out of scraps. Very therapeutic. Want to stab it?"

Eliza set everything on the coffee table. "Okay. Tell me everything so I know exactly how many times to stab this thing."

Mara told her about the private table that wasn't romantic. About Catherine calling it a meeting. The partnership pitch and the weight comment.

"I wore the burgundy dress," Mara said. "I thought it was an actual date."

"Of course you did! Because normal humans don't invite people to romantic restaurants to pitch business deals!" Eliza stabbed the voodoo doll. "What kind of psychopath does that?"

"Apparently, Derek Morrison."

"Derek Morrison is an asshole. He's the human embodiment of circle back." Eliza poured wine. "I bet he has a LinkedIn post drafted about this dinner. 'Excited to announce a potential partnership opportunity.' With that smug headshot where he's wearing a sweater vest. Ugh."

Despite herself, Mara laughed.

"There she is!" Eliza handed her wine. "Okay. Real talk for five seconds, then we go back to mocking Derek. How are you really?"

"Honestly? Relieved."

"Relieved?"

"Yeah. Because now I know." Mara took a sip of wine. "I don't want to date 'appropriate.' I want to date someone who doesn't think I need a six-month optimization plan."

"You want to date Ben."

Mara choked on her wine. "What?"

"Ben. The guy who brings you ibuprofen. Who created the wall of feelings? Who looked like a sad puppy when you said you were having dinner with Derek." Eliza grinned. "Come on, we're done pretending you don't have feelings for him, right?"

"I... maybe. I don't know."

"You know. You've been thinking about him all weekend. Probably compared Derek to him approximately forty-seven times during dinner."

Mara had. Multiple times. "He's my employee."

"He's your Manager of Employee Experience who makes you laugh and notices when you're stress-eating pretzels and tucked your hair behind your ear in a way that made you forget how to breathe." Eliza stabbed the voodoo doll again. "Meanwhile, Derek Morrison thinks you need a personal trainer to be worthy of his business partnership. The choice seems clear."

"It's complicated."

"It's not. You like Ben. Ben obviously likes you. Derek is an asshole. Math is simple."

"Ben hasn't said he likes me."

"Mara. He brought you ibuprofen when you had a headache, which he noticed from across the office through a glass wall. He texted you Friday night that you deserve someone who sees how amazing you already are. The man is basically writing his feelings on a billboard. A very enthusiastic kindergarten-teacher billboard. Probably with gold stars." Eliza poured more wine. "The question is: what are you going to do about it?"

"I don't know. Probably nothing. It's messy. He works for me. There are rules."

"There are also feelings, and life's too short to date men who think you need optimization." Eliza raised her glass. "To dodging bullets in expensive suits."

"To dodging bullets."

They clinked glasses.

They hung out all day and stayed up until midnight. eating cheese and making increasingly ridiculous suggestions for what Mara should say to Ben on Monday. Most of them involved terrible pick-up lines. All of them made Mara laugh.

At 12:30, Eliza left. Taking the voodoo doll with her "for safekeeping."

Mara went to bed thinking about Monday.

About Ben at his desk with his wrinkled shirts and genuine smile. The way he looked at her like she was exactly enough.

Her stomach did a small flip.

Oh no. She was, completely, problematically falling for Ben.

And tomorrow she'd have to see him and pretend she wasn't.

This was going to be a disaster.

***

(Ben's Point of View)

Ben's phone rang while he was making pancakes on Saturday.

His sister Jade.

"Are you dressed? I'm picking you up in thirty minutes."

"For what?"

"Shopping. Real shopping. Not thrift store shopping or whatever sale rack you found those wrinkled shirts on. Actual grown-up professional clothing acquisition."

Ben flipped a pancake. "The shirts you bought me are fine."

"The shirts I bought you are wrinkled every day by ten AM. You pair them with pants that are two sizes too big. We're fixing this. For real this time."

"Jade..."

"Thirty minutes and wear the least offensive thing you own. We're going to Nordstrom and probably three other stores. This is going to take all day."

"I can't afford..."

"I can. Consider it your belated birthday present, Christmas present, and your next birthday. Because this is going to be expensive." She paused. "Also, I'm doing this for Mara."

Ben nearly dropped the spatula. "What?"

"Don't play dumb, you're clearly into her. You talk about her constantly. 'Mara did this.' 'Mara said that.' 'Mara laughed at my broken stapler.' It's adorable and also pathetic."

"I don't talk about her constantly."

164

"You absolutely do. Mom noticed. I've noticed. Even your kindergarten friends have noticed. You're not subtle." Jade's voice softened. "And from what I saw in pictures at that networking event, she's gorgeous, successful, and out of your league in every possible way. So we're fixing the one thing we can control. Your wardrobe."

"My wardrobe is fine."

"Your wardrobe makes you look like you shop in the children's section and then shrink everything in the wash. It's not fine, it's a disaster, and we're fixing it. Thirty minutes."

She hung up.

Ben stared at his phone.

He was not into Mara; he was simply aware of her. Appreciative of her. Respectful of her many excellent qualities as a person and a CEO.

Okay, he was completely into her, had been since day one. But that was fine, totally fine. He could be into his former boss slash current colleague slash friend without it being a whole thing.

Except it was becoming a whole thing. The way he noticed everything about her. The way he watched for her laugh. The way his chest felt tight when she smiled. The way he'd learned Excel just to impress her with data. The way he'd felt physically ill watching her leave for dinner with Derek Morrison last night.

His phone buzzed. Text from Jade.

Jade: *Twenty-nine minutes. I'm timing you. Wear something that doesn't make me cry.*

Ben put on his least wrinkled shirt and waited.

***

165

Six hours later, Ben stood in his apartment surrounded by shopping bags and felt like he'd been through a war.

Jade had been relentless. Store after store. Fitting room after fitting room. She'd made him try on approximately ninety-seven different outfits. Maybe more, he'd lost count.

"Shoulders back," she'd said. "Stand up straight. You're not trying to make yourself smaller, you're trying to look like you belong."

"I'm five-ten. This is as tall as I get."

"It's not about height, it's about confidence. You look like you're apologizing for existing. Stop apologizing."

She'd bought him clothes that genuinely fit. Pants that ended at his ankles instead of bunching, shirts that didn't gap or pull. A blazer that made him look like a professional instead of a kid wearing his dad's jacket.

She'd also dragged him to her hairdresser and eye doctor.

"Contacts," she'd declared. "The glasses are fine, but contacts give you options. Trust me."

He'd argued. Lost. Ended up with a box of contacts and instructions on how to put them in without blinding himself.

Now he stood in front of his bathroom mirror, trying to process what he saw.

The new clothes fit perfectly. Dark jeans that looked intentional. A button-down shirt in soft blue that didn't wrinkle when he breathed. The blazer Jade had insisted on that made his shoulders look broader.

And no glasses. Contacts felt weird. Foreign. But he could see perfectly.

He looked different. Older, more confident, more like someone who belonged in an office with a CEO who wore navy blue suits and ran a thirty-million-dollar company.

He looked like someone Mara might notice.

His phone buzzed. Text from Jade.

Jade: *Send me a picture. I need proof you're not destroying my hard work.*

He took a selfie. Sent it.

Jade: *WHO ARE YOU? Is this what you look like under all those cartoon animals???*

Jade: *I'm showing this to Mom. She's going to cry. Tears of joy and relief.*

Ben: *It's just clothes.*

Jade: *It's not just clothes. It's you finally looking like the grown-up you've been pretending not to be.*

Jade: *Now go get the girl.*

Ben looked at his reflection one more time.

Monday. He'd wear the new clothes to work on Monday and see what happened.

Maybe nothing would change. Maybe Mara would barely notice.

Or maybe something would shift.

He put the clothes away carefully and tried not to get his hopes up.

***

Sunday evening, Mara's phone buzzed with a text from Derek.

Derek: *I think we got off on the wrong foot. Let's talk about the partnership opportunity when you've had time to think it through rationally. Real potential here.*

She blocked his number and felt immediately better. Then she called Eliza back.

"I blocked Derek."

"Good. He's a jerk."

"He texted me about 'thinking it through rationally.'"

"Of course he did. Because clearly YOU'RE the irrational one." Eliza laughed. "Forget him. Focus on Monday. Focus on Ben."

"I'm terrified."

"Good. That means it matters."

CHAPTER 13

Mara arrived at the office on Monday feeling unrested despite having slept for nine hours.

Sunday was quiet, restful. Perfectly fine. Also, lonely. Empty. Wrong in ways she couldn't articulate.

Margaret was already at her desk, as always.

"Good morning, Ms. Wright. Your 10 AM is confirmed, and the Peterson report needs your signature."

Mara thanked her and went into her office.

At 9:03, the elevator dinged, and Ben stepped out.

Mara forgot how to breathe.

He wore dark jeans that fit perfectly. A light blue button-down shirt that looked new. Crisp and unwrinkled. A blazer in charcoal gray that made his shoulders look broader.

And no glasses.

His eyes were just his eyes. Clear. Bright. Blue in the morning light streaming through the windows.

His hair was styled but slightly messy in a way that looked intentional. Professional but not corporate. Put-together but still Ben.

He looked confident, comfortable, like he'd always looked like this, and she'd just never noticed.

He looked incredible.

Mara stared through her glass wall and couldn't look away.

Ben walked to his desk and set down his bag. Tyler appeared immediately. Then Priya. Then Sarah.

The whole office gathered to see the transformation.

Tyler was gesturing wildly. Ben laughed at something. That genuine Ben laugh that lit up his whole face.

But then he looked up. Across the office. Through Mara's glass wall.

Their eyes met.

His expression shifted. Went soft. Uncertain. Like he was asking a question. Like he was waiting for her answer.

Mara's heart hammered in her chest. Her face felt hot. Her hands gripped the edge of her desk.

She should look away. Should focus on work. Should pretend this transformation didn't affect her.

Instead, she just stared.

He smiled. Small. Real. Just for her.

Then Tyler said something that made him laugh and turn away.

Mara sat at her desk and tried to remember how breathing worked.

Ben looked good. Really good. Like someone who belonged in an office. Like someone who'd grown up and grown into himself. Like someone she wanted to know better. Touch. Figure out.

Oh no.

Oh no no no.

This was bad. This was very bad.

She was totally attracted to Ben.

Not just aware of him.

Not just appreciative.

Attracted.

The kind of attraction that made her forget how to breathe. The kind that made her hands shake slightly. The kind that made her want things. Complicated, messy, completely inappropriate things.

She was attracted to her former assistant slash current employee slash friend, who brought her ibuprofen, noticed her stress lines, and made everyone happy just by existing.

The man who celebrated Excel formulas like they were miracles and who looked sad when she said Derek made sense.

She was so screwed.

Mara was still trying to process when Ben knocked on her door.

She jumped. Truly, jumped like a teenager caught staring at her crush.

"Come in," she said. Her voice came out breathless.

Ben entered. Closed the door behind him.

Up close, the transformation was even more obvious. The fitted jeans showed the shape of his legs. The button-down shirt emphasized his shoulders. The blazer made him look professional in a way his wrinkled cardigans never had.

And his eyes. Without glasses, she could see his eyes clearly. The blue. The warmth. The way they crinkled slightly when he smiled.

"Hey," he said, looking uncertain. "New look. Jade's doing. She staged a full wardrobe intervention on Saturday. Dragged me to approximately seventeen stores. I'm not sure I survived."

"You look good," Mara managed. Her voice was barely above a whisper.

Something flickered in his expression. "Yeah?"

"Yeah. Very professional. Appropriate."

"Right…Professional." He said the word like it tasted weird. "That was the goal. Look less like a kindergarten teacher and more like a grown-up. Like someone who belongs here."

"You've always belonged here."

"The cartoon shirts were probably sending the wrong message." He pushed his hands into his pockets. Looking suddenly nervous.

"The contacts are weird. I keep reaching for glasses that aren't there. Might give up on them by Wednesday."

"They look good. You look good," she said again. Then immediately regretted repeating herself.

His expression softened. "Thanks. I was nervous. Jade spent six hours yelling at me about fit and fabric and how to dress like a grown-up. It was traumatic. But worth it I think."

"Definitely worth it," Mara said before she could stop herself.

They looked at each other across her office. The morning sun streamed through the windows, and the city hummed outside, but everything felt suspended.

"I should get back to work," Ben said, not moving.

"You should," Mara agreed. Also not moving.

Neither of them moved.

Ben opened his mouth. Closed it. Something crossed his face. A flicker of something more serious, like he was building up to something that had nothing to do with board presentations or blazers. He looked at her hands on the desk, then back up at her face.

He reached to push up his glasses that weren't there. He touched the bridge of his nose and found nothing.

The moment broke. Whatever he'd been about to say dissolved into a slightly embarrassed laugh. "Still doing that," he said. "The ghost glasses thing."

"I have that board presentation on Thursday," Ben said finally. "The employee satisfaction dashboard. Tyler helped me finish the charts. They look professional. Very Excel-y."

"I'm sure you'll do great."

"Thanks. I'm nervous. I've never presented to a board before. What if I mess up? What if I accidentally call a chart 'fancy graph paper' in front of Gerald?"

"You won't."

"How do you know?"

"Because you care, and you're good at this, and they're going to see that."

He smiled. Soft. Grateful. "Thanks for believing in me."

"Always."

The word came out before she could stop it. Heavier than she meant. More honest.

Ben's eyes widened slightly. "Mara..."

A knock on the door. Margaret appeared. "Ms. Wright, your ten o'clock is ready."

The moment broke.

"Right. Work." Ben backed toward the door. "I'll let you go."

He left.

Mara sat at her desk. She tried focusing on her meeting but failed. All she could think about was Ben in that blazer. Those jeans. Those eyes.

And the way he'd looked at her when she said "always."

***

Tuesday afternoon, Mara walked into the break room for coffee and found Ben reorganizing the tea and coffee station.

"What are you doing?" she asked.

He turned, holding a box of Earl Grey. "Fixing this disaster. Someone organized these by type. That's chaos."

"I organized those by type."

Ben froze. "Oh."

"Last week. because it makes sense. Coffee together. Black tea together. Herbal tea together."

"Right. That's. That's a system." He set down the Earl Grey. "But have you considered alphabetical? Everyone knows the alphabet. Not everyone knows if Earl Grey is black tea or herbal."

"Everyone knows Earl Grey is black tea."

"Do they, though? What if someone wants chamomile and doesn't know which section to check?"

"They check herbal."

"But what if they don't know chamomile is herbal?"

Mara stared at him. "How would they not know that? It's chamomile."

"Tea knowledge isn't everyone's strong suit."

"It's literally one of the most basic teas."

"Okay, bad example." Ben picked up a box of green tea. "But alphabetical is clearer. G for green tea, easy to find."

"But green tea could be caffeinated OR decaf. It should be in both categories."

"That's duplication. Inefficient."

"That's accessibility. Efficient."

They stared at each other across the break room counter.

"You're wrong," Ben said.

"You're wrong."

"Alphabetical is the superior system."

"Type-based organization is objectively better."

"There's nothing objective about it. It's preference-based. Mine is based on universal literacy."

"Yours assumes everyone knows how to spell chamomile."

"Everyone knows how to spell chamomile."

"Do they?"

"Are you seriously suggesting people don't know how to spell chamomile?"

"I'm suggesting it's not as universal as you think."

"It's C-H-A-M-O-M-I-L-E. That's it. That's the whole trick."

"Most people don't think about tea spelling when they're making a cup."

"Most people don't think about type classification either!"

They were standing very close now. The break room felt smaller. The air between them charged with something that wasn't really about tea.

"Fine," Ben said. "We'll test it. I'll reorganize alphabetically. We'll see which system people prefer."

"You're not reorganizing my tea station."

He set down the green tea. Stepped closer. Looked into her eyes. "Look. How about this? You keep your type sections, and I add alphabetical labels. Both systems. Everyone wins."

She looked at him. At his earnest expression. How close he was standing.

"Both systems is redundant."

"Both systems is compromise."

"It's chaos."

"It's collaboration." He smiled. Small. Hopeful. "Come on. Let me make labels. I'm very good at labels now. I've been practicing with my Excel skills. Did you know you can mail merge labels? It's incredible. I made fifty labels for the file room yesterday. Tyler said they were 'unnecessarily thorough but aesthetically pleasing.'"

"You made fifty file labels?"

"The file room was a mess. Now it's beautiful. Alphabetical AND color-coded. Best of both worlds."

Despite herself, she felt a smile tugging at her mouth. "You're impossible."

"I'm creative."

"You're stubborn."

"I'm persistent. There's a difference." He grinned. "Come on. Let me make labels. I promise they'll be professional. No crayons involved."

"You're reorganizing tea that doesn't need reorganizing."

"I'm making the world a better place. One tea station at a time. It's my calling. After kindergarten teaching and Excel mastery, this is clearly my third talent."

She laughed. "You're ridiculous."

"I'm endearing."

"You're rearranging my organizational system."

"I'm enhancing it, think of it as collaboration. Professional collaboration between colleagues who both care deeply about... tea accessibility."

They stood there. Too close. Both smiling. The argument forgotten.

"Fine," Mara said. "Make your labels. Both systems. But if people complain, we're going back to type-based."

"Deal. But when people love it, you have to admit alphabetical is superior."

"That's not going to happen."

"We'll see. I have faith in the universal appeal of alphabetical organization."

He started pulling out his label maker, looking pleased with himself.

Mara grabbed her coffee mug and tried to ignore the way her heart was racing.

They'd just argued about tea organization, and it had felt like flirting.

This was getting out of hand.

***

Thursday evening, Ben appeared in her doorway.

"You're here late?" he said. Leaning against the frame. Looking hesitant.

"I'm about ready to go home. Why are you here?"

"I'm waiting for you to leave so I can walk you to your car. Also, I need to tell you something."

That made her look up. "What?"

He came in, sat in the visitor chair, and fidgeted with his hands. Took a breath.

"Tomorrow's Friday," he said.

"Very observant."

"And I know it's none of my business. But I can't stop thinking about something. About Derek. About him telling you that you need to change." He looked up at her.

His blue eyes serious. "You don't need to change, Mara. You're already everything. Brilliant and funny and kind. You laugh at broken staplers and organize tea and buy cookies for people. You wear fun shoes and hum songs and care about whether people are okay. You're not too much or not enough. You're exactly right."

Her throat felt tight. "Ben..."

"I know you're going to say I'm biased, or that I don't understand the business world, or that image matters. But Mara? The image you're trying to project isn't you. The real you is so much better. The real you makes people happy just by being yourself. And any guy who doesn't see that, who wants to change you, doesn't deserve you."

"What if I'm scared?" she whispered.

"Of what?"

She took a breath. "Of you."

His expression softened. "Why are you scared of me?"

"Because you matter. Because you see me. The real me. Not CEO Mara. Not professional Mara. Just me. The one who color-codes in her head and stress-eats cookies and can't stop humming your alphabet song. And that's terrifying."

They looked at each other across her office. The sun was setting outside the windows, and the office had gone quiet. It was just the two of them and the truth hanging in the air.

"I'm scared too," Ben admitted quietly. "Terrified, actually. You're brilliant and successful and way out of my league. I'm a kindergarten teacher who overwaters plants and makes jam and gets excited about bar graphs. But Mara? I'd rather be scared and honest than safe and pretending."

"When did you get so wise?"

"I've always been wise. You just weren't paying attention." He smiled. "Also, I watch a lot of cooking shows. They're very philosophical. You'd be surprised how much life wisdom you can get from shows about cake."

Despite the intensity of the moment, she laughed.

"There it is," he said softly. "That laugh. That's my favorite sound."

Her heart was pounding. "Ben..."

"You don't have to decide anything tonight," he interrupted gently. "I'm just saying. I'm here. I'm interested. And whenever you're ready, if you're ever ready, I'll be waiting. No pressure. No expectations. Just waiting."

He stood. Wobbled slightly. Caught himself on the chair.

"I should go before I say more weird things. I've hit my weird thing quota for the day. Possibly for the week." He paused at the door. "Have a good night, Mara. Eat some jam tomorrow, think about things. Or don't. Whatever you need."

He left.

Mara sat at her desk and stared at the jar of strawberry jam.

Tomorrow was Friday.

Tomorrow, she could keep playing it safe and keep performing as a CEO should.

Tomorrow, she could walk in at 7:52 like every other morning. Coffee, calendar, glass wall. The same careful distance she'd kept for years, professional and controlled and completely alone.

Or she could stop pretending she didn't know exactly what she wanted.

She already knew, had known for a while, probably. She'd just been waiting for herself to catch up.

She already knew what she was going to do.

***

Friday arrived as usual. Typical day working and trying to stay away from Ben. She knew what she wanted but didn't know how to say it.

Friday afternoon, Mara sat in her office staring at her computer without seeing it.

The week had been intense. Charged. Every interaction with Ben felt weighted, important, like they were building toward something inevitable.

At 3:30, Margaret appeared in her doorway.

"Derek Morrison's assistant called. He'd like to schedule another dinner. Next Friday. Should I add it to your calendar?"

The question hung in the air.

"No," Mara said. "Tell his assistant I'm not available."

Margaret's expression stayed neutral. "For next Friday specifically or in general?"

"In general. Thank you."

After Margaret left, Mara felt something lift from her chest. No more performing. No more pretending.

At 5:00, most people started leaving. Weekend plans with lives outside work.

Ben stopped at her doorway. "Have a good weekend."

"You too."

He started to leave, then stopped, and turned back.

"Mara?"

"Yeah?"

"I'm not going anywhere, just so you know. Whatever you decide, whenever you decide it, I'm still here. Still paying attention, still caring, and still making jam if you want more jam. I have a lot of strawberries."

He left.

Mara sat at her desk and felt her heart race.

Monday. She'd decide on Monday, or maybe now. Maybe she'd already decided and was just too scared to admit it.

She grabbed her phone and typed before she could overthink.

Mara: *What are you doing tonight?*

Three dots appeared immediately.

Ben: *Nothing. Why?*

Mara: *Want to get dinner? Not professional stuff, just dinner.*

The dots appeared. Disappeared. Appeared again.

Ben: *Are you asking me on a date?*

Her thumb hovered over the keyboard.

This was it. The choice. Appropriate or happy, safe or real.

She typed: *Yes.*

Sent it before she could delete it.

His response came fast.

Ben: *Pick you up at 7?*

Mara: *I'll text you my address.*

Ben: *Can't wait.*

Ben: *Wait, I need to ask.*

Ben: *Is this real? Like, you're actually asking me on a date? Not a professional dinner? An actual date?*

Mara smiled at her phone.

Mara: *An actual date.*

Ben: *OMG!*

Ben: *Okay.*

Ben: *I'm going to try to be cool about this.*

Ben: *I'm failing.*

Ben: *I'll see you at 7.*

Ben: *With flowers.*

Pause, then he typed: *Good flowers.*

Ben: *Or maybe bad flowers because I'm nervous.*

Ben: *See you at 7*

Mara set down her phone and tried to breathe.

She'd done it, really done it. She asked Ben on a date.

She was terrified.

She was excited.

She couldn't wait for seven o'clock.

CHAPTER 14

Friday Evening

Mara changed her outfit four times.

The burgundy dress felt too formal. The jeans and sweater felt too casual. The black pants and silk blouse made her feel like she was going to a board meeting.

She stood in front of her closet in her underwear, feeling like a teenager preparing for prom.

This was ridiculous. She was a CEO. She'd negotiated million-dollar deals, she'd fired people, she'd pitched to venture capitalists without breaking a sweat.

But choosing an outfit for a date with Ben felt impossible.

Her phone buzzed on the bed.

Ben: *Leaving now! I should be there in 15 minutes. I'm very excited and very nervous. Mostly excited though.*

She smiled at her phone like an idiot.

She grabbed the jeans and a soft green sweater that Eliza had bought her last Christmas, and she'd never worn because it felt too bright. Then she added the burgundy flats.

She looked at herself in the mirror. Casual. Comfortable. Real. Not CEO Mara. Just Mara.

She left her hair down instead of pulling it back. Put on the rose lipstick and minimal makeup.

At 6:58, her doorbell rang.

She walked to the door. Took a breath and opened it. Ben stood there holding flowers that looked like they'd been through a war.

"Hi," he said, his voice cracking slightly. "These are for you. They were beautiful when I bought them twenty minutes ago, but then I dropped them in the parking lot. I ran them under water in a gas station bathroom to clean them off. Then I realized running flowers under the gas station water was probably worse than leaving them dirty. So now they're clean but also possibly contaminated. I'm off to a great start."

The flowers were daisies. White and yellow. Drooping slightly, definitely worse for wear.

Mara took them and felt something warm bloom in her chest. "They're perfect."

"They're disasters," he said, grinning despite his apparent nervousness. "But they match my energy, so at least we're consistent."

He wore dark jeans and a soft green button-down shirt. His hair was styled but messy in that way that made her want to run her fingers through it. No glasses. Just those clear blue eyes looking at her like she was the only person in the world.

"You look beautiful," he said, his voice going soft.

"You look good too," she managed, trying to sound normal and not succeeding.

They stood in her doorway for a long moment. Just looking at each other. The air between them felt charged.

"So," Ben said finally, rocking back on his heels. "I should tell you about our date. I have a plan, it's a good plan, very romantic. I've been planning in my head."

"What's the plan?" she asked, smiling.

"We're going to play mini golf," he announced, looking proud and nervous and excited all at once.

Mara blinked. "Mini golf?"

"I know, it's not fancy, it's not an expensive restaurant where the portions are tiny, and everything costs fifty dollars. But hear me out." He counted on his fingers. "One, it's fun. Two, it's active, so there's no awkward sitting and staring at each other if conversation gets weird. Three, I'm really good at mini golf, and I want to impress you with my skills. Four, they have good hot dogs. And five, I thought you might be tired of fancy restaurants where people tell you that you need to optimize yourself."

Her throat felt tight. "You thought about all of that?"

"I think about everything when it comes to you," he said simply, then immediately looked flustered. "That sounded less creepy in my head…What I mean is. I wanted you to have fun, real fun, not CEO fun. Just Mara fun."

She grabbed her jacket. "Let's go play mini golf."

His whole face lit up. "Yeah?"

"Yeah."

***

The mini golf place was called Glow Golf Adventure, and it was exactly as ridiculous as it sounded.

Black lights everywhere, neon obstacles, pirate ships, castles, and dinosaurs that glowed green and pink and orange. There was terrible pop music playing too loud, families with kids running around screaming, and teenagers on dates trying to look cool.

It was perfect.

"This place is insane," Mara said, looking around at the chaos.

"I know," Ben said, looking delighted. "Isn't it great? I haven't been here since I was twelve. My birthday party. I threw up after eating three hot dogs and riding the spinning teacup thing outside. It was very memorable. My mom still brings it up at Thanksgiving."

"There's a spinning teacup thing?"

"There is, we're absolutely riding it later. I'm an adult now, I can handle three hot dogs and a teacup. Probably."

They got their clubs and balls at the counter. Ben insisted on the orange ball because "orange is an underrated color." Mara got purple because it glowed the brightest.

"Okay," Ben said, approaching the first hole with intense focus. "I need to warn you, I'm extremely competitive about mini golf. Like, embarrassingly competitive. I take this very seriously."

"Noted," Mara said, trying not to smile.

"I'm going to destroy you, with kindness, but also with superior putting skills." He lined up his shot with exaggerated concentration. "Watch and learn."

He swung. The ball hit the edge of the obstacle, bounced backward, and rolled into the water hazard.

"That was a practice shot," he announced, refusing to look at her.

"Of course it was," she said, biting her lip to keep from laughing.

"I was testing the surface, checking the angles, very strategic. This next one counts."

His next shot went wide, bounced off a pirate ship, and somehow ended up farther from the hole than when he started.

Mara couldn't hold it in anymore. She laughed out loud.

"Oh, you think this is funny?" Ben asked, trying to look offended and crashing completely. "You think my suffering is amusing?"

"I think you're not as good at mini golf as you claimed," she said, still giggling.

"Lies, slander, I'm excellent at mini golf. This course is clearly defective." He gestured at the glowing obstacles. "These pirates are rigged. Look at them, they're mocking me."

"The pirates aren't mocking you."

"They absolutely are. That one just winked. Did you see that?"

Mara stepped up to take her shot. Lined it up carefully. The ball rolled smoothly around the pirate ship, through the tunnel, and dropped into the hole.

Hole in one.

She turned to Ben with an innocent smile. "Beginner's luck?"

His mouth fell open. "No. No way. You've played before. You hustled me. This is a hustle!"

"I've never played mini golf in my life," she said honestly.

"Then you're some kind of mini golf savant. This is very threatening to my masculinity. I'm feeling very threatened right now."

"Your masculinity will survive," she said, walking past him to the next hole.

"Will it, though?" he called after her. "Because I'm currently being beaten by someone who's never played. That's humbling. Very humbling. I may never recover."

By hole seven, Mara was ahead by twelve strokes.

Ben had given up on actually winning and was now focused on making her laugh as much as possible. He narrated each shot like a sports commentator. He did a victory dance when he finally got a hole-in-one. He argued with the glowing dinosaur about proper golf etiquette.

Mara couldn't remember the last time she'd had this much fun.

"Okay, hole eight," Ben said, studying the setup with exaggerated seriousness. "This is where I make my comeback. This is my hole. I can feel it."

A glowing castle with turrets and a drawbridge surrounded the hole. The only way to get the ball in was to hit it up a ramp, through the castle, and down the other side.

"This requires precision," Ben continued, crouching down to examine the angles. "Strategy. Focus. Raw talent."

He swung. The ball went up the ramp, through the castle, bounced off three walls, and came back out the entrance. Rolled right back to his feet.

"The castle rejected me," he said, staring at the ball. "Even the mini golf obstacles think I'm not good enough."

"You're plenty good enough," Mara said, surprising herself with how genuine she sounded.

Ben looked up at her, and something in his expression shifted, went soft.

"Yeah?" he asked quietly.

"Yeah."

They stood there in the glow of the neon castle. Music playing too loudly around them, and kids screaming, but in that moment, everything else faded.

Ben took a step closer.

"Mara, I..."

"WATCH OUT!" someone yelled.

They both turned just in time to see a kid's ball come flying toward them at high speed. Ben jerked backward. Mara stumbled forward. They collided.

Hard.

Ben's arms came up automatically to steady her. Her hands pressed against his chest. They were suddenly very, very close.

Close enough that she could see the flecks of darker blue in his eyes. Close enough to feel the warmth of him. Close enough to see his gaze drop to her mouth.

Her breath caught.

His hand tightened on her waist. She could feel his heart racing under her palm.

Time stopped.

"Sorry!" the kid yelled, running over to grab his ball. "My bad!"

The moment broke.

They stepped apart quickly, both flushed, both breathless.

"That was," Ben started, his voice rough. He cleared his throat. "That was close."

"Very close," she agreed, her heart hammering.

"We should. The next hole. We should go to the next hole." He picked up his club with hands that weren't quite steady.

"Right, next hole, good idea."

They walked to hole nine in charged silence, both hyperaware of every accidental touch, every glance, every moment.

***

After eighteen holes (Mara won by twenty strokes), they got hot dogs and sat at a neon green picnic table outside the mini golf building.

The hot dogs were terrible and perfect; the kind you only get at places like this. Too much mustard, slightly cold buns, and absolutely delicious.

"I have a confession," Ben said, taking a bite of his hot dog. "I may have oversold my mini golf abilities."

"You think?" Mara asked, grinning.

"In my defense, I was very good at mini golf when I was twelve. I peaked early. It's been downhill since then." He wiped mustard off his chin with a napkin. "Although watching you destroy me was oddly attractive. Is that weird? That's probably weird."

"It's a little weird," she admitted, laughing nervously.

"I'm into it, though. Competent women doing competent things is very appealing." He took another bite, seeming to realize what he'd said. "That was flirting…I'm flirting with you. I should probably warn you when I'm doing that since I'm not very good at it."

"You're better at it than you think," she said softly.

Mara set her napkin down and looked out at the neon chaos around them. Kids on the teacup ride. A family arguing over their scorecards. The purple glow of the place catching Ben's face from the side.

"I used to paint," she said. Not really to Ben, just out loud. "Watercolors. I mentioned it recently to someone and he said 'that's a shame' and changed the subject."

Ben turned to look at her. "Who changed the subject?"

"Derek. At the dinner."

"Of course he did." His voice was easy, not sharp. "What did you paint?"

"Mostly landscapes. I wasn't very good at it. But I liked it. There's something about watercolor where you can't fully control it. The paint does what it wants, and you just work with it." She paused. "I'm not usually good at things I can't control."

"I've noticed that," Ben said, in the particular gentle tone he had when something was a joke and also not a joke.

"I haven't painted in three years."

"Why not?"

She thought about that honestly. "I told myself I didn't have time, but I think I just stopped being someone who did things for no reason. Everything had to be productive, or purposeful, or strategic." She looked at him. "Tonight didn't have a strategy."

"I had a strategy," Ben said, mildly offended. "I had five reasons. I counted them on my fingers."

"They weren't strategic, they were just you trying to make me happy."

He looked at her for a moment. "Yeah," he said. "That's basically it."

She smiled.

He looked at her, really looked at her, the way he had in her office. The way that made her feel seen.

"Can I ask you something?" he said, his voice going serious.

"Okay."

"Are you glad? That you said yes to this? To me?" He fidgeted with his napkin. "Because I know I'm not Derek Morrison. I don't have a fancy job, money, or any of the things you're probably supposed to want. I'm just a guy who's bad at mini golf and drops flowers in parking lots. And I just. I want to make sure you're not regretting this."

Mara set down her hot dog. Reached across the table and took his hand.

His hand was warm, strong, and slightly sticky from the mustard. Perfect.

"I'm not regretting anything," she said, meaning it completely. "This is the best date I've ever been on."

"Really?" he asked, looking genuinely surprised.

"Really. Derek took me to expensive restaurants and made me feel small. You took me to mini golf and made me feel tall. There's no comparison."

His fingers tightened around hers. "I'm happy you said yes."

"Me too."

They sat there, holding hands across a neon-green picnic, and Mara thought this might be the most romantic moment of her entire life.

"Want to walk for a bit?" Ben asked, his thumb brushing across her knuckles in a way that made her shiver. "There's a park near here. It's nice at night."

"I'd like that," she managed, trying to sound normal.

He grinned, stood up, and kept holding her hand. They threw away their trash and walked toward the park, fingers intertwined, and Mara's heart beat so loud she was sure he could hear it.

*　*　*

The park was small. A few trees. A playground. A path that wound around a pond that reflected the city lights.

They walked slowly. Not talking. Just being.

Ben's phone rang. Loud. Obnoxious. He pulled it out of his pocket. He looked at the screen, and his expression shifted.

"Oh no. It's my sister. She only calls after nine if it's an emergency." He looked at Mara with apologetic eyes. "I should answer this."

"Of course," she said immediately.

He answered. "Jade, this better be important because I'm on a date and…what? Slow down. What happened to Mom?" His face went pale. "Okay. Okay. I'm coming. I'll be there in twenty minutes."

He hung up and looked at Mara with anguished eyes.

"My mom fell. She's okay. She's fine. But she's at the hospital, and my sister is freaking out, and I need to go. I'm so sorry. This is…"

"Don't apologize," Mara said immediately. "Go, I'll catch an Uber. Is she really okay?"

"Jade says yes. She tripped over her cat and hurt her wrist. But still. Hospital. Mom. I have to go." He ran a hand through his hair, looking torn. "I'm so sorry. We were having such a good time."

"We were," she agreed, squeezing his hand. "Go. Text me when you know she's okay?"

He pulled her into a hug. Fast. Hard. Desperate.

"You're amazing," he said into her hair. "I'll call you later. I promise."

"Go," she said, smiling against his shoulder even though she felt disappointed.

He pulled back. Started backing away toward the parking lot. Nearly tripped over a bench. Caught himself. "I'm fine! Totally fine! Talk to you later!"

He ran.

Mara stood in the park alone, listening to his footsteps fade. No kiss. Almost but not quite.

She got out her phone and ordered an Uber. As she waited, she thought the date had been perfect, absolutely perfect. But it had ended without the kiss she'd been hoping for. Maybe that was okay; perhaps the anticipation was part of it. Or maybe she was just trying to convince herself she wasn't disappointed.

***

Mara was already in bed when her phone buzzed.

Ben: *Mom is OK! Sprained wrist. She says hi. She also says she's sorry for ruining our date with her "dramatic falling." Her words, not mine.*

Mara: *Tell her I'm glad she's okay and her timing is impeccable.*

Ben: *She says your timing comment is "amusing" and she "likes you already."*

Mara: *I haven't even met her.*

Ben: *She saw your photo when I was showing Jade. Then she grilled me for 20 minutes about you while the doctor wrapped her wrist. It was mortifying. She asked if you're Jewish. I said no. She asked when we were getting married and how many grandbabies she is getting. I wanted to die.*

Mara laughed out loud in her empty bedroom.

Mara: *Your mom sounds amazing.*

Ben: *She's a menace, but yeah, she's pretty incredible.*

Mara: *How are YOU?*

Ben: *Tired, wired, still thinking about the mini golf. And the almost-moment at the castle. And the almost-*

moment in the park before my phone rang. I'm starting to feel the universe doesn't want us to have moments.

Mara: *The universe has terrible timing.*

Ben: *The worst, but also, I had a really good time tonight, even without the moments. Just being with you was. Yeah.*

Mara's heart did something complicated.

Mara: *I had a good time too.*

Ben: *Can I see you tomorrow? I know that's probably too eager. I should play it cool, wait a few days, follow some kind of dating rulebook. But I really want to see you tomorrow.*

Mara: *I want to see you tomorrow, too.*

Ben: *Yeah?*

Mara: *Yeah*

Ben: *7 PM?*

Mara: *Sounds great!*

Ben: *Get some sleep. I'll see you tomorrow.*

Mara: *Night, Ben.*

She set down her phone and stared at her ceiling. She tried to process the fact that she'd just had an almost-perfect date that ended with no kiss but somehow felt more romantic than any kiss she'd ever had.

Tomorrow. Just the two of them.

This was either the beginning of something wonderful or she was setting herself up for heartbreak.

Based on how her chest felt, she hoped for wonderful.

CHAPTER 15

Ben picked her up at exactly 7:00 PM, looking determined.

"Hi," he said. "I have a plan. It's foolproof. Nothing will interrupt us tonight."

"What's the plan?" she asked, smiling.

"We're going to my apartment, and I'm cooking dinner. There are no restaurants where waiters can interrupt. No public parks where joggers can show up. No family emergencies because I told everyone I have the plague and am not to be disturbed under any circumstances."

"You told your family you have the plague?"

"Jade said, 'That's dramatic.' I said, 'So is calling me during my date.' She said 'fair point' and promised only to call if someone is actively dying." He offered his hand. "So, my place, pasta, wine, uninterrupted conversation, and hopefully, if the universe has any mercy at all, kissing."

She took his hand. "That sounds perfect."

They drove away from her place and towards Ben's apartment.

Ben's apartment was small. A studio with a kitchen area, a living space, and a bed tucked in the corner. Books everywhere, stacked on shelves, piled on the floor, balanced on the windowsill.

It was warm, lived-in, and completely Ben.

"Sorry about the mess," he said, setting down his keys. "I tried to clean; I gave up on looking sophisticated."

"It's perfect," she said, meaning it.

"Liar. But I appreciate the lie." He gestured to the kitchen area. "Make yourself comfortable. I'm going to cook. This might be my only impressive skill since mini golf was a disaster."

She sat at his counter and looked around. An invitation for an Elementary Teacher's Gala sat on the counter. She played with the pretty paper until Ben glanced over and saw her.

"Want to go?"

"Where"

"To the Elementary Teacher Foundation Gala? They are giving Jake an award for his dedication to the school, and he got me an invitation."

"Sounds like fun, and I get to meet your school friends." She said reading the invitation.

"Perfect, I'll R.S.V.P." he said grinning.

The apartment was smaller than she'd expected. Every surface had books on it. Not decoratively arranged books, not books chosen to look intelligent on a shelf, but books that had clearly been read, left open face-down, stacked sideways on top of other books because there was no other option. A paperback with a broken spine sat on the windowsill next to a plant that was somehow thriving. A library book was on the kitchen counter, marked with a receipt. Three more were stacked on the floor next to the bed like they were waiting for their turn.

Ben was at the stove with his back to her, chopping something with the focused energy of a man who had practiced this particular task approximately eight times. He was explaining the pasta sauce. His grandmother's recipe, which had survived emigration, two moves across state lines, and one very unfortunate incident involving a misread tablespoon-versus-teaspoon distinction that he was still, clearly, not over.

"What's in it?" she asked.

"That's classified."

"You're cooking it in front of me."

"Still classified. You could memorize the steps and replicate it, and then where would I be? I'd lose my only impressive skill. I'm protecting my competitive advantage."

"Your competitive advantage is a pasta sauce."

"My competitive advantage," he said, pointing the wooden spoon with some gravity, "is the only pasta sauce in this city that tastes like a Sunday afternoon in 1987. Very specific, very protected, you'll just have to trust me."

She watched him work. He moved easily in the small kitchen, reaching past things without looking, adjusting the heat by feel. The competence was unexpected and oddly arresting. He was someone who cooked for himself, not for others. Someone who had made this enough times that his hands knew where to go.

She reached over and opened the library book on the counter. A biography. It was heavily annotated in pencil; the margins were full of his handwriting. She read one margin note: "Why does this feel familiar?? look up" with an arrow pointing to a paragraph.

"You annotate library books?" she said.

He turned around and saw what she was holding. His expression shifted into something between caught and completely unapologetic. "It helps me remember what I was thinking."

"You're supposed to return them."

"I do return them, with extra thoughts, future readers can disagree with me if they want. It's a conversation."

"That's not what a library is for."

"Libraries are absolutely for that. They're literally the oldest conversation humanity has, and I'm contributing."

She set the book down, still smiling. "How many of these are yours?"

"The ones on the shelves. The ones on the floor are also mine. The ones on the counter are the library's, technically. There might be some overlap by the bed; I haven't fully sorted it out."

"You have a book problem."

"I have a book enthusiasm. Different thing." He turned back to the stove. "My kindergarteners used to say I talked about books the way other people talked about sports. Which I took as a compliment."

Mara looked at the shelves. There were novels she recognized and ones she didn't. Books on education, on psychology, on urban planning, on fermentation and bread, and the history of salt. A whole shelf of picture books at the end, their spines facing out in careful order, clearly not decorative.

She hadn't expected this, not this version of him. Competent and domestic and full of a life she was only just beginning to see.

"What do you read when you're sad?" she asked.

It came out before she'd decided to say it. He turned around again, this time slower.

"Sad how?" he asked. "Like a bad-day sad or a real sad?"

"Real sad."

He considered this with the seriousness it apparently deserved. "Terry Pratchett. He's very funny, but also about how people try to be good at things. It helps." He tilted his head slightly. "What do you do when you're sad?"

She thought about it. The honest answer was to work or reorganize something. Maybe make a list, or just fill the silence with productivity so the sad thing doesn't have room to settle.

"I don't usually let myself be sad," she said.

"That explains some things," Ben said, not unkindly.

She looked at him across the small kitchen, at the easy way he'd said it, without pressing, without making it into a problem to solve, just received the information and set it down gently.

"Maybe I should read Terry Pratchett," she said.

"I have all of them. You can borrow one anytime." He gestured at the shelf with the wooden spoon. "Fair warning, though. You'll end up annotating it, and then I'll argue with your notes for six months."

"I don't annotate books."

"You would his books, everyone argues with Pratchett eventually. It's respectful."

The sauce began to smell extraordinary.

"Okay," he announced at 8:15, setting two plates on the small table. "Dinner is served. Prepare to be amazed by my mediocre cooking skills."

The pasta was incredible. They ate, talked, laughed, and drank wine.

And Mara felt something settle in her chest. Something that felt like rightness. Like coming home.

"Can I be honest?" Ben asked, setting down his fork and looking at her across the small table.

"Always."

"I'm terrified," he admitted. "Of messing this up. Of saying the wrong thing. Of moving too fast or too slow, or just generally being too much. Because you're, you're you, and I'm just me. And sometimes I can't believe you're sitting in my apartment eating my grandmother's pasta recipe and looking at me like. Like that."

"Like what?" she asked softly.

"Like I matter," he said, his voice rough. "Like I'm not just the guy who accidentally got hired and made a feelings wall. Like I'm someone you actually want to be here with."

She stood up. Walked around the table and sat next to him instead of across from him.

"You do matter," she said, taking his hand. "You matter more than you know. You make me laugh. You make me feel seen. You make me want to be braver, more honest, and more myself. That's not nothing, Ben. That's everything."

He looked at her. His blue eyes were searching hers.

"Mara," he breathed.

"Yeah?"

"Can I please kiss you now? Please? Before something else goes wrong. Before the universe decides to send another interruption. I'm begging the universe right now. Just let me kiss her."

She smiled. Cupped his face with both hands and said, "Yes."

He closed the distance.

Finally.

His lips met hers, gentle at first. Tentative. Testing.

Then she made a small sound, and something shifted.

The kiss deepened. His hand tangled in her hair. Her fingers curled into his sweater, pulling him closer.

He tasted like wine and pasta sauce and six weeks of waiting. His hand slid to her waist, pulled her flush against him.

They kissed a bit more.

When they broke apart, both breathless, he rested his forehead against hers.

"Worth the wait," he managed, his voice wrecked.

"Definitely worth the wait," she agreed, slightly dizzy.

"Can I do that again?" he asked, walking her to the living room.

"Please," she whispered.

They kissed on his couch for what might have been minutes or hours, just lost in each other. Making up for lost time, learning the shape of each other's mouths, the sounds they made, the way they fit together.

When they finally came up for air, both flushed and happy, Ben pulled her against his chest.

"I'm really happy," he admitted. "Like, stupidly happy. Like, can't stop smiling happy."

"Me too."

They stayed there on his couch, wrapped around each other, and Mara thought this was what falling in love felt like.

Terrifying.

Perfect.

Inevitable.

***

Later that evening, Mara said reluctantly, "I should go," even though she was still curled against Ben on his couch.

"Don't," he said into her hair. "Stay. Not like. Not in a weird way, just stay. We can talk or not talk. Or kiss more. I vote for kissing more."

She smiled. "I have to go home."

"Can we meet somewhere? What are the rules for third dates after you've finally kissed?"

"I don't know the rules," she admitted. "I've never been very good at following dating rules anyway."

"Good, because I want to see you tomorrow, and Monday, and basically, every day. Is that too much? That's probably too much."

"It's not too much," she said softly.

He kissed her forehead. Her nose. Her mouth. "Do you really have to leave?"

"I really do."

"Okay. Ben walked her out to the car and drove her home, stopping at the front door of her complex.

He leaned over and kissed her goodnight. Slow and sweet and full of promise.

"Tomorrow," he said.

"Tomorrow," she agreed.

She got out of the car and walked to her apartment with her heart full and her head spinning and the taste of him still on her lips.

***

They spent Sunday together.

Coffee at the bakery. A walk through the city. Lunch at a small café. More kissing on park benches, street corners, and anywhere they felt like it.

They talked about work, about his family, and everything.

"So," Ben said that evening, sitting on her couch, "Tomorrow, work. Us at work, together after this."

"This?" she asked, smiling.

"This whole weekend of dates and kissing and being. Yeah. This." He fidgeted with her hand. "Are we...I mean…What do we tell people? Do we tell people? Do we hide it? What's the protocol?"

"What do you want to do?" she asked.

"I want to tell everyone," He admitted. "I want to walk in holding your hand. I want Tyler to lose his mind. I want the whole office to know that you picked me. But also, you're the CEO. And I don't want to make things complicated for you."

She thought about all the versions of herself. The CEO who ate salads at the counter, reviewed board materials, and never hummed. The woman who chose safe dresses and safe dinners and called it good judgment.

And then this. Ben was on her gray couch, asking what they should tell people, worried about making things complicated for her.

She didn't want to be careful about this.

Don't hide it, don't announce it, just be ourselves and let people figure it out."

"I like that," he said, pulling her closer. "Natural. Honest. Very us."

"Very us," she agreed.

They kissed on her gray couch until it was late, when he had to go home, and they both had work in the morning.

"I don't want to leave," he admitted at her door.

"I don't want you to leave either."

"But we're adults, with jobs, and responsibilities." He kissed her again. "Even though all I want to do is stay here and kiss you for approximately seventeen more hours."

"Very responsible," she teased.

"I'm the most responsible. Very mature. Totally not thinking about all the ways I'd rather spend tomorrow than in meetings." He grinned. "See you at work?"

"See you at work."

He left.

She closed the door and leaned against it, smiling like an idiot.

Monday. Work. Everyone would know just by looking at them.

She found she didn't mind.

CHAPTER 16

Monday morning, Mara walked into the office feeling like everyone could see "I KISSED BEN THIS WEEKEND" written across her forehead.

She'd changed her outfit three times, practiced looking normal in the mirror, and told herself she was a CEO who could handle this. She didn't succeed.

Ben was already at his desk, wearing dark jeans and a gray button-down. He was looking unfairly good.

He looked up at exactly the moment she walked in. Their eyes met. He smiled. Small. Shy. Just for her. She smiled back before she could stop herself. Then, immediately looking away, her heart racing, she walked quickly to her office. Smooth. Very professional. Totally normal.

Margaret was already at her desk. "Good morning, Ms. Wright. Your 11 AM is confirmed. Water with lemon will be on your desk shortly."

"Thank you," Mara managed, slipping into her office and closing the door. She sat at her desk. She took a breath and looked out her window. Ben was staring at his computer with intense focus. Too much focus, like he was trying very hard not to look at her office.

Her phone buzzed.

Ben: *Hi.*

Mara: *Hi.*

Ben: *So. That was awkward...the walking-in thing. I looked at you like a creep. Sorry.*

Mara: *You didn't look like a creep.*

Ben: *I absolutely did. Tyler's staring at me right now with a very suspicious expression. I think he knows.*

Mara: *He can't know. We were very subtle.*

Ben: *We were the opposite of subtle. I smiled at you like you hung the moon. I'm bad at this.*

Despite her nerves, Mara smiled at her phone.

Mara: *What do we do?*

Ben: *I don't know, act normal? Pretend this weekend didn't happen? Impossible because all I can think about is kissing you on my couch.*

Mara: *Ben!*

Ben: *Sorry. Professional thoughts only. Work thoughts.*

Ben: *This is going to be the longest day of my life.*

Tyler's voice carried through the office: "Are you okay, Ben? You've been staring at your screen for five minutes without moving."

Ben jumped. "I'm fine! Very focused! Important work!"

Mara looked away quickly, her face burning.

This was going to be impossible.

***

By 9:54, Mara had accomplished nothing.

She'd opened the same email six times, stared at the quarterly report without reading a single word, and reorganized her pens twice.

She could see Ben at his desk. He kept running his fingers through his hair, adjusting his collar, and glancing at her office when he thought no one was watching.

At 10:15, Tyler rolled his chair over to Ben's desk. Mara couldn't hear what he said, but she saw Ben's face go red. Saw him shake his head and walk away. Saw Tyler grin as if he'd just won the lottery.

Her phone buzzed.

Ben: *Tyler asked if I had a "good weekend." Then he did air quotes. Then he WINKED. I'm dying. This is how I die.*

Mara: *What did you say?*

Ben: *I said, "It was fine," and then my voice cracked like I'm going through puberty again. Very convincing.*

Mara: *He's going to figure it out.*

Ben: *He already knows, look at him, he KNOWS.*

Mara looked. Tyler was at his desk, grinning at his phone, occasionally glancing at Ben's desk and then at her office.

Ben: *Want to get coffee? So, we can talk without texting like middle schoolers?*

Mara: *Is that a good idea?*

Ben: *Probably not, but I really want to see you. Even if it's just in the break room for thirty seconds.*

Mara: *Okay. Five minutes.*

She waited exactly three minutes. Stood up and walked to the break room, trying to look casual.

Ben was already there, making coffee with intense concentration.

"Hi," he said quietly, not looking at her.

"Hi," she replied, walking to the coffee maker.

They stood there in awkward silence. Both making coffee. Both hyperaware of each other.

"So," Ben started, still not looking at her. "This is weird."

"Very weird."

"I don't know how to act around you. At work. After. Yeah." He finally looked at her. His eyes were warm but uncertain. "Do you regret it? This weekend? Us?"

"No," she said immediately. "Do you?"

"Not even a little bit." He smiled. Small. Real. "But I also don't know what we're doing. Like, what this is? What are we? If we're anything official or just... I don't know... Figuring it out?"

"I don't know either," she admitted.

"Okay, that's okay." He poured creamer into his coffee with hands that weren't quite steady. "We don't have to know yet. We can just. Be. Right?"

"Right."

They stood there making coffee, surrounded by the smell of burnt beans and the hum of the refrigerator, and Mara wanted desperately to kiss him again.

"I should get back to work," she said reluctantly.

"Yeah. Me too, critical work, definitely not just staring at spreadsheets and thinking about you." He picked up his coffee. "Mara?"

"Yeah?"

"I really like you, so you know, in case the weekend kissing didn't make that clear."

She smiled despite herself. "I really like you too."

"Good, Okay, I'm going back to my desk now before Tyler takes more photos for his conspiracy board."

"His what?"

"He has a conspiracy board about us. I saw it last week. Very detailed and slightly disturbing." Ben started backing toward the door. "See you later?"

"See you later."

He left.

Mara stood in the break room alone, holding her coffee and smiling like an idiot.

***

At 3:34, Eliza appeared in Mara's doorway.

"Okay," she said, closing the door behind her. "I'm worried, did something happen this weekend?"

"Nothing happened," Mara said, not looking up from her computer.

"Liar, you've checked your phone forty-seven times. You keep staring at Ben through the glass, and you're smiling at spreadsheets. SPREADSHEETS, Mara. You hate spreadsheets."

"I'm just in a good mood."

"Uh huh. And does this good mood have anything to do with a certain person in the office who also can't stop smiling today?"

Mara felt her face heat up. "I don't know what you're talking about."

"You went on a date, didn't you? Please tell me you went on a date. I've been waiting weeks for this. WEEKS."

"We went on a few dates," Mara admitted quietly.

Eliza's whole face lit up. "I KNEW IT. How many? Where? Did you kiss? Please tell me you kissed. If you didn't kiss, I'm staging an intervention."

"Eliza…"

"Details, now, I need all of them."

Mara looked at her best friend. At the genuine excitement on her face.

"We went on three dates this weekend," she said softly. "Mini golf, coffee, dinner at his place. And yes, we kissed."

Eliza squealed. "FINALLY. Oh my god. How was it? Is he a good kisser? He looks like he'd be a good kisser."

"I'm not discussing his kissing abilities with you."

"So, he's a good kisser. Got it." Eliza sat in the visitor chair. "Are you official? Boyfriend and girlfriend? What are you?"

"I don't know," Mara admitted. "We haven't really talked about it. We just, we're figuring it out."

"That's fair, but Mara?" Eliza leaned forward. "You're happy, I can see it, you're actually happy."

"I am," she said, surprised by how true it was. "I'm terrified, but I'm happy."

"Good. You deserve to be happy." Eliza stood. "Also, Tyler knows. Just so you're aware. He knows, and he's been texting the group chat all day with 'evidence.' You should probably prepare for that."

After Eliza left, Mara checked her phone.

Ben: *Eliza cornered you, didn't she? She cornered me ten minutes ago. I cracked immediately. Told her everything. I'm weak.*

Mara: *She cornered me, too. I also cracked.*

Ben: *So, the secret's out. Tyler definitely knows. Probably the whole office knows by now.*

Mara: *Probably.*

Ben: *Is that okay? People know we're. Whatever we are?*

Mara: *It's okay. Is it okay with you?*

Ben: *More than okay. I want people to know. I just don't want to make things weird for you at work. You're the CEO. I'm just the guy who makes plants die.*

Mara: *You're not "just" anything.*

Ben: *You're very sweet. Also, I miss you, which is stupid because you're literally fifty feet away. But I miss you.*

Mara: *I miss you too.*

Ben: *Want to get dinner tonight? After work? We could actually talk about what we are instead of texting about it like teenagers.*

Mara: *I'd like that.*

Ben: *Good. It's a date. Our fourth date. I'm keeping count.*

***

They left work separately. Met at a small Italian place three blocks from the office. Sat across from each other in a corner booth and tried to figure out what they were doing.

"So," Mara said, fidgeting with her napkin. "We should probably talk about this, about what we're doing."

"Good, because I've already told my mom about you, she's very invested."

Despite her nerves, Mara laughed. "Your mom sounds intense."

"She's a lot. But she means well. And she's right. I do have a bad attitude about my chances with you. Because you're amazing and I'm just me."

"You're not 'just' anything," Mara repeated. "You're funny and kind, and you make me laugh, and you see me.

You see the real me behind my CEO mask. That's not nothing, Ben."

He reached across the table and took her hand.

"So we're doing this?" he asked. "Dating? Seeing each other? Whatever we want to call it?"

"We're doing this," she confirmed.

"Even though it's complicated with work and everyone knowing and all of it?"

"Even though."

He smiled. That genuine Ben smile that made everything else fade away. "Can I kiss you? Right here? In public? Even though we don't have an official label yet?"

"Please," she said.

He leaned across the table. Kissed her. Sweet and soft and full of promise.

When they broke apart, they were both grinning.

"Fourth date was a success," he declared. "Established that we're doing this. Kissed in public. Very productive."

"Very productive," she agreed.

They had dinner. Talked. Laughed. Held hands across the table.

And when Ben walked her to her car later, kissed her goodnight against the driver's-side door, and said, "See you tomorrow," Mara felt something flutter in her chest.

She watched him walk to his car, hands in his pockets, that slightly crooked smile still on his face when he glanced back. And she realized with startling clarity: she was already counting the hours until tomorrow.

***

Tuesday Evening Mara was reorganizing her closet when her doorbell rang.

Ben stood there holding a tote bag that looked suspiciously heavy and a container of Thai food.

"Hi," he said. "I brought dinner. And also, books. A lot of books. Too many books. I may have a problem."

She laughed and let him in. "How many is too many?"

"Twelve." He set the bag down with a thud. "In my defense, I was thinking about what we talked about on Sunday. About Terry Pratchett. And reading when you're sad. And I thought maybe you'd want some options for your shelves."

He started pulling books out one by one. Pratchett novels. A biography she'd mentioned wanting to read. A cookbook about bread. A collection of essays. Each one clearly chosen with thought.

"Ben, this is..."

"Too much? It's too much. I got carried away at the bookstore. I told myself just two books, but then I saw this one." He held up a watercolor technique guide. "And you said you used to paint. And then I saw this one about urban gardens, and I remembered you looking at my sad plant, and..."

She kissed him. Quick and soft, cutting off his rambling.

When she pulled back, he was smiling that slightly dazed smile.

"So, not too much?" he asked.

"Not too much. But you know you didn't have to buy me books, right? You could've just brought yours over to read while we watch movies."

"I know. But I wanted to. Besides, half of these are library books I've been hoarding. You're helping me return them by osmosis." He picked up a worn paperback. "This one I annotated heavily. Fair warning. Very argumentative margins."

They ate Thai food on her couch, and afterward, Ben insisted on organizing the books onto her shelf himself.

"It has to be done right," he explained, kneeling by her bookshelf. "You can't just shove them in. Books have feelings."

"Books don't have feelings."

"These ones do. Look, this Pratchett needs to go next to the other Pratchett. They're a matched set. They'd be sad separated."

She watched him arrange and rearrange, muttering about alphabetical versus thematic organization, moving her existing books to make room, creating what he called "proper breathing space."

"You're reorganizing my entire shelf," she observed.

"I'm optimizing," he said, then winced. "Sorry. Bad word choice. I mean, I'm making it better. Making it ours."

"Ours?"

He looked up at her, suddenly uncertain. "If that's okay? Having my books here? I just thought, we spend so much time here, and I'm always wishing I had something to read, and…"

"It's okay," she said softly. "I like having your books here."

His whole face lit up. "Yeah?"

"Yeah, makes it feel more like both of us live here." He stood up, brushed book dust off his jeans. "Well, in that case, I should warn you. I have approximately two hundred more books at my apartment. We might need a bigger shelf."

"Two hundred?"

"I'm rounding down. For your mental health." He pulled her close. "But we can start with these twelve. See how they fit. Make sure they play nice with your books."

"You're ridiculous."

"I'm thorough. There's a difference." He kissed her forehead. "Come on, let's see if that documentary you wanted to watch is any good. I'll even let you pause it when I inevitably fall asleep twenty minutes in."

They settled on the couch, and Mara looked at her bookshelf. Ben's bright spines mixed with her neutral ones. His chaotic annotations next to her pristine pages. His enthusiasm filling her carefully organized space.

It looked right. Like it had always been meant to be this way.

***

On Wednesday, Mara was deep in budget projections when Ben appeared in her doorway holding a paper bag.

"Lunch delivery," he said, walking in without invitation. "Turkish place. Lentil soup and the good bread."

"You didn't have to…"

"You skipped breakfast."

He set the bag on her desk and perched on the edge, easy and familiar. "I have spies that tell me when you forget lunch."

"Margaret is not your spy."

"Margaret is everyone's spy. It's a very efficient spy network." He opened the containers. "Eat."

She picked up the soup. Still warm. Perfect temperature, he'd timed it exactly right.

They talked while she ate. It was an easy conversation with no agenda. He told her about the workplace morale module he was drafting. She told him about a board question she'd been avoiding. He was watching her eat with an expression she'd started to recognize. Soft. Like she'd done something right just by being there.

"Tonight is my old school's spring recital," he said. "Want to come? You'd get to see the kids."

"Yes! I can gather intel on you."

"You absolutely cannot use my kids against me."

"I won't." She smiled. "But yes. I'd like to see where you worked."

Ben leaned forward slightly. She tilted her face up. Their lips were maybe four inches apart.

"Hey Mara, do you have a second to…OH!" They jumped apart.

Tyler stood in the doorway. "Sorry," he said, not sounding sorry at all. "Terrible timing. Don't let me interrupt whatever this was."

He left. Still grinning.

"He took a photo," Ben said, staring at the doorway.

"We weren't doing anything."

"We were doing the face lean, both of us, simultaneously. That's textbook almost-kissing." He stood up, nearly knocked over her mug, and caught it at the last second. "I'm going before Tyler comes back with a film crew."

"He already sent it to the group chat."

"He absolutely did." He grabbed the empty bag. "See you tonight."

After he left, Mara sat with the comfortable weight of the afternoon around her. The soup had been exactly right. It always was.

CHAPTER 17

The elementary school auditorium smelled like floor polish and childhood nostalgia.

Rows of metal folding chairs filled the space, already packed with parents holding cameras, grandparents checking their phones, and siblings squirming impatiently. The stage at the front was decorated with construction paper flowers and hand-painted butterflies. String lights hung from the ceiling, casting everything in warm, slightly chaotic light.

Mara sat next to Ben in the third row. He was nervous, his knee bouncing, his fingers drumming on the armrest.

"You okay?" she asked quietly.

"Yeah, just, I haven't been back since I left. It's weird." He gestured at the room. "I spent five years here. The kids. The teachers. It was my whole life. And then I left for your job, and sometimes I wonder if I made the right choice."

"Do you regret it?"

He looked at her. "Not even a little bit. But I miss them, the kids, they're good kids."

The lights dimmed. Conversation died down. The principal walked on stage to scattered applause.

"Welcome to our Spring Concert!" she announced. "First up are our kindergarteners, who have been working very hard on today's performance. Please give them your warmest applause!"

Twenty-three five and six-year-olds filed onto the stage wearing construction paper flower crowns and butterfly wings that were falling off. They lined up in crooked rows, giggling and waving at parents, and one kid was half-picking his nose.

The music teacher played the opening notes of "You Are My Sunshine" on an out-of-tune piano.

The kids started singing.

It was beautiful and terrible and perfectly off-key. Half of them were too quiet. Three were too loud. One kid was singing an entirely different song. Another was making elaborate hand motions that no one else was.

Next to her, Ben's eyes were wet.

"Are you crying?" Mara whispered.

"No," he whispered back, crying. "I just have something in my eye. Probably dust. Very dusty auditorium."

"It's not dusty."

"It's extremely dusty." He wiped his eyes. "I taught half these kids. That's Emily on the left, she used to cry every morning until I let her be a line leader. And that's Marcus, he ate glue once, and I had to call poison control. And that's Sophia, she drew me a picture of a dinosaur every single day for six months."

"You really loved them."

"I really did, I still do, but the money, the stress, the being exhausted all the time." He turned to look at her. "And I wouldn't have met you if I'd stayed. So, it was worth it."

The song ended. The kids took a bow. Half of them forgot to bow and just waved. One kid did a cartwheel.

Enthusiastic applause.

***

After the concert, they waited outside while parents took photos and kids ran around hyped up on juice boxes and the thrill of performance.

"MR. BEN!"

A small whirlwind in a flower crown slammed into Ben's legs.

He stumbled back, laughing, and picked up the little girl. "Emily! You were amazing! Best flower performance I've ever seen!"

"I sang SO LOUD," Emily announced proudly.

"You did, I heard you from the back row, very powerful voice."

More kids appeared. Mobbing him. Talking over each other. Showing him their butterfly wings and telling him about their day and asking where he'd been.

"I got a new job," he explained, crouching down to their level. "I work at a different place now, with computers and grown-ups."

"That sounds boring," Jacob said.

"It's a little boring," Ben admitted. "But it's also so fun. I like it."

"Is that your girlfriend?" Sophia asked, pointing at Mara.

Ben's face went red. "She's my...We work together."

"Do you LIKE like her?" another kid asked.

"I. That's. That's a complicated question."

"Yes or no, Mr. Ben."

He looked at Mara.

She was trying not to laugh.

"Yes," he admitted. "I like like her."

"ARE YOU GOING TO MARRRRYYYY HER?"

"Okay, that's enough questions about my personal life, who wants to show me their butterfly wings?"

Successful distraction. The kids showed him their wings and then scattered to their parents to get juice boxes.

Sherry appeared, grinning. "You're so obvious, Ben."

"I'm subtle, very subtle."

"You just admitted to liking her in front of seventeen kindergarteners. By Monday, the whole school will know. Parents talk, teachers gossip, you've gone viral in the elementary school community."

"Great. Perfect. My personal life is now educational content." He said, then went on, "Mara, this is a fellow teacher, Sherry."

"Hi, nice to meet you, hope you enjoyed the concert."

"I did thank you."

After they said goodbye to everyone and walked back to the car, Mara took Ben's hand.

"So," Ben said. "This weekend? My mom. My sister. You."

"Should I be nervous?"

"Terrified. My mom's been planning this since I mentioned you existed. She's made a list."

"A list of what?"

"Questions. Topics. Conversation starters. It's color-coded. I saw it on her counter last week." He squeezed her hand. "Also, she's going to ask about grandchildren within the first ten minutes. I'm not joking. I've timed her before. Eight minutes is her record."

"Eight minutes?"

"She asked my sister's boyfriend about his family planning intentions before the appetizers arrived. He lasted three more dates before he fled the state."

Mara laughed. "I can handle your mom."

"Famous last words. She's also going to feed you constantly, like, aggressive feeding. You'll sit down, and suddenly there are seventeen different foods in front of you, and she's asking which ones you want while simultaneously putting them all on your plate."

"That sounds nice, actually."

"It is until you're so full you can't move, and she's still offering dessert. Plural. She makes three kinds. Minimum." He opened her car door. "Oh, and Jade's going to interrogate you about whether I'm a good boyfriend. Fair warning."

"Should I lie?"

"Probably, tell her I'm perfect, she'll know you're lying, but she'll respect the loyalty." He grinned. "But hey, you can survive my mom asking about your stance on circumcision."

"I'm sorry, what?"

"She's very interested in grandchildren' details. Very specific details. I've stopped being surprised." He leaned against the car. "Fair warning: she's also going to ask when we're getting married. Not if. When. She's already planning the wedding in her head. I'm pretty sure she has a Pinterest board."

"We've been actually dating for a week!"

"I know. I told her that. She said, 'When you know, you know.'"

"I'm definitely terrified now."

"Good, healthy fear is important." He kissed her forehead."

"No pressure."

"Tons of pressure, but you can handle it, you run a company. My mom's just one very enthusiastic Jewish woman with boundary issues and strong opinions about brisket."

"Just one?"

"Okay, also Jade. So, two very opinionated women with questions about your intentions with their precious Benjamin." He said his own name in his mother's voice. It made Mara laugh. "See? You're going to be fine. Just smile, eat whatever she puts in front of you, and when she asks about grandchildren, say 'we'll see' and change the subject to literally anything else."

"That's your strategy?"

"It's worked zero percent of the time, but I keep trying." He kissed her. "Come on, I'll drive you home. You need rest before the interrogation."

"You're really selling this."

"I'm managing expectations. My family's a lot. But they're also going to love you, almost as much as I do."

He said it casually. Like it wasn't a huge thing.

Mara's heart did a complete flip.

"Almost?" she managed.

"Okay, not even close, I love you way more, but they'll be solidly in second place. That's still pretty good."

He opened her car door like he hadn't just said he loved her for the first time in a parking lot while discussing his mother's invasive questions.

Mara got in the car, her face burning, her heart racing.

This weekend she was meeting his family.

And apparently Ben loved her.

This was going to be completely terrifying and probably wonderful.

She couldn't wait.

***

Saturday Afternoon- Ben's Mom's House

Ben's mom lived in a small house in the Sunset District, painted cheerful yellow with window boxes full of flowers that were somehow still alive despite the San Francisco fog.

Inside, it smelled like chicken soup, old books, and home. The living room was cramped, full of overstuffed furniture and family photos covering every surface. Embroidered pillows on the couch, a menorah on the mantle. Stacks of New Yorker magazines on the coffee table.

"She's here!" Jade called from somewhere in the house.

Ben's mom appeared from the kitchen wearing an apron that said "GRANDMA'S KITCHEN" despite not actually being a grandma yet. She was short, round-faced, with graying hair and Ben's exact smile.

"Mara!" She pulled Mara into a bear hug before Mara could react. "Finally! Come in, come in."

The kitchen was warm, steamy from cooking. Sunlight streamed through windows that looked out on a small garden. The table was set for four with mismatched plates and cloth napkins.

"When am I getting grandbabies?" Ben's mom asked before they'd even sat down.

"MOM," Ben said, his face turning red. "We've been officially dating for a little over a week."

"So? Your father proposed after two weeks. We were married in three months. When you know, you know."

"That was 1980. Things are different now."

"Love is love. Time doesn't matter." She scooped an enormous portion of brisket onto Mara's plate. "Eat. You're too thin."

Mara caught Jade's eye across the table. Jade mouthed "Sorry" and grinned.

Lunch was chaos.

Ben's mom told lots of stories. Ben's Bar Mitzvah, when he fell off the stage during his speech. Ben's seventh birthday party, where he cried because the magician's rabbit looked sad. Ben's high school graduation, where he tripped while walking to get his diploma.

"Mom, please," Ben kept uttering, hiding his face in his hands.

"What? These are good stories! Mara should know what she's getting into."

"I'm not 'getting into' anything. We are dating." He said.

"Nothing about you is casual, Benjamin. You're the least casual person I know. You alphabetize your spices."

"Organization is important!"

After lunch, Ben's mom pulled out photo albums. Baby pictures and awkward middle school photos; evidence of every terrible haircut Ben had ever had.

"I'm leaving," Ben announced. "I'm going to live in the car, this is too much."

"Sit down, Mara needs to see these."

Mara was laughing so hard she couldn't breathe. Ben at age seven with missing front teeth and a bowl cut. Ben at thirteen, all gangly limbs and unfortunate facial expressions. Ben at sixteen, trying to look cool and failing spectacularly.

"I was a very awkward child," Ben admitted.

"You were adorable," his mom corrected. "Awkward, but adorable. Like a puppy that hasn't grown into its paws yet."

Later, while helping with dishes, his mom turned to Mara.

"He's different with you," she said quietly, her hands in sudsy water. "Happy, he smiles big and talks differently. For five years he came here exhausted, stressed, barely holding on. Now he's. Lighter."

"He's good at his new job," Mara said, drying a plate.

"It's not the job, it's you." She handed Mara another plate. "You're good for him. Whatever you're doing, keep doing it."

"I'm not doing anything special."

"You're loving him, that's special, that's everything." She looked at Mara with Ben's exact eyes. "He's a good boy. Kind. Caring. Sometimes he's too caring. Don't hurt him, okay? His heart is very big and very breakable."

"I won't," Mara said, meaning it.

When they left, Ben's mom hugged Mara again, hard and quick. "Come back soon. Please don't wait for him to bring you back; show up. I'll feed you better food."

In the car, driving back to Mara's apartment, Ben groaned.

"I'm so sorry, she's a lot. The grandchildren thing. The interrogation. All of it."

"She's amazing," Mara said honestly. "I love her."

"She asked about grandchildren within two minutes, I counted, two minutes, Mara."

"I counted too. It was actually ninety seconds."

"Even worse! My mother has no chill. Zero chill. Negative chill." He pulled up to a stoplight, looked at her. "But you liked her?"

"I really liked her."

His smile could have powered the city. "Good. She liked you, too. I could tell. She doesn't usually bring out the photo albums for strangers; that's reserved for people she's already planning to keep."

***

The Ferry Building Farmer's Market was packed with a crowd on Sunday.

Stalls overflowed with produce: bright oranges, deep purple eggplants, and tomatoes so red they looked fake. The air smelled like fresh bread, roasting coffee, and something sweet and fruity. Street musicians played somewhere nearby, the sound of a violin competing with conversations and laughter and the screech of seagulls overhead.

Ben held her hand as they walked through the crowd, stopping at every third stall to examine something. He bought weird vegetables Mara had never heard of: Romanesco broccoli that looked like spirals; purple carrots, and striped tomatoes.

"What are you going to do with those?" she asked, watching him add more to their bag.

"Experiment. Cook. Create culinary magic."

"You're going to burn them and order pizza."

"Probably, but the effort counts." He stopped at a fruit stall. He picked up a pear and examined it with intense focus like he was buying a diamond. "This is a good pear. Very pear-like. Optimal pearness."

"You're ridiculous."

"I'm thorough, there's a difference."

He bought six pears.

At the apple stall, he decided to juggle three apples.

"Ben, don't…"

Too late.

He tossed the first apple up. Caught it. Tossed the second. Caught it. Tossed the third and dropped all three. One rolled into a display of peaches, another bounced off a customer's shoe, and the third dropped straight into the fountain.

"I got it!" Ben announced, chasing the apples.

He leaned over the fountain edge, reaching for the apple floating in the water. He leaned too far and lost his balance. He fell in, not fully, just one leg and most of his torso. But enough that he was soaking wet, dripping, and now holding a wet apple triumphantly.

"Got it!" he announced from inside the fountain.

Mara was laughing so hard she couldn't breathe. She was doubled over, tears streaming, unable to stop.

A small crowd had gathered. Some were laughing, others looked concerned, one person was filming.

"Sir, you can't be in the fountain," a security guard said, appearing from nowhere.

"I was retrieving my apple. It was a fruit rescue! A very important mission."

"Get out of the fountain."

Ben climbed out, dripping water everywhere. His jeans were soaked, his shirt clung to him, and his hair dripped into his eyes.

He looked at Mara, still laughing, and grinned. "Worth it for that laugh."

The apple vendor, an older woman with kind eyes, gave him a towel and a bag of apples for free. "For entertainment value, that was the best thing I've seen all week."

"I aim to please," Ben said, wringing out his shirt.

They walked through the market with Ben leaving a trail of water behind him. Other shoppers gave them a wide berth. A kid pointed and said, "Mommy, why is that man wet?"

"Because I made poor choices," Ben called back cheerfully.

A woman selling jam samples stopped them. "Are you two together?"

"Yes," Mara said before Ben could answer.

The woman smiled. "You're adorable, he's dripping on my booth, but you're adorable."

"I'm very sorry about the dripping," Ben said. "It's involuntary."

They sampled some jams and bought a few jars.

They made it back to Ben's car and got in. Both of them were laughing. There were bags full of weird vegetables and free apples in the back seat, and he was completely soaked.

"I can't believe you fell in a fountain," Mara said, buckling her seatbelt.

"I can't believe you called me your boyfriend to that jam lady."

"I didn't say, boyfriend, I said we're together."

"Same thing. You claimed me. In public. To a stranger." He was grinning like he'd won the lottery. "That's very official."

"Is it?"

"Very official, you can't take it back now, the jam lady knows, so it is legally binding."

She looked at him. Wet and ridiculous and happy. Looking at her like she was the best thing in his entire day, despite him literally falling into a fountain.

"I don't want to take it back," she said quietly.

His expression shifted. Softened. "No?"

"No."

"Good. Because I really like being together. Officially. With the jam lady as witness."

He leaned across the console and kissed her. He tasted like fountain water and laughter.

When they pulled apart, they were both smiling.

"Drop me off at my place and then go to your apartment so you can change," Mara said. "Then come over and we could order pizza, watch a movie?"

"That sounds great, and I can be dry."

They ordered pizza and talked and watched a movie. It was perfect, very easy, exactly what she wanted.

He stayed until the pizza was gone and the movie was half-watched and the Sunday quiet had settled around them.

***

Ben made it to his car before he called Jake. Sat in the driver's seat, keys in his lap, not quite ready to start the engine yet.

He'd almost told her. Three times tonight.

Once during pizza, when she'd laughed at something stupid he'd said and looked at him like he was the funniest person alive. Once during the movie, when she'd curled into his side and he'd thought: *I don't deserve this.* And once at her door, right before he kissed her goodnight, the words practically climbing up his throat.

But he'd swallowed them back down. Every single time.

The street was doing its golden hour thing. Warm light on parked cars and bay windows. Everything looked soft and right, like the whole city had exhaled.

Ben felt the opposite.

He pulled out his phone. Jake picked up on the second ring.

"I need to tell her," Ben said. "About New Year's. The dare. All of it."

"Yeah, you do."

"I tried tonight. I swear I tried. But then she was so happy and I just..." He stopped. Gripped the steering wheel. "After the gala. I'll tell her after the gala."

Silence. Then: "Ben."

"I know, I know, Jake." He said it before Jake could finish the thought he didn't need to hear.

He hung up and stared at Mara's building for a moment longer. Her apartment light was still on. Third floor, second window from the left. He'd memorized it without meaning to.

He could go back up there, right now, tell her everything. Get it over with.

But the gala was next week. A week of her looking at him like that. A week before everything fell apart.

He knew it was the wrong call. Knew it the same way he knew lots of things he did anyway.

Then he started the car and drove home.

CHAPTER 18

Monday morning, Mara walked into the office to find Tyler setting up his phone on a shelf in the break room.

She walked over. "What are you doing?"

"Science," he said, not looking at her. "Historical documentation, don't mind me."

"Tyler."

"Pretend I'm not here, I'm invisible, a ghost, very stealthy."

She made her coffee, hyperaware of the camera, and went to her office.

At 9:15, Ben appeared in the break room.

Tyler sat up straighter at his desk.

Mara watched Ben make coffee while looking toward her office. He was smiling that small private smile.

She got up and walked to the break room. She closed the door and pointed directly at Tyler's hidden camera.

"Hi," she said, laughing.

"Hi," Ben replied. "Is that his phone, or did he upgrade to actual surveillance equipment?"

"Probably both."

"Should we give him what he wants?"

"We've been keeping this secret for a while. I'm tired of sneaking around."

Ben set down his coffee, and she set down her cup.

He cupped her face with both hands. "You sure? Once we do this, Tyler wins."

"Tyler already won."

"Then let's make it official."

He kissed her. Slow and sweet and completely obvious. When they broke apart, Ben rested his forehead against hers. "We're very bad at keeping secrets."

"Terrible at it."

Outside the break room, Tyler jumped up from his desk.

"I GOT IT!" he yelled. "THEY'RE KISSING! EVERYONE COME HERE!"

The entire office converged on Tyler's desk. He pulled up the recording. Hit play. There they were. On camera. Kissing in the break room.

"VINDICATION!" Tyler shouted. "I WIN! EVERYONE PAY UP!"

The office erupted.

Priya yelled, "Finally!"

Sarah exclaimed, "This is the best Monday ever!"

Marcus sighed, "Tyler's going to be insufferable."

Eliza opened the door, grinning. "You two want to come out here and face the mob?"

Mara and Ben emerged holding hands.

The office cheered.

Tyler slow-clapped. "About damn time. How long has this been going on?"

"Since about the second day I was here, honestly. Maybe the first." Ben admitted.

"I knew it day one. You smiled at him weirdly."

"I didn't smile weirdly."

"You absolutely smiled weirdly, very suspicious smiling." Tyler pulled out his phone. "So... Are you together? Official?"

Mara looked at Ben, and he looked at her.

"We're together," she said.

"Officially together," Ben added. "Boyfriend and girlfriend."

The office celebrated.

Margaret appeared with her clipboard. "Should I update your emergency contacts to each other?" she asked.

"Not yet," Mara said. "We've only been together for two weeks."

"Efficiency is key, I'll prepare the forms for when you're ready."

Gerald appeared from his office, looking disapproving. "This won't affect your work performance, I trust?"

"No sir," Mara said. "Completely professional."

"We're very professional," Ben agreed. "The most professional couple in workplace history."

Gerald grunted and walked away.

After the chaos died down, Mara and Ben stood by her office.

"So," he said, still holding her hand. "We're public now."

"Very public."

"How do you feel about that?"

She thought about it. She thought about what she had expected to feel. Some version of anxiety, probably. Second-guessing. She usually ran an internal audit on every decision.

It wasn't there.

"I feel good," she said. "Scared, but good."

"Me too." He squeezed her hand. "Want to have lunch together? Publicly? Where everyone can see?"

"Like a real couple?"

"Like a real couple."

"I'd like that."

They kissed quickly, right there in the office, and Mara realized she'd stopped caring who saw.

***

Tuesday evening, Ben showed up at her door at seven with grocery bags in both arms and his cat lamp tucked under one elbow.

Mara looked at the lamp.

"It's small," he said immediately. "It doesn't take up any space. And I thought, since I'm here half the time anyway, maybe it should be here." He adjusted his grip on the bags. "I can take it back. I just thought it would make your side table less…"

"Bring it in," she said.

He beamed.

She stepped back and watched him carry everything into her apartment. He set the grocery bags on the kitchen counter and placed the lamp on her side table with the careful precision of someone setting down something important.

It was ceramic and roughly the size of a melon, shaped like a fat tabby cat with its tail curled around its base and a small bulb inside that glowed amber.

It looked completely wrong in her gray and white apartment.

She looked at it for a moment again and thought, it looked completely right.

"Okay," Ben said from the kitchen, rubbing his hands together with the energy of someone about to attempt something ambitious. "I'm making pasta again, but a different pasta. An upgraded pasta, I've been practicing."

"You've been practicing pasta."

"I've been practicing pasta. Jake was my test subject. He said it was great, but Jake will eat anything, so that's a low bar. But I think it's genuinely good." He pulled things out of the bags with focused efficiency: tomatoes, garlic, a bunch of basil, a block of Parmesan. "Can I ask you something about your kitchen?"

"You can ask."

"Where is everything?"

"That's not a question."

"It is. I don't know where anything is. Your kitchen is very organized, but the organization is not immediately legible to me." He opened a cabinet and found glasses. Closed it. Opened another and found plates. "See, I expected those to be swapped. You have glasses above the dishwasher but plates above the stove. Why?"

"Because I reach for plates more often at the stove."

"But you reach for glasses more often at the sink."

"I reach for glasses at the counter."

"Which is between the stove and the sink, so either position would be equally efficient, meaning the current system is arbitrary," He stated.

"It's not arbitrary, it's where I put them when I moved in, and I've never had a reason to change it."

"That's the definition of arbitrary." He found a cutting board without asking and set it on the counter. "I won't change anything, I'm just observing, but your system has internal logic that is different from my logic."

"Most things do."

"True." He found a knife without asking, which meant he'd been paying attention to her kitchen even before tonight. He started on the garlic. "Your apartment is very you, by the way."

"Is that good or bad?"

He looked up. "Very good. It's controlled and quiet, and everything is where it's supposed to be, and it smells like you." He seemed to realize what he'd said and looked briefly mortified. "That sounded less strange in my head."

"It's fine," she said, and meant it.

She sat at the counter and watched him cook. He moved more carefully here than in his own kitchen, which she hadn't expected. At his apartment, he was easy and unconscious, reaching past things without looking, narrating whatever he was doing because silence made him itchy. Here, he checked before opening drawers. Set things down gently. Stayed aware of his elbows. He was trying not to break her space.

Something shifted in her chest at that.

"Can I ask you something?" she said.

"Always."

"What are we doing?"

He looked up from the garlic he was mincing. Not startled. Like he'd been waiting for this in the way you wait for something you've been thinking about since Tuesday.

"Specifically, or in general?"

"In general."

He set down the knife and turned to face her properly, leaning back against the counter with his arms loosely crossed. He'd been thinking about this. She could tell because he didn't do the thing people do when they stall, the small throat-clearing, the glance away. He just looked at her and answered.

"I think we're figuring out how to be together," he said. "Without a roadmap. Because there isn't really one for this situation." He looked at his hands briefly. "I've never been someone's person the way I want to be yours. I've had relationships, but not this. Where I'm very sure about the person and very unsure about how not to ruin it."

"You're not going to ruin it."

"I might ruin it. I'm a disaster."

"You're a specific kind of disaster." She chose her next words carefully, because Mara didn't say things she didn't mean. "The kind I think I wanted without knowing it."

He looked at her for a long moment without speaking. Then he picked up the knife and went back to the garlic.

"Okay," he said quietly. "Then I think we keep doing this."

"Cooking in my kitchen?"

"Showing up. Figuring it out, one day at a time."

The pasta was excellent. Better than the first time, which had already been excellent. She didn't tell him that because she could see he was working very hard to seem casual about whether she liked it, and she thought letting him wonder for a few more bites was kinder than she would normally be. She told him on the third bite. His face did something she was going to be thinking about later.

They ate at her kitchen table, which she normally used as a surface for reviewing materials, and which had never, she realized, had two people sitting at it at the same time.

He told her about his projects and she told him about some things with the board. He asked two questions that were better questions than she'd expected, and then a third question that was exactly the right one, the one that cracked the problem open, and she sat there looking at him across her kitchen table thinking: of course. Of course it's him.

At some point, she refilled his wine without being asked. He noticed and smiled at his plate.

At ten o'clock, he gathered his things.

"I should let you sleep," he said at the door, bags in hand. "You have that early call tomorrow."

"I do."

He kissed her. Soft and unhurried, like he wasn't in any particular rush to be anywhere else, which she suspected he wasn't. Then he left.

She listened to his footsteps on the stairs.

She stood in the kitchen for a moment, looking at the clean counter and the two wine glasses drying on the rack. She was still thinking about the board question and the way he'd asked about it, direct and genuinely curious, not performing interest the way people performed interest at networking events.

He'd just wanted to know.

She opened the cabinet next to the sink and moved his wine glass to the left side, separate from hers. She didn't think about why. It just seemed right to have a place for it.

Ten minutes later, her buzzer rang.

"I forgot my phone charger," Ben's voice said through the intercom.

She buzzed him up.

He came back in, retrieved the charger from the outlet by the couch, and then stood in the middle of her living room with it in his hand, looking at the cat lamp glowing amber on her side table.

"It looks good there," he said.

"It does."

He looked at her.

She thought about her carefully controlled apartment. Her gray couch, white walls, and decorative lemons she'd never eaten. The stock photos of beaches in their silver frames. The space she'd designed to show that a successful person lived here, even though that person was rarely actually home.

The cat lamp didn't match any of it.

"Do you want to stay?" she asked.

"Yeah," he said. "I really do."

He put the charger back in the outlet.

***

Wednesday afternoon, Margaret appeared in Mara's office with her clipboard.

"Ms. Wright. I need to update the office directory. What address should I list for Mr. Rosen?"

Mara looked up from her laptop. "His apartment address. Why?"

"I asked him where he wanted the water delivered, and he said, and I quote, 'Oh, just put Mara's address, I live there most days.' Then he walked away before I could clarify." Margaret consulted her clipboard. "However, I need accurate information. The water delivery person needs to know where to leave Mr. Rosen's order."

"He ordered water to my apartment?" Mara smirked.

"Five-gallon dispenser. It's being delivered on Friday." Margaret made a note. "I'll list both addresses for now. But for efficiency purposes, you should clarify the living situation. Duplicate addresses create filing complications."

She left.

Ben had moved in she thought, his toothbrush is in her bathroom. His clothes are in her closet. His cat lamp is on her side table. His water dispenser is arriving on Friday.

They'd become a *we* without ever having the conversation.

And somehow that felt exactly right.

CHAPTER 19

Mara came home Thursday evening to find her kitchen rearranged.

Not slightly rearranged. Completely, totally, systematically reorganized.

The spatulas were in the drawer that used to hold measuring spoons. The measuring spoons were in the drawer that used to hold cooking utensils. The cooking utensils were in the cabinet above the stove. And the spices were lined up on the counter in alphabetical order, each one labeled with a small piece of tape.

Ben stood in the middle of this chaos, looking extremely pleased with himself, wearing one of her dish towels tucked into his jeans like an apron.

"I organized!" he announced, gesturing as if he'd just revealed a masterpiece. "Your kitchen was a disaster! Very inefficient, borderline dangerous."

Mara stared. "You reorganized my entire kitchen."

"I optimized it based on usage frequency and logical grouping." He gestured excitedly. "See? Spatulas near the stove. Measuring spoons in the baking zone. Spices alphabetized for easy access. No more searching for cumin. Just go to C."

"I had a system."

"You had chaos masquerading as a system."

"It worked for me."

"Did it though?" He opened a drawer proudly. "Look! All the wooden spoons together! Organized by size!"

"I could find what I needed before. Because I knew where everything was."

"But your system didn't make sense; it was arbitrary."

"It was based on how I use the kitchen."

"Well, now it's based on how WE use the kitchen. Our kitchen deserves better organization."

Mara took a breath. "Where are MY dish towels?"

"In the drawer by the sink. Makes perfect sense, right?"

"They were in the drawer by the oven, where I use them for hot things."

"But you also use them for drying dishes." He stopped, finally noticing her expression. "You're upset."

"I'm not upset."

"You're doing that thing where your jaw gets tight."

"I'm processing that you reorganized my entire kitchen without asking."

"I was being helpful." His enthusiasm deflated. "You said you wanted me to feel at home here, make it ours. So I made it functional."

"It was functional!"

"It was chaos!"

"It was MY chaos!"

"Well, it's OUR chaos now, and OUR chaos should be alphabetized!" Ben stated a little too loudly.

They stared at each other across the rearranged kitchen.

"The spices were organized by cuisine," Mara said, her voice getting louder. "Asian together. Mediterranean together. Your alphabetical system mixes them up. Cumin is next to cinnamon; those are not the same cuisine!"

"Alphabetical is objective! Cuisine-based is subjective!"

"It was MY logic!"

"Well, OUR logic should be BETTER logic!"

"Your logic is not better, it's just DIFFERENT!"

"Different AND better!"

They both stopped and stared at each other. Then they started laughing.

"Did we just have our first big fight?" Ben asked. "About spice organization?"

"I think we did." Mara looked at the alphabetized spices. "This is ridiculous."

"Extremely ridiculous. We're fighting about cumin placement."

He walked over and pulled her into a hug. "I'm sorry, I should have asked before reorganizing your kitchen. I got excited and didn't think."

"I'm sorry I got annoyed; you were trying to help and the wooden spoons by size are actually genius." She looked up at him. "But the spices need to go back to cuisine-based."

"What if we compromise? Spices by cuisine, but alphabetized within each cuisine?"

"That's actually not terrible."

"I'm brilliant. A genius of kitchen organization."

"You're a disaster who occasionally has good ideas."

He kissed her forehead. "Dish towels by the oven?"

"Yes."

"Spatulas stay by the stove?"

"Fine."

"Look at us compromising. Very mature."

"We just screamed about cumin."

"We had a passionate discussion about optimization. That's very different."

They spent the next hour reorganizing together. Mara showed him why things lived where they did. Ben suggested improvements that made sense. They argued over whisks and compromised on a separate drawer. By the end, the kitchen was a hybrid of both their systems. Part chaos, part optimization. Completely theirs.

"Better?" Ben asked.

"Better," Mara agreed.

He pulled her close. "Still love me even though I caused our first fight?"

"I still love..." She stopped. Froze.

They both went very still.

"I mean," Mara scrambled. "I still like you. Very much. Maximum liking levels."

"Maximum liking levels," Ben repeated, his eyes warm. "Got it. Very high liking occurring."

They both smiled. Both knew what almost happened. Both let it sit there, unspoken but present.

"Thai food?" Ben suggested.

"Thai food sounds perfect."

They ordered in, ate at the table, and Mara thought about how fighting with Ben felt different. It felt safe, like they could disagree and still choose each other. Like this was what it felt like when something was working.

****

Friday, Ben was in the bedroom changing out of his work clothes when Mara came in.

"Can you help me with this?" she asked, turning to show him the zipper on her dress.

He zipped it down slowly, his fingers brushing her spine.

She stepped out of the dress and hung it in the closet. She stood there in her bra and underwear. Burgundy. The matching set.

Ben went very still.

"You're staring," she said, reaching for her sweatpants.

"I'm appreciating, there's a difference." He walked over and put his hands on her hips, gentle but firm. "You're beautiful, you know that, right?"

"I'm starting to."

His thumbs traced small circles on her hips. "I mean it, all of you, exactly as you are."

She looked up at him, at the way he was looking at her, like she was everything.

"Derek said I needed to lose weight before we could be partners," she said quietly. "Said I needed optimization."

Ben put his finger on her lips to shush her, then put his hands back on her hips. "Derek is an idiot who doesn't deserve opinions about anything, especially you."

"He said the most successful wellness CEOs are fit. That I needed to embody the brand."

"The brand is mental wellness, and you embody that perfectly. You built a thirty-million-dollar company while dealing with people like Derek. That's the brand." He pulled her closer. "You don't need optimization. You don't need fixing. You're already everything you're supposed to be."

"You're biased."

"Extremely biased. Completely compromised. Zero objectivity." He kissed her forehead. "But also correct."

She leaned into him, his hands warm on her hips, and realized something. She was standing in her underwear, having a conversation about Derek Morrison, and she wasn't thinking about her body. She wasn't worried about what Ben was seeing. She felt comfortable, safe, and beautiful.

Comfortable. Safe. Beautiful.

"I like that you're here," she said. "That you let me complain. That you put your hands on my hips like you mean it."

"I definitely mean it." His voice was lower now. "These hips are very nice, excellent hips, best hips." He whispered.

She laughed. "Best hips?"

"Top tier. Award-winning. If there were hip awards, you'd win."

"You're ridiculous."

"I'm serious. I have very strong opinions about these hips." He pulled her closer. "And the rest of you, all of it. You're stunning."

She kissed him softly at first, then deeper. His hands stayed on her hips, holding her steady.

The kiss was long and intense and full of heat. They kissed deeper, and she moaned a little when he traced his hand up her stomach.

When they pulled apart, she smiled at him.

A long, slow smile.

Then she grabbed her sweatpants and t-shirt and slowly pulled them on while he watched.

"Thank you," she said.

"For what?"

"For making me feel beautiful, for seeing me, all of me."

"I like all of you. Even the parts that stress-organize."

He kissed her once more, and then he took her hand. "Come on. I'm making dinner tonight. I found a recipe and it looks very simple."

"You're going to burn something."

"I'm NOT going to burn something. I'm going to follow the recipe exactly and create a masterpiece."

"This is going to be a disaster."

"This is going to be FINE."

They walked out of the bedroom and into the kitchen, holding hands and feeling loved.

***

Forty-seven minutes later, the fire alarm went off.

Mara ran from the living room and into the kitchen to find smoke billowing from the oven, Ben frantically waving a dish towel at the smoke detector.

"WHAT DID YOU DO?" she yelled over the alarm.

"I FOLLOWED THE RECIPE!"

"DID YOU CHECK WHAT WAS IN THE OVEN BEFORE YOU TURNED IT ON?"

Ben's face went pale. "Was there something in the oven?"

"SOME TUPPERWARE. I STORE MY EXTRA TUPPERWARE IN THERE!"

"WHO STORES THINGS IN THE OVEN?"

"EVERYONE STORES THINGS IN THE OVEN!"

The building intercom crackled to life. *Attention residents. The fire alarm has been activated. Please evacuate immediately.*

They looked at each other.

"We're going to be those neighbors," Ben said. "The ones everyone hates."

"We're already those neighbors."

They grabbed their phones and keys. Ben was still in socks. Mara didn't have time to tell him.

They ran.

The hallway was full of residents in various states of annoyance and pajamas. An elderly man in a bathrobe glared. A woman in yoga pants carried her cat, who looked personally offended. Mrs. Rodriguez from two doors down appeared in her doorway.

"Is this you?"

"It's us," Mara admitted. "Cooking accident."

"You're the one with the boyfriend who sings loudly?"

"That's also us."

Mrs. Rodriguez shook her head and joined the stream toward the stairs.

Halfway down the stairwell, they found Eliza. She took one look at them, at Ben's sock-covered feet, Mara's guilty expression, and started laughing.

"You set off the fire alarm. You actually set off the building fire alarm." She said laughing.

"There was a Tupperware situation," Ben said.

"A Tupperware situation." Eliza wiped her eyes. "I've been having the most boring day and now this."

Outside, two fire trucks pulled up. The entire building had gathered on the sidewalk, a hundred people in coats, all looking cold and annoyed, all somehow knowing it was them.

The firefighters cleared the apartment fifteen minutes later. Smoke damage, melted Tupperware, one ruined oven.

Everyone filed back in. Mara and Ben rode the elevator up in silence.

The apartment still smelled like smoke and failure. The casserole sat on the counter, beyond saving.

Ben looked at it for a long moment.

"I'm never cooking again," he announced. "I almost burned down the building trying to make you dinner."

He sat on the couch and put his head in his hands. "Your neighbors hate me."

"They already hated you. The loud singing sealed that weeks ago."

He looked at her. "You're not embarrassed?"

"I'm mortified, but also I'm laughing, because this is very you. This is exactly the kind of disaster I signed up for when I agreed to be your girlfriend."

"You signed up for fire alarms?"

"I signed up for chaos. Fire alarms fall under the chaos umbrella."

He pulled her close. "I'm sorry I almost burned down your building."

"Our building. You gave Margaret this address, remember?"

"I did do that. That's romantic."

"It's very us."

They sat there on the couch, windows still open, apartment still smelling like smoke. And Mara thought about how this was her life now. Fire alarms, fountain incidents, and kitchen reorganization fights.

And somehow it was exactly what she wanted.

***

Saturday Afternoon — Luna Café

Mara arrived at the café ten minutes early.

Her mother was already there.

Of course she was, Janice Wright was never late. Being late was disrespectful. Being early was prepared.

"Mara!" Her mom stood, pulled her into a hug that smelled like expensive perfume and judgment. "You look wonderful, sweetheart. That blouse is very flattering."

Flattering. The word that meant *hides your flaws well.*

"Thanks, Mom."

They sat at a small table by the window. Her mom ordered a salad without dressing and water. Mara ordered a sandwich, turkey and brie with chips. Her mom's eyes flicked when she said chips. She didn't say anything. Didn't need to.

"So," her mom said, arranging her napkin precisely on her lap. "Tell me about Ben."

"He works at my company. Manager of Employee Experience. We met when he was accidentally hired as my assistant. He used to be a kindergarten teacher. It's a long story. We've been dating for almost two and a half weeks."

"An assistant?" Her mom's smile didn't waver, but something shifted in her eyes. "That's nice. And he treats you well? You're happy?"

"Very happy."

"Good. That's what matters." She paused. "How much does he make in his new position?"

"I don't know. That's not really…"

"It's important, financial stability matters, you've worked so hard to build your career, and you need someone who can match that."

Mara's sandwich arrived. Warm bread, melted cheese. She took a bite. Her mom watched, then smiled. "You're so lucky you can eat whatever you want."

There it was.

"I'm hungry," Mara said.

"Of course! You work so hard." Her mom sipped her water. "I've just been reading about this wonderful program. Not a diet, a lifestyle change. My friend Carol tried it and…"

"I'm not interested, Mom."

The door chimed. Ben walked in fifteen minutes late, looking slightly windblown. His hair was a mess, and his shirt was wrinkled. He spotted their table and waved.

Mara wanted to cry with relief.

"Sorry, I'm late!" he said, arriving breathless. "My meeting ran over, and traffic was terrible. Hi, I'm Ben." He stuck out his hand to Mara's mom.

Janice stood, shook his hand, and evaluated him in approximately three seconds. Former assistant, wrinkled shirt, messy hair. Mara could see the calculation happening.

"Janice Wright. So lovely to finally meet you, Mara's told me so much about you."

"All good things, I hope." Ben sat down next to Mara. Under the table, his knee pressed against hers. Warm. Solid. Present.

"Of course, she's very smitten."

Ben's face went slightly pink. He looked at Mara. She widened her eyes in a look that said: *Help me.*

He pressed his knee harder against hers in response.

Janice put him through the full interview. Career goals. Financial sustainability. Family background. Ben answered every invasive question with complete honesty and zero self-consciousness, which Mara found both mortifying and deeply endearing.

"And what attracted you to Mara?" Janice asked finally.

Ben's whole face softened. "Everything. Her competence, her kindness, the way she tries so hard to be appropriate when all I want is for her to be herself." He looked at Mara. "She's brilliant and funny, and she reorganizes things when she's stressed, and she laughs like she's surprised joy is allowed to exist. She's the best person I've ever met."

Mara's face was burning. Under the table, she squeezed his hand so hard it probably hurt.

Janice watched this exchange with an unreadable expression. "That's very sweet." She paused. "And you're supportive of Mara's health and wellness? Encourage her to make good choices?"

Mara kicked him under the table. Hard. A warning.

Ben's eyes flicked to her. She shook her head slightly.

"Health is important," Ben said slowly. "Being happy is important. Mara's both of those things, so I'm not sure what you're asking."

"Mom," Mara said, her voice sharp. "Don't."

"I'm just…"

"You've been making comments since I sat down." Mara set down her sandwich. "I know what you're doing, and I need you to stop. I feel happy, genuinely happy for the first time in years, because I'm with someone who thinks I'm enough exactly as I am. I'd like you to be happy about that too."

The table went quiet.

Janice dabbed at her mouth with her napkin. "Well, I'm glad you're happy. That's what matters."

The conversation shifted, became lighter. Janice asked about work. Ben told a story about Tyler's elaborate documentation system that made everyone laugh. Mara finished her sandwich, including the chips, and didn't care what her mother thought.

When they said goodbye in the parking lot, Janice hugged Mara. "He's very sweet," she said quietly. "A bit messy, not very polished, but sweet."

"He's perfect," Mara said.

"If you're happy, I'm happy." She didn't sound happy, but she smiled, got in her car, and drove away.

Ben and Mara stood in silence in the parking lot.

"Your mom is intense," Ben said finally.

"I know, I'm sorry."

"Don't apologize. She's your mom; she cares about you." He turned to face her. "But she's wrong. About all of it." He put his hands on her face. "You're perfect exactly as you are. Anyone who can't see that is an idiot, even if that person is your mom."

"I don't care what she thinks," Mara said. And for the first time, she meant it completely.

She kissed him, right there in the café parking lot.

"Thank you for coming," she said. "For being honest, and for defending me."

"Always. Even against terrifying mothers with strong opinions about chips."

They got in the car and drove home, Ben's hand finding hers before they'd even left the parking lot.

CHAPTER 20

A week later, Mara stood in her bedroom staring at the emerald dress hanging on the closet door.

The Elementary Teacher Foundation Gala was in two hours.

"You're staring at it as if it might attack you," Eliza said from the doorway. She'd appeared twenty minutes ago with wine and unsolicited advice, which was basically Eliza's love language.

"I'm deciding if I can pull it off."

"You can pull it off. We literally bought it specifically because you looked stunning in it." Eliza walked over and examined the dress. "Green is your color. It makes your skin glow and is very expensive-looking. Ben's going to lose his mind."

"That's not why I'm wearing it."

"It's absolutely why you're wearing it. You want him to look at you like you hung the moon, there's nothing wrong with that."

Mara changed into the dress. Eliza zipped her up. They both looked at the mirror.

The emerald green hugged her curves in ways that made her want to celebrate and hide at the same time. The neckline showed collarbones she usually kept covered. Her dark hair looked richer against the green. Her skin glowed.

She looked beautiful.

"Wow," Eliza said quietly. "Yeah, Ben's definitely going to malfunction."

"Stop."

"I'm serious. His brain is going to short-circuit, blue screen of death, cannot compute." Eliza stepped back and examined her with a critical eye. "You look like someone who runs a thirty-million-dollar company and doesn't need anyone's approval. Wear that energy."

"I'm terrified."

"Good, terrified means you care. Now put on the heels and let's make you gorgeous."

Thirty minutes later, Mara heard the doorbell.

Ben had gone back to Jake's apartment to get ready, claiming he needed moral support to figure out how bow ties worked. Now he was here to pick her up like they were going to prom instead of a foundation gala.

Eliza answered the door.

Mara heard Ben's voice from the bedroom. "Is she ready?

"She's in the bedroom. Go tell her she's beautiful, I have to leave anyway." Eliza grabbed her bag. "Have fun at the fancy gala and don't let anyone make you feel small."

She left.

Ben appeared in the bedroom doorway.

He was wearing a tux, an actual tux. Black jacket, white shirt, bow tie that was only slightly crooked. His hair was attempting to rebel against whatever product he'd used to tame it. He looked nervous, handsome, and completely out of his element.

He looked at her and his mouth fell open but no sound came out.

"Hi," Mara said.

"You're..." He stopped. Started again. "I can't... Words aren't working…My brain stopped making words."

"Is that good or bad?"

"It's the best. You're the most beautiful thing I've ever seen, like ever, in my entire life. Including that sunset from Twin Peaks and that time I saw the ocean at dawn. You're more beautiful than all of that."

She laughed. "You're very dramatic."

"I'm very honest. You broke my brain. I'm going to fall into seventeen things tonight just looking at you." He walked closer, his eyes never leaving her face. "Mara. You're stunning."

"You look handsome, too, very sophisticated."

"I look like I'm playing dress-up, this bow tie is strangling me." He pulled at it nervously. "But you, you look like you were made for this dress. Or the dress was made for you. I don't know how fabric works, but whatever's happening here is magic."

He handed her flowers. Sunflowers. Bright and impossible to ignore.

"You brought flowers."

"I'm courting you. Very formally. With flowers and compliments and a rental tux that costs more than my car payment."

She kissed him. Careful not to mess up her lipstick, but unable to help herself.

"Ready?" he asked.

"Ready."

They left the apartment and walked to his car. Ben opened her door like they were in a movie.

"This is very fancy," Mara said.

"I'm being a gentleman; Jake gave me a whole lecture about gala etiquette. Apparently, there are rules, many rules, and I'm going to break most of them accidentally."

"Just don't fall into anything."

"No promises. You in that dress is very distracting. A safety hazard. I should file a report."

They drove toward the Fairmont Hotel, and Mara thought about how two months ago she'd been alone. CEO Mara, who didn't date employees, or fall for kindergarten teachers, or wear emerald dresses that made her feel beautiful.

Now she was holding hands with the wrong Ben, who turned out to be exactly right, wearing a dress that hugged every curve, heading to a gala where she'd meet his friends and maybe, finally, tell him she loved him.

She had no idea that in three hours, everything would be destroyed.

For now, it was just Friday night. A fancy dress. And a man who looked at her like she was magical.

***

The Grand Ballroom at the Fairmont Hotel looked like something out of a fairytale dipped in gold. Crystal chandeliers the size of compact cars hung from the vaulted ceiling, casting light across polished marble floors. Round tables draped in ivory linens dotted the space, each centerpiece an explosion of white roses and eucalyptus. A string quartet played something classical in the corner. Waiters in crisp white jackets glided between clusters of formally dressed guests carrying champagne on silver trays.

There were signs with 'WellPath,' Mara's competition and Derek's company, all over the venue. It must be his foundation sponsoring the event she thought.

Ben stood at the entrance, his hand clasped in Mara's.

He looked significantly calmer than she'd expected. Still nervous, but not the "about to walk into my own execution" energy he'd had two weeks ago when they'd bought the tux.

"You okay?" she asked.

"I'm good, weirdly good." He straightened his shoulders. "I belong here. We belong here. I've been practicing that in the mirror."

"You practiced in the mirror?"

"Jake made me, he said I needed to stop apologizing for existing in fancy spaces." Ben squeezed her hand. "So, I'm not apologizing. I'm just going to walk in there, celebrate my best friend, and try not to spill anything on this rental tux."

"Very mature."

"I'm growing as a person, slowly, with setbacks. But growing."

They walked into the ballroom hand in hand.

"BEN!" Jake's voice cut through the refined murmur like a foghorn. He appeared through the crowd wearing a tux that somehow looked both perfectly fitted and utterly wrong on his large frame. "You made it! And you brought Mara! She's real! I was starting to think you'd made her up!"

"Why would I make up a girlfriend?" Ben asked, accepting Jake's enthusiastic hug.

"Because you talk about her constantly in a way that seems too good to be true. Like 'my girlfriend is brilliant and beautiful and funny and perfect,' and we're all like

263

'sure, Ben, your imaginary perfect girlfriend.'" Jake turned to Mara, his grin infectious. "But you're real! And you're actually here! With him! On purpose!"

"On purpose," Mara confirmed.

Maya appeared next, her pink hair styled into an elegant updo, her dress a deep purple. "Oh my God, you look stunning. Ben, you didn't mention that your girlfriend looks like she should be on a magazine cover."

"I mentioned it," Ben protested. "Multiple times. I have literally not stopped mentioning it."

"Fair," Maya conceded. "You do talk about her a lot. Excessively, even." She smiled at Mara. "You two are adorable together, like disgustingly adorable. I want to hate it, but I can't because it's too genuine."

Sherry joined them. Her dress was an elegant navy. "Finally, the famous Mara, Ben has shown us approximately eight hundred photos."

"Eight hundred is an exaggeration," Ben said, his face going pink.

"It's not an exaggeration," Jake said. "We've seen the photo evidence, you're obsessed."

"I'm appropriately enthusiastic about my girlfriend."

"You're unhinged about her, there's a difference."

They talked for several minutes. Ben's friends surrounded them with warmth that made Mara's chest feel tight. They asked about her work, her company, her life, but not in the evaluating way her mother had. They asked because they genuinely wanted to know. Because she mattered to Ben, and therefore she mattered to them.

But then Mara caught a flash of movement in her peripheral vision that made her entire body tense.

Derek Morrison stood about twenty feet away near the bar, champagne in hand, talking to a woman in a red dress with the easy confidence of someone who believed the world was designed for his comfort. He was wearing a tuxedo that made every muscle stand out, his hair perfectly styled, his smile charming and completely devoid of genuine warmth.

He must have felt her staring because he turned, his eyes finding hers across the space, his expression shifting into something that might have been surprise or might have been calculation dressed up as surprise.

Ben noticed the change in her immediately, his hand tightening around hers. "What's wrong?"

"Derek's here," she managed.

"Where?" Ben's voice had an edge she'd never heard before.

"By the bar, dark tux, talking to the woman in red."

Ben turned casually, like he was just scanning the room, then turned back with his jaw set. "Want to leave? We can leave. Jake will understand."

"No. I'm not letting him ruin this." She squeezed his hand. "I'm here with you. He doesn't matter."

"He doesn't matter," Ben repeated firmly. "You're with me, I'm with you, Derek can go synergize himself off a cliff."

She laughed despite herself and felt some of the tension drain from her shoulders.

"We should find our table," Jake said, checking his watch. "The awards ceremony starts in twenty minutes. They asked me to sit up front since I'm being honored, which means I can't hide in the back like I want to."

"You deserve this," Ben said, his voice carrying genuine emotion. "You're an amazing teacher, the kids are lucky to have you."

"Thanks, man." Jake's eyes went slightly bright. "Means a lot coming from you."

They found their table near the front, close enough to the stage to see Jake's nervous fidgeting. The table was set with more silverware than any person reasonably required, crystal wine glasses catching the light, name cards in elegant calligraphy.

Ben pulled out Mara's chair for her and then sat down next to her. He put his hand on her knee under the table.

"You're doing great," she whispered.

"I haven't spilled anything yet. New personal record."

The lights dimmed slightly. The Superintendent of Schools took the stage, welcomed everyone, and thanked the event sponsors. He launched into a speech about the importance of dedicated educators. The awards ceremony moved quickly with five teachers honored, Jake among them. He walked to the stage looking terrified and proud, accepted his plaque, and gave a short speech about patience, creativity, and loving children even when they ate glue.

Ben watched with undisguised pride, clapping so hard his hands must have hurt.

When Jake finished, Ben was on his feet immediately, clapping louder than anyone else. "That's my friend!" he said to no one in particular. "That's my best friend, and he deserves every bit of recognition he's getting!"

Several people at nearby tables smiled. One woman wiped her eyes.

After the ceremony, the ballroom opened up for mingling and dancing. The string quartet was replaced by a small jazz band. People were moving between tables, congratulating the honorees, networking, doing the delicate social dance these events required.

"Want to dance?" Ben asked, standing and offering his hand.

"You're going to step on my feet."

"Absolutely, multiple times, but I'll apologize each time, and you'll laugh at me, and it'll be romantic in a clumsy, disaster-prone way."

They moved to the dance floor. Ben pulled her close, one hand at her waist, the other holding hers. They swayed to the music.

True to his word, he stepped on her feet twice in the first thirty seconds.

"Sorry," he said immediately, his face flushing. "I told you I was bad at this."

"You're perfect at this," she said, and meant it in ways that had nothing to do with dancing.

They moved together, not graceful but genuine, and Mara let herself sink into the moment. The weight of his hand at her waist, the warmth of his palm against hers. The way he looked at her like she was the only person in the entire ballroom.

"Thank you for coming tonight," he said quietly. "For meeting my friends. For being here. For all of it."

"There's nowhere else I'd rather be."

"I'm so happy you exist," he said, pulling her slightly closer.

She almost said it then. Almost said the three words that had been sitting on her tongue for weeks.

But the song ended, and people started clapping politely. The band transitioned into something more upbeat.

"I need a drink," Ben said. "You want something? White wine?"

"White wine sounds perfect."

"I'll be right back, don't let Derek near you, I'll fight him. I've never fought anyone in my life, but I'll figure it out. YouTube has tutorials for everything."

"Please don't fight Derek."

"Fine, but I'm thinking about fighting Derek. Very aggressive thoughts."

He kissed her cheek and headed toward the bar.

Mara watched him go, smiling to herself, thinking about how much she loved him. How much he protected her. How right he was.

***

Ben stood in line at the bar, which had somehow accumulated to about fifty people all having the same idea about needing alcohol to survive formal events.

The woman in the sequined dress ahead of him was loudly complaining about something to her companion. Ben was trying to be patient, reminding himself that good things came to those who wait, when he heard Jake's voice cutting through the ambient noise.

"Remember New Year's?" Jake was saying, his words slightly slurred in a way that suggested he'd been celebrating his award with enthusiasm. "When we got Ben so drunk he could barely stand and then dared him to apply for that CEO assistant job?"

Ben's head whipped around so fast he nearly gave himself whiplash.

Jake was standing about fifteen feet away with Maya and Sherry, all three clustered near a high-top table, wine glasses in hand, clearly reminiscing.

"Oh my God, yes!" Maya's laugh carried across the dance floor. "Two hundred dollars! Best money we ever spent! He was like 'I'm gonna revolutionize corporate snack inventory management' and we were crying laughing!"

Ben started moving toward them, panic rising in his chest, but the bar line was packed and he couldn't get through without causing a scene.

"The application was so ridiculous," Sherry added, giggling. "He said 'conflict resolution' and meant 'mediating crayon fights' and 'crisis management' meaning 'preventing glue consumption.' I can't believe anyone actually hired him!"

"And then he actually fell for her!" Jake was saying, his voice carrying. "Like genuinely fell in love! We thought he was just going to do it for the money and quit, but no! Plot twist! He met her and immediately turned into a disaster of feelings!"

"It was very sweet," Maya said. "Watching him completely lose his mind over this woman he was supposed to be trolling, very rom-com."

"The dare that turned into true love," Sherry said dramatically, raising her wine glass. "Two hundred dollars well spent! We're basically Cupid!"

Ben finally broke free of the line, abandoning his mission to get drinks, moving toward his friends with single-minded purpose.

But he was too late.

"Fascinating story."

Ben froze.

Derek Morrison stood just behind Jake's group, champagne in hand, two fresh drinks balanced in his other hand as he'd just come from the bar. His expression was one of delighted interest that made Ben's stomach drop.

"I couldn't help but overhear," Derek continued, his voice smooth and pleasant. "You're Ben's friends?"

"That's us!" Jake turned, completely oblivious to the danger. "You know Ben?"

"I know Mara, his girlfriend." Derek's smile was all teeth. "We work together, I'm Derek Morrison, small world."

The temperature around their little group dropped approximately forty degrees. Maya's eyes went sharp. Sherry's smile disappeared. Jake looked like he'd just realized he'd wandered into a trap.

"Oh," Jake said, his enthusiasm deflating. "You're that Derek."

"I'm that Derek," he confirmed pleasantly. "And you were just talking about how Ben applied for Mara's assistant position on a drunken dare? For two hundred dollars? After you got him drunk specifically to make him do something ridiculous?"

The silence that followed was so profound Ben could hear his own heartbeat thundering in his ears.

"That's not..." Maya started, but Derek was already moving away, his champagne still perfectly level, his expression that of someone who'd just found exactly what he was looking for.

Ben got to the table. "Shit. Shit shit shit."

Jake's face had gone pale. "Ben, I'm so sorry. We were just reminiscing; we didn't know he was there. We didn't mean..."

"I know, it's not your fault, this is my fault, I should have told her weeks ago." But his voice sounded distant to his own ears.

He turned, scanning the ballroom for Mara, and found her immediately. She had that effect on him, pulling his attention like gravity.

She was at their table, and Derek was sitting in Ben's seat, leaning close, talking with animated interest while her face went progressively more closed, more guarded, more hurt with each passing second.

Ben started moving, pushing through the crowd with less care for politeness than he should have, but he already knew he was too late. He could see it in the set of Mara's shoulders, in the way her hands were clenched on the table, in the careful blankness of her expression that meant she was trying desperately not to fall apart in public.

He reached the table just as Derek was standing and enjoying his victory.

"Ben!" Derek said warmly, like they were old friends. "I was just having the most interesting conversation with Mara about how you two met. Fascinating story, I'll leave you both to discuss it. Enjoy your evening."

Derek walked away.

Ben slid into his chair, his heart hammering so hard he thought it might actually break through his ribs.

"Mara..." he started.

"Is it true?" Her voice was quiet and controlled, but he could hear the tremor beneath. "You applied for the job on a dare? Your friends bet you two hundred dollars to apply?"

The ballroom felt too loud suddenly. The jazz band sounded too cheerful. The laughter from other tables was too bright and careless.

Ben wanted to lie, wanted to deny it, wanted to explain in a way that would make this okay, but he knew how much Mara hated liars.

All he could manage was: "Yes."

The word landed between them like a grenade.

Mara felt something inside her chest shatter with a sound only she could hear.

"Yes," she repeated, tasting the word. "Yes. You applied for my job, for my assistant position, on a drunken bet!"

"It started that way," Ben said quickly, his words tumbling over each other. "But the second I met you, the second I saw you, it stopped being about the dare. It stopped being about anything except you."

"When were you going to tell me?" The question came out sharper than she intended. "Were you ever going to tell me? Or was this just going to be your funny little secret? The story you told at parties? 'Remember when I got hired on a dare and accidentally fell for the desperate CEO?'"

"It wasn't like that." He reached for her hand, but she pulled away. "Mara, please. I know how this looks. I know how bad this sounds, but I fell for you, really fell for you. The dare stopped mattering the moment I walked into your office."

"But you didn't tell me." She stood, needing to move, needing to do something with the energy crackling under her skin. "Six weeks. We've been together for six weeks. We're living together, and I've met your mother. You've met mine too, and you never once thought to mention 'oh by the way, our entire relationship started as a joke and a lie?'"

"It wasn't a joke!" Ben stood, his voice rising enough that people at nearby tables were starting to notice. "The dare was stupid. I was drunk and broke, and my friends bet me money to do something ridiculous. But YOU were never part of the dare. Us falling for each other was never part of it."

"How am I supposed to believe that?" Her voice broke on the last word, betraying her despite every effort to maintain composure. "How do I know any of it was real? The feelings wall, the coffee deliveries, the pancakes, all of it, was any of it real, or was it all just part of some extended joke you were doing?"

"All of it was real." He moved closer, and this time she didn't step back. "Every single moment was real. The way I felt about you from day one was real. This...us... everything we built together, it's the most real thing in my entire life."

"You lied to me." The words came out more quietly now, more defeated than angry. "For six weeks, you lied to me. Every day you didn't tell me was another lie."

"I didn't lie. I just..." He stopped, ran both hands through his hair, destroying whatever style he'd managed. "I didn't tell you, and that was wrong. I know that was wrong, but I was scared. You told me you hated dishonesty, and I was afraid. I was terrified that if I told you, you'd think exactly what you're thinking right now, that it was all fake. That I didn't care about you. That you were just some bet I was trying to win."

"Weren't I?" The question hung between them, sharp and cutting. "Wasn't this whole thing just a silly bet? See if you could make the desperate plus-size CEO fall for the cute kindergarten teacher? Good story for your friends?"

"No!" The word came out fiercely, almost angry. "God, no. Mara, you're everything to me. You're the first thing I think about when I wake up and the last thing before I sleep. You're the person I want to tell about my day. You're the person whose laugh I'd literally do anything to hear. You're the person I..."

He stopped abruptly, the words dying in his throat.

She knew what he'd been about to say. Could see it written across his face.

"What?" she demanded, needing to hear him say it, needing to hear him finish even though it would probably destroy her. "I'm the person you what?"

"LOVE!" he said, and the word landed like a blow despite being spoken with desperate tenderness. "I love you. I'm in love with you, and I have been since the feelings wall, since you told me about your coffee order, since you made fun of my organizational system. Since you laughed at my fountain incident, wore my shirt to sleep, and let me bring you Turkish food every day. I love you, and I should have told you weeks ago, but I was scared and stupid, and I'm sorry."

Mara felt tears burning hot behind her eyes. "You don't get to say that now. You don't get to say it for the first time right now, here, when I just found out our entire relationship started as a lie."

"Your friends dared you to make fun of corporate culture, to mock CEOs, and laugh at people like me." The words tasted bitter. "And you wrote an application describing your kindergarten teaching as office skills. 'Conflict resolution was crayon fights.' 'Snack inventory management.' You made fun of my job and of me."

"I made fun of corporate culture," he corrected, and even now he was being honest in a way that hurt. "I made fun of job listings that require bachelor's degrees for answering phones. The application was a middle finger to a system that felt designed to exclude people like me. It wasn't about you. I didn't even know you existed."

"But you applied, you took the interview, and you accepted the job." She crossed her arms, holding herself together. "You spent weeks working as my assistant, knowing it all started as a lie."

"I know that sorry isn't enough. I know I hurt you. I know you have every right to walk away right now and never speak to me again." His voice dropped quieter, more vulnerable. "But I'm asking, begging, for a chance to make this right. To prove that what we had was real. To show you that I'm not the guy who lies anymore. I'm the guy who tells you everything, even when it's terrifying."

Mara stood there, tears finally spilling over despite every effort to contain them, looking at this man who'd just said he loved her for the first time in the worst possible moment.

And she didn't know if she could believe him.

"I need to go," she managed, grabbing her purse from the table with shaking hands. "I can't do this. Not here. Not now. I need space to think."

"Let me drive you home." He was following her as she moved toward the exit. "Please don't leave like this, let me at least make sure you get home safely."

"I'll get an Uber." She was walking faster now, pushing through clusters of people who were probably wondering what drama had unfolded. "I need space, Ben. I need time to process this without you standing there telling me you love me and expecting that to fix everything."

They'd reached the grand entrance, the same doorway they'd walked through hours ago, holding hands, full of optimism.

The valet was already moving to get an Uber, responding to the obvious distress of a crying woman in formal wear.

Ben caught her arm gently, carefully. "Please, just tell me if there's a chance, tell me if we can fix this. Tell me I didn't destroy the best thing in my life because I was too much of a coward to be honest."

She looked at him. Really looked at him. At his face that she'd memorized. At his eyes that were red with tears. At the bow tie that had come undone at some point and now hung loose around his neck.

"I don't know," she said honestly, and watched something die in his expression. "I don't know if we can fix this. I don't know if I can trust you again. I don't like dishonest people. I need space, and you're too close for me to think clearly."

"Okay." He dropped her arm immediately, stepping back. "Okay. Space, time, whatever you need. I'll go to Jake's place."

He screwed up and he knew it.

CHAPTER 21

The apartment greeted her with cruel familiarity, Everything was exactly where it should be. Everything was organized, clean, and full of Ben.

Ben's books created rainbows on the shelves. His cat lamp glowed on the side table, casting warm light across the space. His toothbrush sat next to hers in the bathroom holder. His dish towel hung in the kitchen. His shoes were by the door.

Mara stood in the middle of the living room, still wearing the emerald dress, mascara running down her face, and looking at the evidence of their life together. Everything they'd built over these weeks. Everything that had felt so real and solid and true.

Everything that had started with a lie.

Her phone buzzed in her purse.

Ben (11:47 PM): *I'm so sorry. Please let me explain properly. Please give me a chance to make this right.*

She stared at the message, her chest aching.

Another buzz.

Ben (12:03 AM): *The dare was real. I won't lie about that. But everything after was real, too. Everything we built was real. You're the most real thing in my life.*

The tears started again, hot and angry and hurt.

Ben (12:34 AM): *I love you. I should have said it weeks ago. I should have said it every day. I should have said it before, I love you, and I'm so sorry I hurt you.*

She read it three times. Each word cutting deeper.

That didn't change the facts. Ben had lied, he'd hidden something fundamental about their relationship, and now she was supposed to just forgive that because he said he loved her?

She changed out of the emerald dress carefully and hung it in the closet, like maybe someday she'd want to remember tonight.

She put on his shirt. She hated herself for it, but put it on anyway, the shirt still smelled like him. She climbed into bed.

The apartment was completely silent. She lay in the dark and listened to the absence of it.

Her phone buzzed again.

She fell asleep crying into his pillow, her phone on the nightstand with unread messages she couldn't bring herself to answer.

She dreamed of standing on a stage with everyone laughing at her. Everyone aware of what happened and laughing, wondering how she could be such an idiot.

***

Friday Night — Jake's Apartment

Ben sat on Jake's couch in his ruined tuxedo. His bow tie was undone, and his face was blotchy from crying. He was staring at his phone like maybe if he looked at it hard enough, Mara would respond.

She didn't.

Jake emerged from his bedroom in sweatpants and a t-shirt that said "Teachers Make the World a Better Place" and surveyed the wreckage of Ben with the expression of someone trying to figure out how to help when help seemed impossible.

"She's not responding," Ben said, his voice rough from crying and shouting and desperately trying to explain himself in a ballroom full of people who'd heard every word. "I told her I love her, and she's not responding."

"Give her time." Jake sat on the coffee table across from him, close but not crowding. "She just found out something huge; she needs space to process."

"I screwed up." Ben dropped his phone and put his head in his hands. "I screwed up so badly. I should have told her weeks ago, I should have told her on day one."

"You should have," Jake agreed. "But you didn't. And now you're here, so what are you going to do about it?"

"What can I do? She won't even read my texts."

"Well, sitting here feeling sorry for yourself isn't going to fix anything." Jake leaned back. "You really love her?"

"More than anything."

"Then you need to figure out how to prove it, how to show her it's real." Jake stood and headed toward the kitchen. "But first, you need to sleep and hydrate. You look like death. Like death in a rental tux."

"I can't sleep. Every time I close my eyes, I see her face when I admitted it was true." Ben's voice cracked. "She looked so hurt, Jake. Like I'd destroyed her."

"You did hurt her. You lied by omission for six weeks. That's a real thing that happened." Jake returned with water and aspirin. "But the question isn't whether you hurt her, the question is whether what you had was real enough to survive it."

"Was it a joke?" Ben asked quietly. "Does she think we made her the butt of our joke?"

"We had you apply for a job as a joke; that's what happened. Everything after that was real. You fell for her. She fell for you. That wasn't part of the dare." Jake sat back down. "The dare was stupid. But it doesn't erase what came after."

"She thinks it does."

"She thinks it does RIGHT NOW because she's hurt and processing, and that Derek guy planted a bunch of poison in her head." Jake pointed at him. "You need to give her time to work through that, and then you need to show her, really show her, that what you had was real."

"How?"

"I don't know, you're the one who fell into a fountain for her. You're the one who gave out gold stars and brought her cookies every day. Figure out your grand gesture." Jake grinned slightly. "Just maybe don't fall into any more fountains, your track record with water features is concerning."

Despite everything, Ben almost smiled. "No fountain promises."

"That's the spirit." Jake stood. "Now sleep. Tomorrow, you can start figuring out how to win back your girl. Tonight, you simply survive."

Ben changed into the spare clothes he'd left at Jake's apartment months ago. They smelled like Jake's laundry detergent, not the stuff he and Mara used, and it felt wrong.

Everything was at Mara's apartment. His books, his toothbrush. His entire life was carefully integrated into hers, and now he was on Jake's couch in borrowed sweatpants, texting messages that went unanswered.

At 2:30 AM, when he still couldn't sleep, he sent one more message.

Ben: *I know you're not reading these. I know you need space. But I love you. And I'm not giving up on us. Take all the time you need. I'll be here when you're ready.*

The message showed as delivered but not read.

He fell asleep on Jake's couch with his phone clutched in his hand, still waiting for a response that didn't come.

***

Saturday passed in a blur of crying, staring at her phone, and wearing Ben's shirt like maybe if she kept it on long enough, it would make this hurt less.

It didn't.

Mara tried to work. Opened her laptop, stared at spreadsheets that made no sense. She closed her laptop. She tried again a little later but eventually gave up.

Eliza texted around noon.

Eliza: *You alive?*

Mara: *Barely.*

Eliza: *Want company? I want to hear all about the fun you had at the Gala.*

Mara: *Want to be alone.*

Eliza: *Why, what's going on?*

Mara: *We broke up.*

Eliza: *What! What happened?*

Mara: *Long story, I'll tell you later, I just want to be alone.*

Eliza: *That's a terrible idea, but I'll respect it. Text me if you need anything. Or if you want me to slash Derek's tires. I know a guy.*

Mara: *Please don't slash anyone's tires.*

Eliza: *The offer stands.*

Sunday was worse.

She made coffee and stood at the kitchen counter looking at the spice cabinet. They were organized in the compromise system they'd built together the night of the kitchen fight: her cuisine-based sections, his alphabetical labels within each. Her logic and his, merged into something neither of them would have done alone. She reached for the cumin and put it back without opening it. She didn't have anything to cook. She just needed to see if she could touch it without feeling anything.

She couldn't.

She thought about packing his things. Putting them in boxes and texting him to come get them. She made it approximately five minutes before she had to stop because touching his books made her cry.

This was ridiculous; she was a CEO. If she could run a thirty-million-dollar company and survive Derek Morrison's inappropriate comments, she could survive a breakup.

Except it didn't feel like just a breakup, it felt like losing a piece of herself she hadn't known was missing until Ben filled it.

Sunday evening, she finally opened his text messages.

Read them.

Cried harder.

Didn't respond.

***

Mara arrived at work Monday morning at 8:15, hoping to slip in before anyone noticed.

Tyler was waiting at her office door.

Of course he was.

"You look terrible," he said, which was becoming everyone's greeting of choice.

"Thank you, Tyler. Very helpful feedback."

"No, I mean, you look like you've been crying for three days straight. Your eyes are puffy, you're wearing the same blazer you wore last Monday, and you brought your own lunch, which means you stopped at the deli instead of having Ben do it for you." He pulled out his phone. "So, what happened? Where's Ben? Why do you both look like someone died?"

"We're taking a break."

"A BREAK?" Tyler's voice rose several octaves. "You don't TAKE BREAKS. You're MARA AND BEN. You're the office romance that restored my faith in love!"

"Well, we're taking a break. Figuring things out. Giving each other space."

"What happened?" Tyler leaned forward. "Did he do something? Did you do something? Did Derek do something because I swear to God if Derek..."

"Derek told me something about how Ben and I met. Something Ben should have told me weeks ago." Mara unlocked her office. "That's all I'm saying, please don't interrogate me."

"For the record? Whatever Ben did, he's completely miserable about it. I've never seen someone look so devastated while trying to be professional."

After Tyler left, Mara tried to work. She could see Ben's desk from her office. It was empty. He arrived early but wasn't at his desk, which meant he was probably hiding somewhere trying to avoid her.

Her chest ached.

Ben appeared in her doorway. He looked terrible, genuinely terrible. His eyes were red and swollen. His hair was a disaster. His clothes were wrinkled. He looked like he hadn't slept in days, which he probably hadn't.

"Hi," he said, his voice rough.

"Hi," she managed.

They stared at each other across the space of her office, and Mara felt everything she'd been trying to suppress for five days rise in her throat again. Love and hurt and confusion and missing him so much it physically hurt.

"I just wanted to say..." He trailed off, seemed to lose his words. "I'm going to respect your space. I'm not going to bother you or push you or make this harder. But I needed you to know that I'm still... I meant what I said Friday night. All of it. I love you, and I'm sorry, and I'm here whenever you're ready to talk. If you're ever ready to talk."

"Okay," she whispered.

He nodded, then he turned to leave. He stopped. "Also, I need to get some clothes from the apartment. Can I come by when you're at work? I don't want to ambush you or make things weird."

The apartment. Not "our apartment" anymore. Just "the apartment."

"You can come by," she said. "Your key still works."

"Okay. Thanks." He left, and Mara watched him walk back to his desk, sit down, and put his head in his hands for approximately ten seconds before forcing himself upright and pretending to work.

This was going to be impossible.

***

Wednesday, Ben stood outside Mara's office at lunch, holding two containers of lentil soup and the good bread from the Turkish place.

He'd walked there on autopilot. He ordered her usual, paid, and walked halfway back before realizing this was the stupidest possible idea.

She'd said she needed space, she'd made it clear she wasn't ready to talk, and here he was, standing outside her office with lunch as if nothing had changed.

Like they were still them instead of two people trying to figure out if there was still a "them" to be.

He stood there for a full minute, frozen, while people walked past giving him strange looks.

"Mr. Rosen."

He turned to find Margaret standing behind him, clipboard at precisely ninety degrees, expression neutral.

"I appear to be stuck," he said.

"I can see that." She glanced at the Turkish food, at Mara's office, at his face that probably looked as devastated as he felt. "Would you like me to deliver that to Ms. Wright? You could return to your desk and preserve both your dignity and her requested space."

"Would you?" The relief was immediate. "That would be... thank you. Thank you so much."

Margaret took the food from him with careful efficiency. "Go sit down, Mr. Rosen. Try to do some actual work. Moping is unproductive."

He fled back to his desk, collapsed into his chair, and tried not to watch through the glass as Margaret entered Mara's office.

***

Margaret knocked twice on Mara's door frame and entered without waiting for permission.

"Ms. Wright. This arrived for you." She set the Turkish food on Mara's desk with precise placement.

Mara looked up from her laptop, saw the familiar containers, and her face crumpled.

"From Mr. Rosen," Margaret added unnecessarily.

"Of course it is." Mara's voice was barely a whisper. She stared at the containers like they were a puzzle she couldn't solve. "He brought me lunch."

"He brought lunch," Margaret confirmed. "Then stood outside your office for sixty-three seconds, unable to decide whether to enter or not. I relieved him of the dilemma."

"Thank you, Margaret." Mara's eyes were filling with tears.

Margaret stood there, watching her boss desperately trying not to cry over lentil soup, and made a decision that went against every professional instinct she'd honed over thirty-three years of office management.

She sat down in the visitor chair.

Mara looked up, surprised. Margaret never sat down uninvited.

"My husband and I separated once," Margaret said quietly. "Thirty-two years ago. We spent three weeks apart. The worst three weeks of my entire life."

"What happened?"

"He was laid off from his job. Didn't tell me for six weeks. Too proud. Thought he could fix it before I noticed." Margaret's hands rested on her clipboard. "I found out from a neighbor. She mentioned seeing him at the grocery store during work hours. Asked if he was feeling better. I had no idea what she was talking about."

"That's awful."

"It felt like a betrayal. Not the job loss, I didn't care about that. The lying. The hiding. Three weeks of pretending everything was fine when it wasn't." Margaret's expression remained neutral, but her voice carried weight. "I asked him to leave. I told him I needed space to figure out if I could trust him again."

"How did you..." Mara trailed off. "How did you get past it?"

"I asked myself one question." Margaret met her eyes directly. "Did I believe he loved me? Everything else was noise. The lying, the hiding, the breach of trust. Those were problems we could work on if the foundation was solid. But if I didn't believe he loved me, if I thought the whole relationship was built on lies, then there was nothing to save."

"And you believed he loved you?"

"I did, despite the lying, despite the pain, I knew he loved me. I knew he'd made a terrible decision out of fear and pride, not malice." Margaret stood, smoothing her skirt. "So, I asked him to come home. We worked on trust. We worked on communication. We've been married forty-one years now. The separation was thirty-two years ago. I can barely remember what it felt like to doubt him."

She moved toward the door. "Do you believe he loves you, Ms. Wright?"

"I don't know," Mara whispered. "I don't know what's real anymore."

"Then that's what you need to figure out." Margaret paused at the threshold. "Not whether the beginning was perfect, and not whether he made mistakes, but whether you believe, fundamentally, that what you built together was real."

She left.

Mara sat alone with her lunch, Margaret's question heavy in her chest.

Did she believe he loved her?

She thought about six weeks of gold stars and lunch breaks. About the way he'd looked at her when she said "our apartment" for the first time. About his face when she'd met his mother, nervous and hopeful. About three days of crying in his shirt and staring at his toothbrush.

She opened the lentil soup, it was still warm, perfect temperature. He'd timed it exactly right, just like he always did.

She started crying again over good bread and the realization that maybe Margaret was right.

Maybe the question wasn't whether he'd made a mistake.

The question was whether she believed what came after was real.

***

Friday morning started normally. Then at 11:50 AM, the office fire alarm went off.

The sound was roaring. A piercing shriek that seemed to come from every direction, echoing off the walls, making everyone jump.

Mara ran out of her office to find smoke billowing from the break room, and Ben standing in the middle of the smoke looking absolutely horrified.

"WHAT DID YOU DO?" she yelled over the alarm.

"I WAS MAKING LUNCH!" Ben yelled back, frantically waving his hands at the smoke detector like that would somehow help. "THE MICROWAVE CAUGHT FIRE!"

"HOW DID THE MICROWAVE CATCH FIRE?"

"I DON'T KNOW! I PUT IN THE LENTIL SOUP! I PRESSED THE BUTTONS! I FOLLOWED THE INSTRUCTIONS!"

Tyler appeared, phone out, filming. "This is GOLD. Pure GOLD. Ben Rosen has set off his SECOND fire alarm in TWO WEEKS!"

"SECOND?" several people asked.

"He set off Mara's apartment building alarm two weeks ago!" Tyler announced to the gathering crowd. "Casserole disaster! Whole building evacuated! Very illegal."

"It wasn't illegal!" Ben protested, still getting soaked by the sprinklers. "It was an accident! A series of unfortunate cooking events!"

The building intercom announced:

"ATTENTION. FIRE. FIRE. FIRE. PLEASE EVACUATE IMMEDIATELY. THIS IS NOT A DRILL."

"We have to evacuate," Mara said.

"Again?" Ben added miserably. "We have to evacuate again. I'm that guy. The fire alarm guy. This is my identity now."

They grabbed their phones and headed for the stairs. The entire office was evacuating, everyone looking annoyed, confused, or entertained depending on their relationship to Ben.

Gerald appeared from his office looking like someone had personally insulted him. "Mr. Rosen, did you set off the fire alarm?"

"It was a microwave accident, sir."

"A microwave accident."

"The lentil soup bowl wasn't microwaveable, and chose to melt. I had no control over the situation."

They made it outside. The entire office stood on the sidewalk. Some in coats, some without, but everyone looking irritated.

Two fire trucks pulled up.

Again.

Firefighters jumped out looking way too prepared for action.

Tyler was narrating everything into his phone. "Day five of the breakup, Ben has set off another fire alarm attempting to make Mara lunch. The man is not the best cook, but he keeps trying. It's tragic and hilarious. Mostly hilarious."

A firefighter approached. "Who set off the alarm?"

Everyone pointed at Ben.

"You again?" the firefighter asked.

"Again?" Ben looked confused.

"We responded to your apartment building two weeks ago. Casserole incident. You don't remember me?"

"Oh God. You were there for that, too?"

"I was. You have a pretty good disaster resume for one person."

"I'm very talented, multifaceted, a disaster renaissance man."

The firefighters went inside to check the breakroom and emerged fifteen minutes later.

"Microwave fire contained, you can go back in." The firefighter looked at Ben. "Maybe stop cooking. For everyone's safety."

"That's the plan. I'm embracing my limitations. Accepting my role as a permanent takeout customer."

The office filed back inside. Ben stood on the sidewalk, coughing from the smoke, looking miserable.

Mara's phone buzzed.

Eliza: *Did your boyfriend set off ANOTHER fire alarm?*

Mara: *How do you know about this? You're at a conference?*

Eliza: *Tyler posted it. It's already going viral. #FireAlarmBen is trending in our building's Facebook group.*

Mara: *Oh God.*

Eliza: *Your boyfriend has a very specific love language, and it's smoke detectors. This is the second time in two weeks. At what point do we call it a pattern?*

Mara: *He was trying to make me lunch.*

Eliza: *He was trying to burn down your office while making you lunch. There's a difference.*

Mara: *I have to go.*

Eliza: *Just saying. A man who sets off multiple fire alarms trying to feed you is either deeply committed or deeply incompetent. Possibly both.*

Mara looked at Ben, still standing outside, looking like the saddest disaster she'd ever seen.

He'd been trying to make her lunch again, even though they were broken up and she'd asked for space. He kept trying to take care of her in the only way he knew how.

And she started laughing, couldn't help it, the whole situation was so ridiculous, so perfectly Ben, that she couldn't keep the laughter contained.

Ben heard it. Looked over and saw her laughing.

He smiled that soft smile that was just for her.

And Mara realized, with sudden, overwhelming clarity, that she was going to forgive him.

Maybe not today.

Maybe not this second.

But eventually.

Because the alternative, living without him, felt worse than working through the hurt.

***

Back at her desk, Mara sat staring at her phone. She'd spent five days trying to figure this out alone. Five days of wearing his shirt, avoiding his books, and talking to his cat lamp. Five days of missing him so much she couldn't function.

She needed to talk to him. Really talk, just the two of them, without an audience.

She pulled out her phone. Typed a message. Deleted it. Typed it again.

Finally settled on:

Mara: *Can we talk? Tomorrow? I'm not saying I'm ready to fix everything. But I'm ready to talk.*

The response came back immediately, like he'd been holding his phone waiting for five days straight.

Ben: *Yes. Whenever you want. Wherever you want. Thank you. Thank you for giving me a chance to explain.*

She started typing: *My apartment at 2 but* stopped. The apartment felt too loaded. Too full of their shared life. Too much like stepping back into something before they'd figured out if there was still something to step back into.

Mara: *Where should we meet? Somewhere neutral.*

The typing dots appeared and disappeared several times. She could picture him on Jake's couch, agonizing over the right answer.

Ben: *The park? Buena Vista? It's quiet on Saturdays. We could talk without interruptions. But if that's too public or weird, we can go somewhere else. Coffee shop? Literally anywhere you're comfortable. I'll come to you. Whatever you need.*

The park. The place he'd taken her when she was stressed. Where he'd told her about teaching and why he'd left. The bench overlooking everything.

Neutral but meaningful. Public but quiet. Their place but not their home.

Mara: *The park works. 2 PM?*

Ben: *I'll be there. Thank you, Mara. Thank you for this chance.*

Mara: *Don't thank me yet. Just bring honesty, all of it. Everything you should have told me six weeks ago.*

Ben: *I promise. Everything. No more hiding.*

She set down her phone and looked around at his books, his lamp, his toothbrush, his entire life still integrated into hers.

Tomorrow they will talk. Tomorrow she will listen. Tomorrow, she would decide if what they built together was worth the risk of trusting him again.

But tonight, she would put on his shirt and sleep in their bed and try to prepare herself for whatever came next.

CHAPTER 22

Ben stood in Jake's living room at 11:34 AM on Saturday, surrounded by four poster boards, three bags of hand-cut gold stars, and approximately seventeen different types of anxiety.

The poster boards were propped against the couch, each one titled in his messiest kindergarten-teacher handwriting, decorated with hand-drawn star borders:

Board 1: "You Interviewed the WRONG Ben" Board 2: "You Hired the WRONG Ben Anyway" Board 3: "You Fell for the WRONG Ben" Board 4: "...Because I Was ALWAYS the Right Ben for You"

Each board was covered in gold stars, hundreds of them, each one labeled with a date and a memory. He and Jake got up early, shopped for supplies and were now cutting stars out, Ben was writing memories and organizing them chronologically.

Ben picked up one from the pile.

Day 1: You smiled at me during the interview. I forgot what question I was asking.

Jake grabbed another from the couch.

Day 1: I answered the phone wrong. You didn't fire me. First sign you were special.

"This one's good," Jake said, reading the next star.

Day 3: *You organize sticky notes by color AND urgency. I fell a little bit in love.*

Ben held up another.

Week 1: *I memorized your lunch order in one day. Turkish lentil soup, the good bread, split between lunch and afternoon.*

"You're such a disaster," Jake said, but he was smiling. He picked up the next star.

Week 2: *You let me reorganize your supply closet.. You trusted me with your space.*

Ben kept sorting through them, reading each one, his chest getting tighter with every memory.

Week 3: *I fell into the fountain at the Ferry Building trying to get an apple. You laughed so hard you couldn't breathe. I knew I was done for.*

Week 4: *First kiss, my whole world shifted.*

"God, you really documented everything," Jake said, looking at the pile. There were so many stars. Too many stars. Every moment from six weeks compressed into construction paper and Sharpie.

Week 5: *You met my mom. Survived the baby questions and the embarrassing stories. I knew you were it.*

Week 5: *Kitchen fight about spice organization. Almost said I love you.*

Week 6: *You stood in burgundy underwear discussing Derek. I called your hips 'best hips.' Meant every word.*

Week 6: *I set off your building's fire alarm while making casserole. You laughed instead of leaving me. That's when I knew.*

Jake set down the star he was holding and looked at Ben seriously. "You ready?"

"No, absolutely not, I'm terrified." Ben ran both hands through his hair. "This is either going to be the most romantic thing I've ever done or the most humiliating."

"It's going to work," Jake said firmly. "You've always been too much: Too emotional. Too honest. Too big with your feelings. And she fell in love with that. She doesn't want understated, she wants YOU."

"What if it's not enough? What if she can't forgive me?"

"Then at least you'll know you tried. At least you showed up and were honest." Jake walked over and put both hands on Ben's shoulders. "But I don't think that's what's going to happen. I think she's going to see all this and know it's real."

Ben wanted desperately to believe him.

He looked at the poster boards, at the hundreds of gold stars, at the evidence of six weeks of falling completely, irrevocably in love.

"Okay." He took a breath. "Okay. I need to get to the park. Set up the trail. I have two and a half hours."

"Go win back your girl with kindergarten craft supplies."

***

Ben arrived at Buena Vista Park carrying poster boards, bags of stars, and a heart rate that suggested imminent cardiac arrest.

The park was moderately busy. Joggers. Families with kids. Dog walkers. People sitting on benches reading.

297

There were more people than he'd hoped for, but that was fine. Public meant witnesses. Public meant accountability.

He started at the park entrance, placing the first gold star on the ground with shaking hands.

"Start here. Follow the stars. -B"

Then he began laying the trail. One star every few feet, creating a path toward his thinking place, the bench overlooking the city.

Each star told a story.

He placed the first one carefully. Each a few feet up the path.

A jogger stopped, picked up one of the stars, and read it. "Did you drop this?"

"No, I'm making a trail for someone. A romantic trail."

The jogger set it down carefully, reading the text with a soft smile. "That's really sweet, good luck."

"Thanks. I need all the luck."

Ben kept placing stars, his hands steadier now. The trail wound through the park, past the playground, around the dog area, and up the hill.

A woman walking her dog stopped to read a few stars, then looked up at Ben with such warmth he almost started crying.

"Someone's very lucky," she said.

"I'm the lucky one," Ben managed, his voice rough. "If she forgives me. If this works."

"She'll forgive you. Anyone who inspires this much love is worth forgiving."

Ben nodded, not trusting his voice, and kept placing stars.

By 1:30, the trail was complete. A winding path from the park entrance to his bench, each one a memory, a moment, a piece of falling in love.

At the bench, he arranged the poster boards against the back. Then scattered more stars on the ground, creating a heart shape.

He stepped back and surveyed his work.

It was too much, way too much, she was going to think he'd lost his mind.

His phone buzzed.

Jake: *How's it going? Are you spiraling?*

Ben: *What if she doesn't come?*

Jake: *She'll come. She texted you. She WANTS to talk. Now breathe and wait.*

Ben sat on the bench, surrounded by his poster boards and gold stars, and watched the trail winding down through the park.

It was 1:27 PM. Twenty-three minutes until she was supposed to arrive. Twenty-three minutes to either save his relationship or watch it end in a pile of construction paper.

***

Mara stood in her apartment wearing jeans and Ben's sweatshirt, trying to convince herself to leave.

She'd been ready since noon and changed outfits four times. She put on makeup, washed it off, put it back on 3 times.

Now it was 1:45, and she needed to leave in five minutes to get to the park by 2, and her feet felt glued to the floor.

What if this didn't work? What if they talked and she still couldn't trust him? What if the hurt was too big?

Her phone buzzed. Eliza.

Eliza: *You're still going, right? Not chickening out?*

Mara: *I'm going. Leaving in 5 minutes. Panicking but going.*

Eliza: *Good. Listen to what he says. Truly listen. Not the Derek voice in your head. Not your mom's voice. HIS voice. And then decide.*

Mara: *What if I can't forgive him?*

Eliza: *Then you can't, but at least you'll know. At least you'll have tried.*

Mara grabbed her keys, her phone, her courage.

Left before she could change her mind.

The walk to Buena Vista Park took twelve minutes. Her heart is racing, her palms are sweating, and her mind is running through every possible version of this conversation.

She'd practiced what she wanted to say. How she'd ask the hard questions. How she'd explain that trust mattered.

But all her practiced speeches disappeared the moment she reached the park entrance and saw it.

A gold star is sitting on the ground: yellow construction paper, hand-cut with slightly wobbly edges.

She bent down, picked it up, her hands shaking.

"Start here. Follow the stars. -B"

Her breath caught. She looked up, following the path, and saw more stars. A trail of them winding through the park.

"Oh no," she whispered. "What did you do?"

She picked up the next star.

Day 1: You smiled at me during the interview. I forgot what question I was asking.

Her chest felt tight. She moved to the next one.

Day 1: You said, "Make yourself at home." I wanted to stay forever.

"Ben," she breathed, and started following the trail faster, collecting stars as she went, reading each one through tears.

Day 4: You let me bring you ibuprofen. It was the first time I took care of you.

People in the park were noticing her now. A woman smiled as Mara passed, tears streaming down her face, clutching gold stars. A jogger slowed, watching with interest.

She kept walking, kept collecting, kept reading.

Week 2: You let me reorganize your supply closet. You trusted me with your space.

Week 3: I fell into the fountain at the Ferry Building trying to get an apple. You laughed so hard you couldn't breathe. I knew I was done for.

She laughed through the tears at that one, remembering. The fountain, the wet apple, and his completely soaked dignity.

Week 4: You claimed me to the jam lady at the farmers market. Made us real before we were ready.

Week 4: First kiss. My whole world shifted.

She was half-walking, half-running now, following the trail up the hill, collecting memories as her vision blurred.

Week 5: You met my mom. Survived the baby questions and the embarrassing stories. Still chose me.

Week 5: You let me leave my toothbrush in your bathroom. My heart exploded.

Week 5: Kitchen fight about spice organization. Almost said I love you. Said 'maximum liking levels' instead -like a coward.

Week 6: You said, 'our apartment.' I cried in the supply closet after because it was real.

Week 6: You wore my shirt to bed. I wanted to tell you I loved you, but I didn't have the courage.

Week 6: You stood in burgundy underwear discussing Derek. I called your hips 'best hips.' Meant every word.

Week 6: I set off the fire alarm while making casserole. You laughed instead of leaving me, that's when I knew.

The trail wound around the playground, past the dog area, up toward the overlook. She saw Ben standing there surrounded by poster boards and hundreds of gold stars scattered on the ground in a heart shape, looking terrified and hopeful and so perfectly himself that her heart broke and healed all at once.

She stopped at the edge of his gold star heart, clutching the stars she'd collected, tears streaming down her face, unable to speak.

He didn't speak either for a long moment. Just stood there looking at her with those blue eyes she'd memorized, his hands shaking at his sides.

Behind them, a small crowd had gathered. The woman who'd smiled at Mara on the trail, the jogger, and a family with kids. People who'd followed or noticed.

"Hi," he finally managed. "You came, I was terrified you wouldn't come."

"You made a trail of gold stars through the park," she said, her voice breaking. "How could I not come?"

He took a breath, seemed to gather himself, then stepped forward to the very edge of the star circle; close enough that she could see the tears already forming in his eyes.

"Before I show you any of this..." He gestured at the poster boards behind him. "Before I do the whole grand gesture thing, I need to say something. I need to apologize. Really apologize. Not the panicked sorry from the gala or the desperate texts. An actual apology."

She nodded, unable to speak, clutching her collected stars.

"Mara, I'm sorry." His voice cracked, and tears spilled over. "I'm so sorry I lied to you. Not a direct lie, but a lie by omission, which is just as bad. Worse, maybe, because you trusted me and I chose not to tell you something that mattered."

He wiped at his eyes roughly, not trying to hide the tears.

"I was scared. That's not an excuse, but it's the truth. I was terrified that if I told you about the dare, you'd think everything was fake. That you'd leave before I could prove how real this was for me. But that fear doesn't justify the lying, nothing justifies it." His hands were shaking so badly he shoved them in his pockets. "You deserved honesty from the beginning. You deserved to know I applied for your job on a drunken bet. You deserved to make informed decisions about us instead of finding out from Derek."

"Ben..." she started, but he shook his head.

"Please. Let me finish. I've been practicing this for six days." He pulled his hands from his pockets and held them out slightly. "I broke your trust. That's the worst thing I could have done because trust is the foundation of everything. And I know I can't just apologize and expect you to forgive me. I know I must earn that trust back. I know it might take weeks or months, or maybe you'll never fully trust me again. But Mara, I want to try. I want to spend however long it takes proving to you that you can trust me. Proving I'll be honest even when it's hard. Proving I'm worth the risk."

The crowd was completely silent now, everyone holding their breath.

"I should have told you the first day. The first week. Any moment before Derek could weaponize it." His voice was raw. "But I was a coward. And you paid the price for my cowardice. And I'm so, so sorry for that."

He took one more step forward, close enough now that she could see every detail of his face.

"I know 'sorry' isn't enough. I know I hurt you. I know you have every right to walk away right now." His voice dropped quieter. "But I'm asking, begging, for a chance to make this right. To prove that what we had was real. To show you that I'm not the guy who lies anymore."

He held out his hands, palms up.

"So that's my apology. I'm sorry I lied. I'm sorry I hurt you. I'm sorry I made you doubt something real. And I'm sorry it took losing you to be brave enough to be completely honest."

Mara stood there, tears running down her face, looking at his outstretched hands.

Six days ago, she'd stood in a ballroom and felt her world shatter. Six days of anger and hurt and confusion and missing him so much it physically hurt.

And now here he was, standing in a heart made of gold stars, apologizing with his whole heart on display.

She looked down at the stars in her hands. Memories he'd cataloged. Moments he'd noticed. Proof that he'd been paying attention to every detail of her life.

She thought about Margaret's question: Do you believe he loves you?

She thought about weeks of coffee deliveries and the reorganization of the coffee station. About the way he looked at her when she said, "our apartment." About his face when she met his mother. About six days of crying in his shirt and staring at his toothbrush.

She stepped forward into the circle of stars, closing the distance between them, and placed her hands in his.

His fingers immediately closed around hers, desperate and warm and shaking.

"I forgive you," she said.

***

His entire face transformed with shock. "You what?"

"I forgive you." She squeezed his hands, holding tight. "What you did was wrong. Hiding the truth really hurt me, it made me doubt everything. You know how much I hate dishonest people, but these stars..." She glanced down at the trail, at the circle surrounding them. "You remember everything. Every moment. Every detail. Only someone really falling would notice that I organize sticky notes by urgency. Only someone truly seeing me would remember the fountain, the jam lady, the fire alarm. Only someone who loved me would hand-cut hundreds of stars and label them with dates."

"I notice everything about you," he said, his voice rough with emotion. "I can't help it. You're all I see."

305

"And that's why I forgive you." She stepped closer. "Because the dare was two months ago. Everything after, all these memories, all these moments, that was real. I felt it. I lived it. And I'm choosing to believe it was real for you, too."

"It was real." Tears were streaming down his face now. "God, Mara, it was the most real thing in my life. Every single moment, every gold star, all real."

"Then show me." She glanced at the poster boards behind him. "Show me the rest of it. Show me why you're the right Ben."

He let out a shaky laugh, wiping at his face with one hand while still holding hers with the other. "Okay. Okay. So. I used to be a kindergarten teacher. Gold stars were kind of my thing." He gestured at the absurdity surrounding them. "They still are, apparently."

He reluctantly released her hands and turned to grab the first poster board.

You Interviewed the WRONG Ben.

"My friends dared me to apply as 'the wrong Ben,'" he said, his voice getting stronger now, more animated. "Wrong background, wrong experience, wrong everything for a tech CEO's assistant. They bet me two hundred dollars I wouldn't do it. And they were right! I WAS the wrong Ben for that job."

He pointed to the stars covering the board.

"I goofed up answering your phone on the first day. Who does that? The wrong Ben does that. I reorganized your supply closet without asking. Wrong Ben behavior. I brought you ibuprofen like some overly familiar weirdo. Very inappropriate.

The crowd had grown larger now, maybe fifty people watching, completely absorbed.

Ben set down the first board, picked up the second.

You Hired the WRONG Ben Anyway

"And you HIRED ME ANYWAY!" His voice rose with emotion, tears still streaming but grinning through them now. "Even though I was clearly a disaster! Even though I had zero corporate experience! Even though every professional instinct should have told you to hire literally anyone else!"

More stars, more memories displayed.

"And I kept being the wrong Ben! I brought you lunch every day, even though that's not in the job description! I noticed when you were stressed and CARED! I asked if you were okay and WAITED for the answer! I reorganized your entire life because I couldn't help myself! I DEFENDED you to Derek even though it wasn't my place!"

He grabbed the third board, his energy building.

You Fell for the WRONG Ben.

"And then you FELL FOR ME!" He was almost shouting now, tears streaming, but grinning through them. "You should have fallen for someone from your world, someone successful and appropriate, someone like Derek who spoke fluent corporate! Someone who DOESN'T fall into fountains chasing apples, someone who DOESN'T set off MULTIPLE fire alarms trying to make you lunch or dinner, someone who DOESN'T cry when you give him drawer space!"

Someone in the crowd laughed, delighted.

"You should have chosen someone appropriate!" Ben continued, his voice carrying across the park. "Someone your mother would approve of! Someone who knew which fork to use! Someone who wouldn't be embarrassed by being a DISASTER at basic adult functions!"

He set down the third board and picked up the final one, his hands steadier now.

Because I Was ALWAYS the Right Ben for You
The crowd held its breath.

"But maybe, just MAYBE, I was the RIGHT kind of wrong." His voice dropped, became quieter but more intense, speaking directly to her even though fifty people were listening. "Maybe you NEEDED someone who didn't fit your carefully controlled world, someone who challenged your 'appropriate, ' someone who made you laugh in supply closets and convinced you to take lunch breaks and fell into fountains, making you smile."

Mara's breath caught because he was right.

"Maybe you needed someone who saw YOU. Not CEO Mara. Not the perfect polished version everyone else sees, but the woman who secretly loves chaos even though she pretends she doesn't. Who laughs like she means it, really laughs and laughs loud, and who makes room for shelves of books and weird lamps even though they don't match her aesthetic because deep down, she WANTS to like me."

She felt tears streaming down her face.

"Maybe you need someone who would notice you bite your lip when you're stressed and bring you ibuprofen without being asked. Someone who would notice your favorite lunch order because paying attention to you felt like the most important thing in the world. Someone who would reorganize your spice cupboard and make it BETTER because he couldn't stand seeing you struggle."

He set down the final board and stepped forward.

"The dare was real, I won't pretend it wasn't. Two hundred dollars and drunk decision-making, and my idiot friends thinking it would be hilarious." His voice was thick with emotion. "But everything AFTER, everything on these boards, that was real. Every gold star is a moment I fell more in love with you. Every memory is proof that this stopped being about the dare the second I met you."

He pulled out three more poster boards from behind the bench.

The crowd gasped.

"These are from the last two weeks. Moving in together. Meeting your mom. The gala. The fight. The past six days of missing you so much I couldn't function." He gestured desperately at the pile. "I RAN OUT OF SPACE! There were too many moments! Too many times, I fell more in love with you! I couldn't FIT them all!"

Someone in the crowd made a sound, a half sob, half laugh.

"You want to know if it was real?" Ben's voice rose again, carrying across the park. "I have SEVEN POSTER BOARDS covered in HUNDREDS of GOLD STARS documenting every moment I fell for you! I hand-cut these stars and labeled them because I needed you to KNOW! I needed you to SEE that this wasn't a joke or a game or anything except me completely losing my mind over how incredible you are!"

He took her hands again, his grip desperate.

"You hired the WRONG Ben. But I was always the right Ben for YOU. The Ben who sees YOU, the Ben who loves YOU exactly as you are, the Ben who makes you laugh and brings you lunch and reorganizes your chaos because that's how I show love. The Ben who's standing in a public park, covered in kindergarten craft supplies, because subtle isn't my style, and you deserve BIG. You deserve GRAND. You deserve someone who loves you SO MUCH he makes a complete fool of himself with gold stars to prove it."

The words hung in the air between them.

Mara looked at him. At this man who loved so loudly, so publicly, so entirely without restraint. At the poster boards covered in memories. At the hundreds of gold stars. At the trail winding through the park. At the wrong Ben, who was exactly right.

"And I know I already apologized," he said, his voice cracking. "But I need to say it one more time. I'm sorry I made you doubt this. I'm sorry my cowardice hurt you. I'm sorry for everything. But Mara..."

He dropped to his knees in the circle of gold stars, still holding her hands, looking up at her with tears streaming.

"I LOVE YOU!" he shouted, loud enough that his voice echoed. "I'M IN LOVE WITH YOU! I've been in love with you since day one! Since you asked if I was okay and CARED about the answer! Since you trusted me with your space and your vulnerability and your carefully guarded heart!"

The crowd gasped collectively. Several people are crying openly now.

"I love you, and I'm SORRY I didn't tell you about the dare sooner! I'm sorry I was a COWARD! But I'm not hiding anymore! I'm KNEELING in a PUBLIC PARK surrounded by GOLD STARS telling YOU and FIFTY STRANGERS that I LOVE YOU!" His voice was raw, desperate. "I love your competence and your kindness! I love how you organize the world! I love that you make room for my chaos! I love that you laugh like joy is surprising! "I love that you're brilliant and fierce and so much more than the title on your door!"

Then he stopped shouting.

The crowd went still, trying to catch what came next.

He dropped his voice so low it was just for her, barely above a breath, the fifty people around them leaning in and hearing nothing useful.

"Maximum liking levels," he said.

Mara's breath caught.

"In the kitchen, after the spice fight, you were so scared to say it, and you said that instead." His hands tightened around hers. "I heard it. I kept it. I've been keeping it since that night."

He looked at her the way he had in that kitchen. Not for the crowd. Not for the strangers and the cameras and the kids running through the gold stars. Just for her.

Then he looked up, and his voice broke back open.

He was fully crying now, his whole body shaking.

Mara stood there looking down at him, kneeling in gold stars, his hands holding hers like a lifeline, his face wet with tears and desperate hope.

And felt everything she'd been holding inside for six days burst out.

"AND I LOVE YOU!" she shouted back.

The crowd erupted.

Ben's eyes went wide. "What?"

"I LOVE YOU, BEN ROSEN!" Louder now, so everyone could hear. "I love your chaos and your ridiculous grand gestures! I love that you fell into a fountain! I love that you made me laugh when I'd forgotten how! I love your gold stars and your terrible cat lamp and the way you set off fire alarms trying to make me dinner."

She pulled him to his feet, not gently, yanking him up with enough force that they both stumbled, catching each other in the middle of the heart made with stars.

"I love that you noticed my coffee order after one day! I love that you wanted to beat up Derek and make it BETTER! I love that you see ME, truly SEE me, when everyone else sees a title!" Her voice was breaking, tears streaming. "I love that you're the WRONG BEN who turned out to be EXACTLY RIGHT!"

"Say it again!" He was grinning now, crying and grinning and looking at her like she hung the moon.

"I LOVE YOU!"

"AGAIN!"

"I LOVE YOU I LOVE YOU! I LOVE YOU!"

He wrapped his arms around her waist, lifted her up, spun her around in the circle of gold stars while the crowd absolutely ERUPTED. Cheering, clapping, whistling, crying. Kids jumping up and down. Adults hugging each other. Someone's dog is barking enthusiastically.

"I LOVE MARA WRIGHT! EVERYONE HEAR THAT? I LOVE HER, AND SHE LOVES ME BACK, AND I'M THE LUCKIEST DISASTER IN SAN FRANCISCO!" He shouted to the sky.

When he set her down, they were both dizzy and laughing and crying, his hands cupping her face, her hands fisted in his shirt, gold stars stuck to both of them.

"Can I kiss you now?" he asked, his voice dropping to just for her. "In front of all these people? Very publicly?"

"You Better kiss me after making me walk through A HUNDRED GOLD STARS!"

"Can't take it back! Too late, you already said you love me FOUR times. It's legally binding. The crowd is witness."

But he was already leaning in.

He kissed her, and the crowd went WILD.

It wasn't gentle, it wasn't tentative, it was six days of missing each other and six weeks of falling in love and the pure relief of being forgiven and trusted and loved back.

It became passionate and loving and a little bit steamy.

When they finally broke apart, both breathless, grinning, and covered in tears and gold stars, the crowd was still clapping.

"We're definitely going viral," Mara said, laughing.

"Worth it." Ben shouted to the crowd, "I'D DO IT A THOUSAND TIMES! I LOVE HER!"

"I love you too," she said, softer now, just for him.

"Forever, if you'll have me, if you'll trust me again. If you'll let me prove every day that this is real."

"You already proved it." She touched his face, her thumb brushing away tears. "These stars. These memories. The apology. All of it. You proved it, Ben. I trust you. I believe you. I love you."

Someone in the crowd shouted, "KISS HER AGAIN!" and they both laughed.

"Demanding audience," Ben said.

"Should we give them what they want?"

"Absolutely."

He kissed her again, and this time it was softer, sweeter, full of promise and future and the absolute certainty that they were going to be okay.

When they pulled apart, the crowd was still there, still watching, still celebrating with them like they were part of something beautiful.

"Take me home," she said. "Our home. With your rainbow books and terrible cat lamp and seven poster boards we need to figure out where to put."

"We'll hang them. All seven. Cover the entire apartment in evidence that I love you." He started gathering the poster boards while people came up to congratulate them. "Although the kids took most of the trail stars. We might have distributed our love story across the entire park."

"There goes our documentation." She said lightheartedly.

"We don't need documentation; I remember every moment." He pulled her close, watching kids running around with his hand-cut stars, scattering them across the grass like confetti. "Besides, now there are gold stars all over the park. Pieces of our love story scattered around. That's pretty romantic."

"That's littering."

"That's distributed romantic evidence, very different. Educational. We're teaching children about love."

They gathered what they could, posed for photos with strangers who'd witnessed the whole thing, and answered questions about their story. The woman who'd smiled at Mara on the trail approached, tears streaming down her face.

"That was the most beautiful thing I've ever seen," she said. "Thirty years ago, my husband proposed to me in this park, right on that bench. You just reminded me why I said yes. Thank you."

"Thank you for watching," Mara managed, her own tears starting again.

They finally made it out of the park, poster boards in hand, gold stars stuck to their clothes and in their hair, surrounded by the evidence of their chaotic love story.

"Ready to go home?" Ben asked.

"Our home," Mara corrected.

"Our home. Our life. Our everything." He kissed her quickly, tasting like salt and happiness. "Our perfectly imperfect, wrong-turned-right, chaotic but real relationship."

"I wouldn't change a single thing," she said, and meant it.

They walked home together through San Francisco, carrying poster boards and memories and the absolute certainty that the wrong Ben had been exactly right all along.

***

They got back to the apartment at 5:30 PM, both covered in gold stars that refused to unstick, both laughing, both completely happy.

Ben immediately started trying to figure out where to hang the poster boards.

"Living room wall?" he suggested, holding up Board #1.

"That's too much."

"Bedroom?"

"Still too much."

"We could hang them in the hallway. Make a gallery? Very artistic."

"We live in an apartment building. The hallway is a shared space."

"Our home office then. When we eventually have a home office. Long-term planning."

They settled on leaning them against the wall in the bedroom for now, a temporary solution that would probably become permanent because that's how everything happened with them.

Mara changed out of her jeans into sweatpants. Ben changed into the clothes he'd left in her closet weeks ago that had become their closet.

They ordered Thai food and ate on the couch surrounded by his books and her organization and their combined chaos.

"I set off two fire alarms in two weeks," Ben said through a mouthful of pad thai.

"You did."

"That's probably a record. Possibly an achievement. Definitely concerning."

"Very concerning, you're banned from all cooking."

"I already banned myself. Lifetime ban. Self-imposed for public safety."

"Good call."

They ate in comfortable silence, his foot hooked around her ankle, her head on his shoulder.

"I can't believe you made seven poster boards of gold stars," Mara said.

"I can't believe you followed the trail. I was so scared you'd get to the park, see the first star, and just leave."

"How could I leave? You labeled every single one with dates and memories."

He kissed her. "True. But the gold stars are pretty great."

Later, lying in bed, Ben turned to face her.

"Thank you," he said.

"For what?"

"For forgiving me. For believing me. For loving me back even though I'm a disaster who sets off fire alarms."

"You're my disaster," she said. "And I love you, all of you, even the fire alarm parts."

"Even the fire alarm parts. That's true love right there."

"The truest love."

He pulled her close. "I'm never lying to you again. About anything. Even small things. Total honesty from now on."

"Good."

"Even if it's embarrassing."

"Especially if it's embarrassing."

"I used your expensive face cream last week because I ran out of moisturizer."

"I knew it! I could tell because the container was half empty."

"You knew?"

"I always know. You're not subtle."

"I'm extremely subtle. Very covert. A mystery."

"You're the least mysterious person I've ever met. You wear your heart on your sleeve and your thoughts on your face."

"That's fair." He kissed her. "I love you."

"I love you too. My wrong Ben who's exactly right."

They fell asleep tangled together, gold stars still stuck in their hair, surrounded by evidence of their chaotic love story.

And Mara thought about how two months ago she'd been alone and appropriate and controlled. How she'd hired the wrong person and fallen for the wrong guy and built a relationship on a foundation that started as a lie.

But somehow it had all become exactly right.

The wrong Ben.

The right love.

The perfect chaos.

It was exactly what she needed all along.